A SELECT GROUP

A SELECT GROUP

Blaine C. Readler

A SELECT GROUP

Visit us at: http://www.readler.com

E-mail: blaine@readler.com

ISBN: 978-0-9992296-1-3

Printed in the United States of America

To Monica.

ACKNOWLEDGEMENTS

Many thanks to the editing prowess of Jennifer Silva-Redmond, for calming the storm of overwrought exclamations, and for whacking the first two original chapters. Trust me, you don't need them.

www.jennyredbug.com

MTB's fearless proofing surgically sliced out a myriad of embarrassing typos and grammatical blunders. Hat's off to you, dear. May your red pen never run dry of ink.

Once again, Jackson Finley adroitly transformed a literary theme into a compelling image:

www.jwfinley.com

Our bloody nature, it can now be argued in the context of modern biology, is ingrained because group-versus-group was a principle driving force that made us what we are.
—E. O. WILSON, THE SOCIAL CONQUEST OF EARTH

An eye for an eye only ends up making the whole world blind.
—MAHATMA GANDHI

Chapter 1

Kelly pretended to be serene, but I knew her too well. She was irritated that I was leaving the group, even though she was sleeping in another man's bed. Willy Hendricks, the Sultan, the spiritual leader, also smiled serenely as he pulled up to the bus stop, but in his case, I knew the satisfaction was genuine. After all, it was his bed.

I slid open the door of the beat-up old van and hauled my two bags out as Kelly and the Sultan came around to say goodbye. The people waiting at the bus stop shelter glanced curiously at Willy's bare legs beneath his short white sarong. He gave me a hug, placed his palm on my forehead, and intoned, "May you resonate with Klaatu." Kelly gave me a hug, and whispered in my ear, "He has the patience of Klaatu."

I knew what she was saying. One of the many exemplary qualities of Klaatu was supposed to be perseverance. She was bragging about Willy's stamina, something the whole Pod knew about indirectly—from moans and shouts in the night—and most of the women knew first hand.

Kelly had been something of a witch from the beginning, but she'd been a seductive dish, and I couldn't resist.

Willy the Sultan drove off with my girlfriend of three months, and I picked up my bags and faced the miscellany of waiting passengers, all suddenly studying their shoes or gazing off. I would be spending a lot of time with some of these people, but I had no clue which ones yet. Three buses later, only two remained, a thin young woman with a large bag at her feet, and a balding middle-aged man sitting on the bench reading a magazine. I would catch her watching me until I glanced over. She wasn't what most guys would call pretty, but there was an elusive animation about her that spoke of depth and humor.

She finally gave me a quick little grin and said, "I presume you're here from the ad?"

"Participants wanted for university study?" I quoted from memory. "Must be available full time, long term, and hold a valid passport? Room and board provided?"

"That's the one. And don't forget the $110 per week stipend."

"I didn't want to sound desperate."

Her grin widened. "But you are?' she suggested.

"No!" I said. Her smile welcomed honesty. "A little. Let's just say the opportunity is irresistibly convenient. How about you?"

Her brow scrunched a moment. She wanted to return the honesty. "No. Not desperate. But like, you, I guess—an irresistible opportunity." She gave me a warm smile and held out her hand. "Ellie," she said.

I took her small, warm hand and shook it. "Caleb," I replied. "Welcome to the experiment."

Her eyebrows went up. "You know that it's an experiment?"

"No. Not at all. I guess a study doesn't necessarily mean an experiment."

I suddenly felt self conscious, and rubbed my fingers unconsciously over my short, stubby hair. I hadn't been willing to shave my head like the other men of the Pod, but found that a quarter inch was almost worse. I wanted to explain to Ellie that this wasn't the normal me, that I would look a lot better when it grew back.

Instead, I quipped, "So, what's a nice girl like you doing in a place like this?" which made my face feel hotter.

Her grin told me she noticed. "I just finished up my undergrad degree here at the university—biology," she explained. "I got out of sync. Otherwise I would have graduated in the spring. I guess you could say that I'm experiencing a crisis of faith about my career path. I'm supposed to be taking some more pre-med classes. My father's a doctor, and my family has always assumed I'd follow in his footsteps. My boyfriend—actually, he sort of thinks he's my fiancée—is taking an intern position in Boston, and I'm supposed to follow him next fall and start med school there. I just need some time out to think about things. I thought this was as good a way as any."

"Why do you and your boyfriend disagree about being engaged?" I asked, then felt myself blushing even deeper.

Ellie chuckled. "I always thought it was a foolish risk when guys propose to their girlfriends in public. But I understand now why they do it, consciously or otherwise. Brad—my boyfriend—arranged to have his proposal broadcast to the world on the gigantic message board at a Padre's game. There I was, sitting with mustard on my cheek and beer dribbling down my chin, and all of a sudden the organ music bursts into some upbeat anthem, and there's my name and his proposal, and me—my face—live on half of the board, mustard, beer, and all."

"So you thought you had no choice," I said.

"Was I going to take another big bite of hotdog and shake my head no with cheeks bulging?"

"No, I guess not."

"Damn right, not. After the hoopla died down and everybody turned their attention back to the game, I told him we'd talk about it later. Later never seemed to arrive."

She eyed me. "Your turn. Want to explain who Klaatu is?"

"Ah, you overheard the Sultan's blessing."

"He's a sultan?"

"Only to the Pod members of the Planet X welcome party."

She waited.

"They're a bunch of pseudo-science nuts," I explained.

Her eyes grew wide. "You seemed to be part of it."

"Was. Past tense. And not really."

Her brow went up. "You're, like, an agent planted by the FBI?"

"No. An idiot planted by his sex drive. My girlfriend—ex-girlfriend—wanted to join. We came out from New Jersey to California a month ago. I thought I could get a job doing sailboat deliveries. I figured she'd get over this whole Planet X nonsense, like she'd done before. I didn't figure on Willy."

"Willy?"

"The Sultan."

"I see," she said, nodding. "Let me guess—he's handsome, but he's also extremely charismatic and completely convincing in his earnest, spiritual approach."

"You know him?" I asked, feigning shock.

She laughed. "I know his species. Some women are attracted to men like that as flies are to a dung pile. He represents the silverback alpha male of the troop."

The balding man looked up at this, but immediately dropped his eyes back to his magazine.

"Willy doesn't pound his chest and roar," I said, "but probably only because he hasn't thought of it."

My attention was drawn to feet pounding toward us. A young man, maybe college age, was tearing along the sidewalk, his thick black hair flopping across his face. A bulging backpack forced him to bend forward as he ran, and he also carried a duffel bag clutched to his chest. When he reached us, he gasped for air and tried to talk, but gave up and waited until he caught his breath. "Did I make it?" he finally asked no one in particular.

We glanced at each other.

"The university study. Isn't that why you're here?" he asked, looking at each of us in turn.

Ellie nodded and introduced herself. "And this is Caleb," she said, and I shook the young man's hand. His grin was infectious.

"Hi," he said. "I'm Rudy."

"And I suspect he's waiting as well," Ellie added, pointing at the balding man reading a magazine.

The man looked up from his magazine and said, "Sheath," and before anybody could extend a hand, he went back to reading.

We looked at each other and exchanged surreptitious shrugs.

"Somebody from the university is supposed to pick us up, right?" Rudy said.

"That's what I was told," I confirmed.

"Is that right?" Ellie asked. "I was simply told to come here. There was no mention of a ride."

I replayed the phone conversation I'd had with the university person. "No, you're right. I was just told to come here. I assumed it was to be picked up."

"It is a bus stop," Rudy pointed out. "A place where people get picked up."

"An understandable assumption," Ellie agreed, nodding. She seemed to genuinely want to eliminate any sense that missing the detail implied dullness.

"Guys," Rudy said, easing his pack down to the sidewalk and slumping onto the bench, "I gotta sit down before I fall down."

I liked his quick transition to casual familiarity.

There was plenty of room, so I sat down as well. Ellie leaned against the edge of the Plexiglas wall and folded her arms across her chest. "Looks like we'll be together for awhile," she said. "We might as well get comfortable." She told Rudy about her misguided fiancée and post-graduate hiatus, and I summarized my previous five years: two as a business major, two tooling around Florida and New Orleans, and finally an aborted year in the journalism department. I wrapped up by relating my exit from the Pod and failed chance to meet Klaatu, the prophesied emissary from Planet X.

"Wasn't Klaatu the alien in the movie *The Day The Earth Stood Still?*" Rudy asked.

"Amazing coincidence, eh?" I replied dryly.

Ellie nodded at Rudy. "Okay, your turn."

Rudy explained that he'd been attending the community college while working full time. He'd been doing okay—good grades, keeping his head above water—but he'd burned himself out. He'd lost perspective about what it was all worth. He needed a reset to regain his motivation. He told us that he loved tinkering with electronics, but that it was real work focusing on the theory.

Ellie gestured toward Sheath. "How about you?"

The balding man finally put his magazine down and looked at her. "I think the whole thing is disgraceful abuse."

The place where people get picked up was suddenly very quiet.

"Uh, why do you say that?" I asked Sheath.

"Do you know where they're taking you?" he asked me. His eyes were afire with passion.

"Well, no, but—"

"Do you know how long they'll want you?" he asked, looking at Ellie.

She shook her head slowly, reservedly.

"How about you?" he said to Rudy. "Do you have any clue what they want you for?"

Rudy smiled, as though he was keen for the game. "Maybe we like the uncertainty."

Sheath looked hard at him. "So, it's just a nice adventure?"

"Adventures aren't supposed to be nice," Ellie said.

Sheath glared at her, but I detected a glint of appreciation.

This middle-aged man who had been until now nearly invisible was suddenly a dominant force, and I instinctively wanted to push back.

"So, why are you here?" I asked.

The glare he gave me was not so appreciative. "I was curious. I was curious what kind of fools would answer such an ad."

My cheeks were hot, and I struggled to find words.

"I guess you've found us," Ellie said quietly.

Judo uses the attacker's own momentum—step aside and steer him to a fall of his own doing. It would have worked with any other man, but Sheath never stumbled. "I guess I have. Evolution has failed to weed out the simple fool." He folded his magazine, got up, and walked away.

I'd like to believe that I recognized the portent, but hindsight can never be objective.

Silence ruled the Plexiglas cage for awhile until conversation between the three of us slowly emerged from hiding. We discovered that Rudy was something of an inventor. He'd developed a proto-type for a device he thought could change the lives of much of the third world, and he'd brought it along. He dug it out of his pack and showed us. It was a simple idea, yet he had crafted it well. It was the size and shape of a hard cover book, and one side was completely composed of perfectly fitting blocks of solar cells, while the other side hosted an array of LEDs. The user simply lay the tablet in the sun, photo-cells upward during the day. At dusk, the device was retrieved, and provided workable light for a few hours. Rudy called it the Phial, after the light from the phial of Galadriel that Frodo used against Shelob, the giant, evil spider. He'd coated the entire device in thermoplastic polyurethane. It was completely waterproof, and nearly indestructible, with no moving parts, not even external knobs or switches. He showed us how he'd even built in a radio. It could be activated and tuned using any small piece of iron, as the electronic controls reacted magnetically through the polyurethane.

Ellie gently took the Phial from him and held it in both hands, admiring the smooth finish. "Rudy," she said, "I think you may be a genius."

I added my heartfelt agreement, but there was a tiny corner of that heart that was jealous. There was something about Ellie I found difficult to define. She didn't so much look at you when you spoke as into you, as though she was connecting at a deeper, nonverbal level. If your words were important enough to speak, then they were important enough to be given her complete attention. In return, since your words were being received with such care, you felt a responsibility to provide them proper deliberation before launching. Even bantering about trivial subjects was suddenly time well spent out of your allocated time on this Earth.

We talked about many things as bus passengers wandered in and departed in plumes of diesel fumes. Time passed quickly, and as I had nothing else to do but wait for a change of life, I would have been happy to spend the rest of the afternoon with my new friends, but eventually Ellie looked at her watch and said, "It's an hour past the pickup window. I guess it's not going to happen. Maybe tomorrow."

"I don't think I can lug all this stuff another day," Rudy said. "If nobody shows up today, I'm calling it quits."

At that very moment, a van was slowing and pulled over to the curb fifty feet away.

"What the …?" Rudy said.

I saw the reason for his consternation. The man who stepped out was Sheath.

Chapter 2

Sheath's manner had changed. Instead of dourly indifferent, he was upbeat, smiling and waving when he saw us. The three of us looked at each other, but nobody spoke. His clean, pressed slacks and trim, buttoned-up polo shirt spoke of easy affluence.

"Ready to go?" he asked as he walked up to us.

"Go where?" Ellie asked.

"To the university. For a briefing."

"About what?"

"You didn't need to know what when you answered the ad, nor when you came today, ready to go."

"What were you doing …?" Her voice trailed off.

"He was spying on us," I concluded.

She looked at Sheath for confirmation, but he waved it off, as though I was nitpicking. "Come on," he said, gesturing us along, "we have another pickup."

Rudy shrugged and picked up his pack and duffel bag. I grabbed my bags, but Sheath held up his hand. "Not you."

I blinked. "Huh?"

"Sorry," he said. "You won't be going."

"Why?"

"You're just not."

He'd sat and listened to our conversations. I tried to remember what I'd said. "Is it because I was part of a nut cult? If so, you have to believe me that I—"

"You're just not," he interrupted.

"It's a matter of motivation," Ellie said. "Isn't it?"

That was unfair—I felt very motivated.

Sheath gave her a slight grin. "We're not going to discuss that here. Now let's go—just the two of you."

Ellie gave her head a little shake. "It's because Caleb's desperate, isn't it?" she said, throwing me a quick glance of apology. "He needs this, but Rudy and I have a choice."

Sheath lifted his shoulders for a second.

"Well, if Caleb isn't going, then neither am I or Rudy."

Rudy looked surprised at this, but quickly nodded in agreement.

Sheath held out his hands. "It's your choice." He waited a second, then turned and walked away.

Rudy panicked, and made as if to follow, but Ellie frowned, and caught his arm. We stood, suspended in the tension of the moment. When he reached the van, Sheath turned to us. His grin had disappeared. But his face loosened and he waved us to follow.

"All three?" Ellie called.

He smiled sardonically and nodded.

We scrambled to gather our gear and nearly tripped over each other in our dash to get to the van.

ж ж ж

We made another pickup where Danny and Sheryl, husband and wife, joined us. Sheryl leaned in to whisper, "Do you know what this is all about?" We shook our heads in solemn unison.

Sheath drove off, and I noted again the marked change in his demeanor from earlier. Now he smiled and joked, calling out as he pulled away, "We're off to see the wizard!"

I had noticed that when he met Danny and Sheryl, he didn't introduce himself as Sheath. I asked Danny about this, but before he could respond, our driver called out the answer. "Burrows! Professor Burrows. Sheath was an alias."

Ellie and Rudy looked at me with surprise. "So, you were spying on us," I said.

He glanced at me in the mirror. "Let's say I was interviewing you incognito. None of you have anything to hide, do you?" He looked at us again, and from the back, I could see his grin widen. "I wouldn't think you'd want to set off on this venture with hidden baggage," he added.

"How can we know?" Ellie said. "We have no idea what it's all about."

"That's true," Burrows agreed. And that's all he would say.

Burrows hadn't wanted me along. Perhaps Ellie's argument made some sense—I was the only one actually desperate for the opportunity. I tried to rewind our conversations, though, the ones that Burrows heard, searching for something else that would have marked me as undesirable.

Maybe it was my crew cut. I looked a little like the kid playing the banjo in Deliverance.

ж ж ж

At the university, Burrows wound his way through the campus and parked in a small lot behind the theatre arts building, then escorted us around the corner and through a side door that let to a small lecture hall. There were perhaps a dozen others there milling about and talking, and I saw that tables had been set up on one side, heaped with folded piles of cloth.

A tall, slim, middle-aged woman walked onto the stage and clapped her hands briskly, calling for us to take seats. Her graying hair was tied back functionally, yet with professional precision. She introduced herself as professor Margaret Plath, department head of the psychology department. All business, she explained that we were volunteering to participate in a study program that she was heading. Details would follow once we signed the paperwork. She instructed us to stand one at a time and state our given name and age for the group. The first to stand was a frizzy-haired girl who started in with a mini-bio, but was immediately interrupted by Plath, who clapped sharply and reminded her that she was to give her first name and age only. Everything else about us and our lives was not relevant for what was to follow.

Rudy leaned over to whisper, "I guess we screwed up at the bus stop."

This elicited more brusque claps from Plath and a reprimand to please be quiet so that we could get on with it.

At this point, Burrows walked onto the stage. Plath introduced him as a member of the university's anthropology department, and said that he would be assisting her in the study. She explained that we wouldn't be under individual observation, rather, it was group dynamics that were important. She emphasized that this wasn't a test, and that there wasn't any right or wrong way to participate. We should view this as a little vacation getaway—just be ourselves.

"Much more than that," she said, "I can't really go into at this point. For obvious reasons, participants can't know too much about what is being studied."

"Other than that we're counting on you to be cooperative," Burrows added, smiling.

Plath gave him a hard look.

Rudy leaned over again. "If the rat knew it was in a maze," he whispered, "it might climb over the wall and run away."

Plath clapped once, sharply, and Rudy jerked back into place.

"I can't give you details," she went on, "but I can promise that what I do tell you will be the truth."

A man with long hair raised his hand and said, "That doesn't quite jive with a certain Mr. Sheath."

The three of us looked at him. Apparently we weren't the only ones.

"What do you mean?" Plath asked.

"I mean," the long-haired man replied, "how Mr. Burrows was pretending to be some guy named Sheath."

She shook her head. "I still don't understand."

"You don't know? He pretended to be a participant. He spied on us."

Plath glared at her colleague, who continued to smile warmly, as though we were talking about somebody else completely. "We'll talk about that offline," she said to him.

She turned back to the group. "Does everybody have their passports? Let's see them."

There was a lot of rummaging and shuffling, and a few minutes later, everybody was holding their little booklets in the air.

"Okay," she said, "you won't need them. You can hang onto yours if you like, but I would recommend passing them forward. I'll keep them in my office safe until we get back."

The long-haired man raised his hand again. "Then, why did we have to bring them?"

She shook her head and flicked her hand in dismissal. "It's administrative. I'll explain later—"

"It's an easy way to weed out indigents," Burrows explained, talking over Plath.

The psychology department head glared at Burrows. "Can I talk to you?" she demanded through tight lips, and waved him away off the stage to the right. We sat quietly as words echoed and tumbled over each other somewhere in the depths of the theatre wings. I couldn't make out what was said, but the tone was angry.

A few minutes later they returned, and Plath handed out packets of paper. She said nothing. Burrows was still smiling, again as though Plath's anger had been directed at someone else. I took mine, and saw that each consisted of half a dozen sheets stapled together.

"As you can see," Plath began, "the lawyers have a hand in nearly everything. These are waivers and agreements. In a nutshell, you will be agreeing to hold the university harmless, no matter what happens. I want to direct your attention specifically to page four, near the bottom. This paragraph directs that all details about this study will be kept in strictest secrecy. At some point in the future, this gag-provision will be lifted, but until then, mum's the word. Do you understand? Your signature means that you agree."

She waited until we were all bobbing our heads agreeably.

"Now, I have to tell you that the living conditions are going to be … well, Spartan. Some of you will probably find them uncomfortable. Some may find the activities more than they bargained for. Now's the time to leave if you don't want to chance it."

The long-haired man raised his hand as he continued to read his packet. "What about this section covering civil damages?" he asked, looking up. He looked down again. "It says here that we could be held liable for damages if we divulge protected information."

She waved it off. "More legalese. Don't worry about it. As I understand it, the university would have to show monetary damages, and I don't see how that could be possible."

"I wouldn't take it too lightly," Burrows added, his smile gone now. "If you agree to participate, you're in one hundred percent—lock, stock, and barrel. You could find yourself in real trouble if you stray."

Plath was watching him with clenched jaws. I was expecting her to drag him off-stage again, but the tension was broken by a young woman with cornrows. "How long will it last?"

Plath stared at Burrows a moment longer, seeming to decide whether to throw a punch, before she finally turned to the girl. "I can't tell you exactly. It depends on how things proceed. I am confident that it will be more than two weeks, but most likely not a full month." She clapped her hands again, as though gathering the attention of a pack of circus dogs. "Okay, study the agreement, sign it, and put it on the table. If you want to call your family one last time, now's your last chance."

Burrows nodded. "That's right—no cell service on Laguna Mountain. And there's no turning back after that!"

Plath seemed to count to ten. "We're not taking them hostage, James."

Burrows just smiled amiably.

Chapter 3

I'd given up my cell phone as something seditious when I'd joined the Pod, so I stood and watched as everybody else milled aimlessly about talking on theirs for five minutes until Plath clapped again for the pack to heel.

"Okay," she instructed, "you are not going to need the clothes you packed. We're providing clothing for you. On the tables along the wall you'll find a plastic bin with your name on the front. You will remove from your bags whatever personal effects you will need—grooming supplies, medicine, books, and so forth. Please note that access to electricity will be very limited, so don't bother to bring hair dryers or irons. No need for phones or ipads, either. Transfer these personal items into the duffel bag that has your name—you'll find those behind the bin. In the duffel bag, you'll find clothes you'll be wearing for the duration of the study. Place the clothes that you brought as well as your cell phones in your bin. The bins will be kept safe until you return."

She looked around at us. "Any questions?"

A few hands went up, but most people headed for the tables, lugging the bags they had so carefully packed that would mostly not be needed. Rudy stood looking down at his bulging pack and bag. He saw me watching. "I'll need two bins for all this stuff."

I rummaged through my bag and extracted my toothbrush, deodorant, three books, and five dark chocolate bars. I put all of these in the duffel bag, and gazed one last time at the electric razor and travel clock/radio. I hadn't packed a hair brush. I didn't expect to be gone long enough to need it.

Plath's roundup clap filled the room. "Okay," she called, "time to go. This will be your last bathroom break for a couple of hours, so take advantage. Everybody on the bus in five minutes. If you're not on, you don't go. Chop-chop!"

A harried-looking middle-aged man appeared and grabbed an armload of duffel bags, which he carried out the door. I motioned to Ellie and Rudy, and we each grabbed a load and followed him to where he was loading them into the luggage compartment of the university bus. I noticed that Plath looked at us with a raised eyebrow. I wondered if we were doing something wrong, breaking some unspoken rule. She was a psychologist, and this was a study. I remembered David Steinberg's old bit where he played a psychiatrist who steered his patients to a particular chair and then shouted, "Psychopath!"

Five minutes later the harried man was at the wheel and the bus pulled off. We wound our way onto Interstate 8 heading east.

Ellie and Rudy sat together, and I sat immediately behind them, leaning forward to be part of the conversation. The bus had a festive feel. People were laughing and talking. There's a certain freedom in putting your life in somebody else's hands. It was like taking off on a school-sponsored trip, which, I noted, it was.

"Blue's not my best color," Ellie said.

"Blue?" Rudy asked. "Mine were green. What about you, Cal?"

"You mean the prison uniforms? Mine are blue."

Rudy looked crestfallen.

"Why the long face?" Ellie asked.

"It probably means I'm in a different group."

"Not necessarily," she said. "The color of the clothes doesn't have to mean that—"

"It does," the man with the long hair said. He was in the seat in front of Ellie and Rudy, and he turned around. He was the one who had called Burrows out on his Sheath spying. "There's just two colors, and they're divided evenly."

"How do you know?" Ellie asked.

He had an angular face and faint acne scars. "I observed." His eyes carefully studied us, and I saw that he would have.

Ellie shrugged. "So, maybe they didn't have enough of one color."

The long-haired man shook his head. "Not if Burrows is part of it."

"What do you know about Burrows?" I asked.

He turned his searching eyes on me, and I had the urge to sit up straight and make sure there was no spinach caught between my teeth. "What I was able to learn in ten minutes before they took our phones away. He comes from old Boston money. Apparently headed west when he butted heads at Harvard—"

"Harvard?"

"He was a protégée of E. O. Wilson, but there was a falling out. I wasn't able to learn the details."

"E. O. Wilson," I repeated. The name was familiar.

"Sociobiology," Ellie explained.

Right. She'd just finished her undergraduate degree in biology.

"Yeah, apparently," the man agreed. "You're familiar with it? Somehow societies are influenced by our genes?"

"The 'socio' here refers more specifically to social behavior of people—all animals, really. The idea is that everything else about us—the organization of our bodies, the operation of our immune systems, our instincts—meaning our emotions—all of this is defined by our genes, molded over time by natural selection. So, why do we expect our behavior to be any different?"

His eyes followed her words like a cat stalking a mouse. "But societies are just human behavior averaged over large numbers," he said.

Ellie smiled. "Indeed. Sociobiology extends to the structure of societies, but only as a second order effect. Do you have a background in biology?"

He shook his head, but didn't elaborate. "Society is the manifestation of human behavior operating as an amalgamation within groups."

"You're kidding," she accused. When he continued looking at her, she added, "About not having a background in biology, I mean."

He shook his head again. They were brusque little wags, the minimum to halt your flawed line of reasoning. "It's a quote from Burrows."

"What else did you learn?" she asked.

He thought a moment. "Burrows published papers on group theory."

"Mathematics?"

The abrupt head-shake again. "People in groups—that kind of group theory."

Ellie nodded slowly. "The idea that people have some amount of predictable behavior as part of groups didn't originate with him."

"Isaac Asimov," I said.

Everybody looked at me.

"The Foundation Trilogy. You know, the Second Foundation. Psychohistory."

"Science fiction," Ellie confirmed.

"Yeah. But he came up with this around, like, WWII."

"Right," Ellie agreed hiding a little grin, and then turned back to the long-haired man. "So, what about it? Did his papers propose specifics about groups?"

The man's eyebrows contracted in thought. "I didn't catch it. The jargon was gobbledegook." He shrugged. "Something about dominance and cooperation operating in counterbalance." He directed a little head shake at himself. "I didn't really get it."

We learned that the man's name was Albert—not Al, and not Bert, Albert. That's about all we learned, other than that his mother had been a maid, and his father had come across the southern border illegally thirty years before. What he himself had been doing to support himself and why he'd signed up for this study was left locked behind the little perfunctory head shakes.

"What about Plath?" Ellie asked. "Did you look her up as well?"

"No. Burrows is the one to watch."

"But Plath is running the show. She was reprimanding him."

"She thinks she's running the show. Burrows obviously does whatever he wants."

The frizzy-haired girl was watching us from across the aisle. "James has a right to," she broke in.

Albert turned his exploring gaze on her, and she leaned back a little, as though he might take a swing.

"He's basically funding the whole project," she said, defensively.

"How would you know that?" Albert asked.

Her frizzy head lifted, vindication was at hand. "Our families are friends."

"You know him personally?" Albert asked.

"Not me specifically. Of course not. Our families."

"I don't get it."

"Our *families*," she repeated. "My uncle belongs to the same club as Burrows."

They watched each other a moment. "That's it?" Albert finally said. "They go to the same American Legion?"

Frizzy Head's eyes went wide with shock, then narrowed. "Very funny. Ha, ha."

"I'm not trying to be funny," Albert replied, and I wondered if he ever was.

Her smug grin was a winning hand about to be laid down. "Perhaps you've heard of the Somerset Club," she said.

"Haven't," he replied with the brusque head-shake.

His curt reply seemed to let some of the air out of her inflated head. "It's only about the most exclusive club in Boston—in all of America! You have to be invited to join."

"You can't go fishing with *my* uncle unless he invites you." Albert said. "Maybe we can have a competition to see who has the most exclusive family."

Her nose tilted up. "Sour grapes."

He nodded. "I'd expect that expensive grapes eaten for the sole reason that they're expensive must be sour."

She pursed her lips and turned away, muttering something about the decay of American values.

Albert looked at me, and—completely out of the character that I'd been building in my mind—winked. It wasn't a twitch, but a genuine, sharing a little secret wink. It lasted one second, and was gone. I wasn't sure if I'd imagined it.

He looked down at something in his lap, and I thought he was done with us, but then he held up some papers and pointed at one line buried deep in one of the longer paragraphs. "I'll bet you didn't notice this," he said.

I saw that he had one of the packets we had all signed. "You didn't hand yours in?" I asked.

"This was an extra."

I refrained from pointing out that Burrows had specifically walked around gathering extra copies.

"'Signee agrees to follow directives as provided by administrative staff,'" he read. "'Since failure to do so could jeopardize the fundamental viability of the program and the safety of other participants, signee agrees that under such circumstances, the staff may take whatever means may be deemed appropriate to impose cooperation.'"

Albert looked at us, but nobody spoke. Frizzy Hair stared out the window, snorting little protests from her side of the aisle.

"I gotta learn to read these things before I sign," Rudy finally declared. "That sounds like we're enlisting in boot camp."

"They always tell you to read it carefully, but then don't give you time," I added.

"Would it have made a difference?" Ellie asked.

I chuckled. "No, I guess not. I wouldn't have liked it, but I would have signed anyway."

"It might have made a difference," Albert said. "If we had raised the point, they would have had to address what they meant by 'whatever means deemed appropriate' to the group. Since we wouldn't have signed yet, the answer would have established specific bounds and become de facto part of the agreement."

Silence again.

"You're a lawyer?" Rudy asked.

Albert snorted. "The rules of law are mostly logic. The *practice* of law is mealy-mouthed CYA, manipulation, and side-stepping the truth."

"Hey!" Rudy exclaimed looking out the window. "What the …?"

I saw. We were exiting Route 8 for Route 15 north.

"Can you get to Laguna Mountain from the 15?" Ellie asked, forehead furrowed. "Maybe through Julian and the Cuyamaca

Mountains," she said, answering her own question. "But that doesn't make sense. It's, like, twice as far."

"Maybe there's a traffic problem on the 8," Rudy offered. "Maybe a wildfire."

"They never said we were going to Laguna Mountain," Albert reminded us, searching our eyes in turn.

"Sure they did," I protested. "Burrows said that there's no cell reception … ah, I see. Shit. He didn't actually say we were going there. Do you really think he was misleading us?"

"What did we all do right after he said that?"

I thought about it. "Oh, geez! Everybody made their last phone calls. Our families think we're off to Laguna Mountain."

"Where're we really going?" Rudy wondered.

"Good question," Albert agreed, turning his gaze to Frizzy Hair.

She noticed him. "Don't be so paranoid," she rebuked. "You're in good hands with Doctor Burrows."

"So, we're in Burrows' hands, not Plath's?"

"Oh, you know what I mean."

"Do *you*?"

Her look was defiant, but also hesitant.

"The meaning we're ultimately going to care about," he went on, "is 'whatever means may be deemed appropriate.'"

"Oh, pooh," she shot back. Her tone was dismissive, but her brow contracted in consternation.

Albert watched her a while before returning to his study of the packet.

"Maybe we're going to Disneyland," Rudy suggested.

Nobody carried the joke further. We just watched the flat expanse of Miramar Air base flashing by.

Chapter 4

Rumors coursed up and down the bus about the destination. I had a good guess when we left Route 15 at Temecula and headed east, and then north on 371 through Anza. I pointed to the line of peaks filling the horizon ahead of us. "The San Jacinto Mountains?" Ellie asked.

As the highway carried us up out of the desert flats, trees began to appear, scattered pines at first, growing more dense with maple, oak, and manzanita added to the mix as we passed Lake Hemet. When we finally turned off on to a winding mountain highway, everybody agreed that our destination had to be the little alpine town of Idyllwild. Ten minutes later we arrived—and passed on through.

"This doesn't make any sense," Ellie said, "The highway doesn't go anywhere past this point."

"It has to go *somewhere*," Rudy objected.

"I mean, it just eventually goes back down out of the mountains. About twenty miles from here it comes down to Banning—in the pass that connects LA with Palm Springs."

"Palm Springs!" Rudy said. "Yeah! I could do Palm Springs."

"No! It doesn't make *sense*! There's easier ways to get there. This would be like going upstairs, crawling out a window, and climbing down the drainpipe to get to your car."

Rudy shrugged. "Maybe it's just to throw us off track."

"What track? We're all on the bus together. We have no cell phones."

Albert spoke up without turning around. "Plath warned that the conditions were going to be rough," he reminded us.

"'Spartan' was the word she used," Ellie agreed. "But they can't just dump us somewhere in the wilderness," she protested.

Albert didn't respond. There was nothing to add.

Minutes later, the bus slowed and turned laboriously onto a dirt road that climbed through the rocky terrain on switchbacks. We bounced around in our seats like ice cubes in a cocktail shaker. After a while I developed a headache from all the jostling.

"Where in God's name are they *taking* us?" Ellie yelled, her voice jerking up and down with each bone-bouncing bump.

"Looks like they're going to dump us in the wilderness after all," I said, sounding drunk as I clung to the seat back.

"We're going to need oxygen masks soon. I feel nauseous."

The Pod had gone on a hiking trip in these mountains—a chance to let the spirit of Klaatu feel the unadulterated breath of Earth—and I knew that Idyllwild was at five thousand feet. We'd climbed maybe another two thousand since then. "I don't think altitude sickness starts until at least ten thousand feet," I said. "We've got a ways to go."

"I wasn't thinking about altitude sickness, my inner ear is suffering from shell shock."

Just then the bus jerked to a halt. The world continued to bounce around, but I knew the motion was just in my head.

"Oh, no!" Ellie cried, and I saw what she was looking at. Ahead of us the road seemed to go vertical. We'd already negotiated some inclines that I wouldn't have thought possible in a bus, but this would take a miracle.

The bus engine went silent. Dust from the road floated up around the windows to be caught and carried away in the breeze. The harried university staffer cum bus driver stood up and grabbed the metal post next to his seat, obviously considerably shaken himself. He opened the door, called out, "Everybody off!" and stepped out.

The bus erupted with seventeen voices all jabbering at once. We filed out into the dry, crisp air, and it seemed as though a veil had been lifted between the Earth and sun. Shadows were delineated by sharp divisions between near blackness and the eye-squinting blaze of sunlight. Old-growth pines surrounded us, continuing up the mountain side in an unbroken green sea as far as could be seen. Majestic silence reigned, broken only by the gravelly caw of a raven, echoing among the valleys and rock faces.

"Holy shit!" Rudy exclaimed, gazing around.

"You've never been to the San Jacintos?" Ellie asked.

He shook his head, peering wonderingly at the peaks thrusting still higher above us.

"Come on!" called the harried staffer as he grabbed duffel bags from the guts of the bus and tossed them onto the pine needles. "Find yours and then step aside."

I'd just dragged mine next to Ellie and Rudy's when we all turned at the sound of another engine whining in a low-gear from below. A minute later dust billowed up over the crest of the road, and a Jeep Wrangler emerged, so dust-coated it looked like it had materialized from the coalescing particles. It jerked to a halt, and Plath and Burrows got out, both grinning as though, like Rudy, they'd never been to the most northern, and highest, of the Peninsular Ranges.

The harried staffer, who we now learned was named, appropriately enough, Harry, seemed relieved. He hurried down and climbed into the driver's side of the Jeep. Plath and Burrows disappeared into the pines along a path that I hadn't noticed. Plath came back and waved to us. "Come along!"

We hefted our bags, fell haphazardly into single file, and moments later were surrounded by soft darkness, broken by dappled, trembling spots of sunlight dancing on the needle-carpeted forest floor. The path angled up, sloping away from the road, made a switchback turn, and continued up. The sound of the Jeep attacking the last steep climb broke the peace of the mountain. In five minutes, we'd climbed another hundred feet in altitude and met the road again just as we topped a ridge and came to a level plateau. We learned that this four-acre stand of tall pines was called Camp Valley, but it was more like a ledge, where, after a thousand foot plunge from the peak, the mountain paused for a moment before falling away another thousand-feet beneath us. The name harked back to a time generations before when this had been a Boy Scout camp, before Boy Scouts began camping in local parks.

Much of the camp was hidden among the trees, but off to the right I could see a small platoon of colorful one-man tents scattered among the tree trunks like a little forest-elf festival. To the left, at the other edge of the plateau was another, larger tent, gray with a peaked roof, like the company-command army tents I'd seen in old WWI pictures.

In the center of the camp, a hundred feet in front of us, were two tiny cabins. Each was maybe twelve feet by twelve feet and looked brand-new—cedar walls, shingled roofs, and small windows. They even sported doll-house-sized porches.

Plath approached from the cabins. "Welcome! You have arrived! The sun will set in an hour, and it gets cold almost immediately, so you'll want to get settled and ready as quickly as you can. I have some unfortunate news, however. You will be staying in cozy cabins, like these," she said, gesturing towards the two lone examples. "Regrettably, they weren't ready in time. But, as they say, when handed a lemon, make lemonade! The cabins are all here— they're pre-fabricated, and just need to be assembled. This will give you a chance to get acclimated and acquainted with each other."

Rudy leaned towards Ellie and me and whispered, "It's a slave labor camp!"

"The manufacturer claims that a team of four skilled workers can assemble one in a single day," Plath explained. "Since presumably none of you are carpenters, it may take twice that long. Once completed, each cabin will house three of you. That makes for rather tight quarters, but surrounded by all that the mountain has to offer, I doubt you'll be spending much time indoors anyway."

I thought that no matter how much splendid nature surrounded you, three people squeezed into what amounted to a child's bedroom was going to be challenging.

What about showers?

And toilets?

And television?

Plath was explaining the temporary arrangements. "We only had one large tent. So half of you will be staying there, and that will be all of you with green clothes. Those of you with the blue clothes will have your own, individual tents off there," she said, pointing at the elf festival.

Rudy looked totally dejected now. "Great. Communal boot camp with a bunch of strangers. I'm going to get a wedgie for sure."

"It's only temporary," Ellie said. "Maybe the three of us can arrange to share a cabin."

I liked that idea. I liked it a lot.

Ellie and I, following six others, headed off for tent city. We talked about who might have already claimed the first two cabins, but quickly concluded that Plath and Burrows obviously had one each. With rank comes privilege, and we didn't rank. Ellie wondered what we were going to do about food, and I had a moment's panic that maybe I was supposed to bring my own. When we arrived, we found that there was only one tent left unclaimed, and it was the smallest.

"There's only seven tents!" I exclaimed indignantly. "What the hell!"

"You take it," Ellie said, glancing around for some alternative.

"Don't be silly," I replied. "You'll obviously get the tent, but why aren't there enough?"

"Why do I automatically get it? Because I'm a girl?"

A loaded question. "No," I scoffed, searching for a suitable lie.

I had it. "Because Pod disciples of Planet X sleep on the floor to build character. I'm used to it."

"That's all the more reason you should have the tent. You've earned it."

"Oh, fiddle. We'll still be here arguing about it when the sun goes down. I'm going to go talk to Plath—this is unacceptable."

"You going to demand your money back?" she called as I stalked away.

I came up short, surprised to find the psychology professor standing not far away, watching us. I stomped over. "There's not enough tents!" I said.

"I see," she responded.

"Well, what are you going to do about it?"

"What makes you think there's anything I can do?"

"It's your game."

"Is that why you came? As a game?"

"No. It's an expression—you know that. You can't just abandon us out here in the woods!"

"I'm not abandoning you. I'm right here."

This was going nowhere. She was talking like a ... like a psychologist. "You know the answer," I accused.

"I do?"

"I think you do, but you want me to figure it out for myself."

"That would be convenient."

"So you do know the answer."

"I didn't say that. Look, what's the problem? I mean fundamentally?"

"The problem is that there's not enough tents!"

"Yes. I agree. There's not enough tents if each person claims for themselves just what they found."

I looked at her. She was obviously handing me the answer. I just wasn't getting it.

"What exactly is a tent?" she asked patiently.

"Now we're exploring philosophy?"

She just looked at me, waiting.

"A tent is something that provides protection from wind, rain, and bugs," I said.

"It doesn't have to be something you take out of a nice box that you bought, though, does it?"

"Of course not."

I turned around and gazed across the red, blue, and yellow festival. No two tents were the same. Some were a simple traditional triangle with a zippered flap for a door, while a few were modern domes, supported by external metal tubing. One consisted of a complex triple dome structure with tubing support. Of the six tents, two included a rain fly—a separate waterproof cover strung over the main tent. The triple-dome mansion also sported an awning above the entrance.

I guessed what she was getting at. "Right," I said, and headed back. "Hey, guys," I called. Heads emerged from the tent openings.

"We're short a tent. But I think I can piece one together if I could use your rain flies and maybe that awning over there."

A squat, curly-haired woman immediately began removing her rain fly, and the boy in the other tent—he barely looked eighteen—asked if I thought it would rain. I didn't know, but he began taking his down anyway.

The occupant of the mansion tent emerged as well. He was a man I'd noticed in the initiation meeting—on the short side, but handsome and solid, all muscle—with well trimmed hair and an easy, if slightly patronizing, smile. The words Iron Man came to mind. I wasn't surprised that he'd managed to claim the primo lodging.

Iron Man smiled at me, but made no move towards his awning. Instead, he held up his hand to the other two. "Hold it." He turned to me. "Late bird misses the last worm, eh?"

He said this as though commiserating with me. It might have seemed empathetic, except that *he* had made himself the obstacle.

"We're short one tent," I pointed out. "*Somebody* had to be the last one."

"Right," he said, as though I had supported his point.

"I just need the two rain flies and—"

"Heads-up! Blue team!" he called to the group, cutting me off. "We've got a late comer here!"

Heads popped out of the rest of the tents like gophers.

"I'm not exactly late, and if I could just get—"

"We need to pull together to drag his butt out of the fire!" Iron Man announced, stepping out into the center of the gathering circle. He stood with his hands on his hips, surveying the troops. "Unless anybody has something else not obvious, we'll use these two rain flies and my awning. It's simply a question of looking out for every member of the group, no matter how capable."

I felt my face getting hot. I'd met his type before, and avoided them when possible. Forget Iron Man, I now bestowed the label Passive Bully. I was about to protest, when there was a touch on my arm. It was Ellie, and she rolled her eyes and shook her head.

I stood by, seething, as Jeremy—I'd gathered that was his name—directed the construction of my jury-rigged tent. They used his awning for the flooring, and overlapped the rain flies to create the main tent. Twenty minutes later, he held out his hand to demonstrate the gift that the group was presenting to me. I struggled to contain my annoyance. Anything but gratitude would have played into his hand, since at this point, he'd convinced the group that they had indeed saved my butt.

I glanced off towards the little cabins. Plath had been watching the tent raising unfold, but she was now gone. There was no way she could have orchestrated that—all the same, I imagined the tree trunks glowing in the setting sun to be a maze, and I a mouse.

Chapter 5

Burrows called us to dinner, but told us to first change into our "project clothes." Changing in a tent that barely had enough room to sit up was a challenge. On top of that, something was painfully poking my tailbone. I reached under the awning that formed my floor, and dug out the irritant. It was a gun! It didn't weigh nearly enough, however, and I saw that it was in fact just a plastic toy. I wondered what Boy Scout merit badge would have required that.

I finally crawled out and stood up, only to find that the medium that I had been sized for meant that the legs were too short and the sleeves too long. I knew what Soviet-era Russians felt like after coming home from the state-run "store."

At least they were blue.

Ellie was waiting for me, and though her uniform didn't fit any better, the package inside was cuter. I started off towards the cabins, but she told me that we were supposed to take along our street clothes.

"Why?" I said. "You think it'll be more difficult to escape without them?"

"Maybe simply for safe-keeping?" she suggested.

I collected my clothes and we finally started off, only to be called to a halt by Jeremy. He had the other five blues gathered around him, and he motioned us over. "What's up?" I asked when we reached them.

"We'll go together as a group," he replied and started off.

Any other time, I would have let it go, but the last half hour had been one sour pickle after another. "Who made you leader?" I called.

The other five blues who had begun to fall in behind him turned in surprise at my unexpected—even rude—challenge. Jeremy turned, wearing his patronizing smile. "Nobody," he replied congenially. "Would you like to be the leader of our group?"

"No! We don't need a leader! This isn't a Boy Scout troop!"

He contemplated this, never losing his smile, and nodded agreement. "You're right," then waved his hand for everybody to follow him. The leader.

"Don't let him get your goat," Ellie said softly beside me. "That's exactly what he wants."

I took a deep breath and nodded. That she sympathized with me, that she knew what bothered me about him, allowed me to believe that it was indeed he who was the jerk, not I.

Ellie and I brought up the rear when we reached the meal tent. We hadn't seen it when we had arrived, as it stood at the very back of the plateau, a hundred yards beyond Plath and Burrows' cabins. There were no tables. It was just a camp kitchen where participants came to collect their food. Plath was holding court, explaining the eating rules. The light was fading as the sun fell behind the ridge to the west, and she wasn't wasting time on us stragglers. "... so this evening will be just cold sandwiches."

The boy who'd donated his rain fly explained softly, "Normally the evening meal will be hot."

"The project budget didn't accommodate the cook we'd planned on," Plath went on, "so the hot meals—breakfast and dinner—will be prepared by you, the participants. We'll alternate days between green and blue—green will go first tomorrow. Once we get the cabins built, we can develop structured kitchen duty schedules, but for now, you can work out among yourselves how to manage it. Okay, it's going to get chilly quickly now. If you haven't found them already, there's a fleece jacket and stocking cap in each of your duffel bags. Any questions?"

"Yeah," a green shouted. "Why the uniforms? They suck!"

As Plath went on to explain that the uniforms were part of the program, and that there were many things she couldn't divulge, a quiet voice from behind us said, "I told you—it's a slave labor camp."

It was Rudy. I was glad to see him.

"How's it going in green-land?" I asked.

"Albert's organized the tent."

"What do you mean?"

"Men on one side, women on the other, a tarp hung down the middle."

"Sounds logical."

"Not if you want to see women changing."

Ellie gave him a playful shove.

He wrapped his arms around his torso, tucking his hands in his armpits. "It's damn cold! See you later." He took one of the sandwiches Harry was handing out from a large cooler, and trotted off towards green-land.

Ellie and I took sandwiches—turkey with mustard—and bottles of water, and headed back to blueville. It *was* getting chilly, damn cold, in fact. My hands were shaking as I took bites. Waves of shivers washed through me. The air seemed to go from pleasantly mild to arctic within minutes after the sun went down.

I finished the sandwich, said goodnight through chattering teeth, and crawled into my charity tent. I pulled out stacks of folded uniforms from the duffel bag until I found the jacket and hat. Even with these, I was still cold, so I took off the jacket, yanked on two more layers of uniform, then replaced the jacket and hat.

Something plopped on the ground just outside the opening. I stuck my head out and saw a cloth bag lying there. The ever-busy Harry was walking around, tossing identical bags in front of the other tents. I dragged the offering inside and found, glory of glories, a sleeping bag—from the feel, a good one. If ever there was evidence that a God existed who interacted in our personal lives, I decided that this was it.

About to crawl into the bag and curl into a tight, warm ball, I heard Rudy outside again. I was torn. But then I heard Ellie laugh, and I knew I had to go out with them. I liked Rudy, and I wanted Ellie to like him as well—I just didn't want her to like him more than me.

When Rudy saw me, he held out his arms and asked, "What do you think?"

In the fading light, I wasn't sure what he was talking about. "Uh, your clothes fit as badly as mine?"

He glanced down, looking a bit distraught, then shrugged. "What else?"

"Here's a hint," Ellie said. "They're not green."

They weren't green. They were blue. "Oh! Yeah!" I said. "What happened? Albert kick you out of the commune for peeking at the women?"

"I didn't give him the chance—I traded places."

"With who?" I said.

"With whom," Ellie corrected.

"Thanks, mom." I turned back to Rudy. "So whom's clothes do you have?"

Ellie rolled her eyes.

"Jack. He was in that tent there," Rudy said, pointing at one of the more affluent domes. "He said he likes having other people around, but I think he's afraid of mountain lions."

"Mountain lions?" Ellie's voice rose to a squeak.

"Don't worry," I assured. "They're more afraid of you—"

"Than I am of them? I doubt that very much."

"I thought you'd been to the mountains before?"

"Mountain lions don't smash through car windows."

"You've never been camping?"

"Look, let's put this to bed—I'm not an outdoors, woodsy kinda girl, okay? I've never slept outside, other than my friend's yard when we got really drunk. And even then, when I woke up in the middle of the night, I crawled into my car."

"Don't worry," Rudy said. "I'll take care of you."

"What are you talking about?" I said. "You've never been in the mountains either. I'll take care of you both."

"My heroes," Ellie crooned, holding her arms out to both of us. "So, you guys will run out and fight the mountain lion when it comes?"

"Absolutely," I said.

"You bet," Rudy said.

She looked at us. "You guys are lying, aren't you?"

"It's like promising to run out and catch the meteor when it falls into the camp," I said. "I can't take any more of this cold—my teeth are getting frostbite. I'll see you two in the morning," I chattered, and crawled into my tent. I felt a stab of pain in my butt. It was the damn toy gun. "Here!" I said, tossing it out through the flaps. "Maybe the lion will think it's real."

I lay in my sleeping bag listening to Ellie and Rudy talking and laughing, and thought that in the interest of protecting my claim, I should go out and join them.

Then I fell asleep.

ж ж ж

I awoke the next morning to the sound of heated arguing. I tried to crawl deeper into my sleeping bag. Although the sun had risen, it wasn't high enough to deliver any warmth through the maze of tree trunks. It was Plath. And Burrows. They were arguing.

This was too juicy to miss, so I wiggled out of the bag and found my shoes. One advantage to sleeping outside in the cold is that you're already dressed when you get out of bed. Ellie was up, sitting on the ground pretending to tie a shoe that was already tied. Plath and Burrows stood fifty feet away, and Rudy slouched nearby looking embarrassed.

"The whole point was that the selection was random," Plath said. "You can't allow adjustments. Co-inclined behaviors will clump."

"Oh, now," Burrows said in a reasonable tone, "a certain amount of fluidity won't hurt. Besides, this tends to remove cross-group bonds."

Plath glanced at Ellie and me, and took Burrows elbow to lead him a little distance away. I couldn't make out the words until Plath began shouting. "I don't give a damn about the funding!" she yelled. "I am directing this project, whether you like it or not!"

Burrows remained cool, and I couldn't hear his reply. It was his turn to take her elbow, and he led her back towards their cabins.

Rudy looked at us, shrugged, and came over.

"Looks like you got busted," I said.

He made a sour face and nodded towards the other tents in our festival. He squatted down next to us. "Dana snitched on me. What a bitch."

"Who's Dana?"

"She was the snob who sat across from us on the bus. You remember." Rudy waved his hands as though imitating a little girl. "My uncle's in the Somerset Club. So *there*!" he sang in a little girl's voice.

"Frizzy hair," I said.

"Frizzy hair growing from a frizzy brain."

"Now, now," Ellie said. "You don't know the circumstances."

"The circumstances are that they're going to make me go back to the Gulag tent."

"Oh, it can't be that bad."

"Altitude makes you fart more. There's not a lot of air in that tent."

"Rudy!"

"Well, it's true."

We all jumped at the sound of a blaring, raucous air horn—the kind boaters and exuberant sports fans use.

"What's that about?" Ellie wondered.

It came from the back of the camp. "Maybe it's a call for us to come."

"Maybe it's breakfast," Rudy said hopefully.

Other participants began streaming towards the back of the camp, so we joined the migration. I realized how hungry I was when I smelled the beautiful aroma of pancakes and sausage. I nearly broke into a trot.

The kitchen tent was complete chaos. The smell was exciting everybody's stomachs, and we jostled to be closer. Despite Albert's directions, barked in frustration, his three green workers behind the counter were literally tripping over each other's feet. The camp kitchen was outfitted with three separate two-burner propane stoves, and each worker had their own stove. This meant that they were bumping elbows, spilling batter, and even dropping sausages.

To be fair to Albert, we, the excited stomachs, didn't give him a chance to iron out the process, to convince his charges to work assembly-line style. We paid the price with either cold or blackened meat, and either runny or blackened pancakes. The fake maple syrup was fine, though, so we used that to smother the defects. We found various rocks to sit on while we ate, and watched as Plath, who had been standing off to the side watching the whole fiasco, stepped out and clapped her hands to get the pack's attention.

"When you're finished, you'll take your plate and utensils over to the basin and wash them. Hang on to them—they will be yours from now on. There are no replacements."

She gazed around at us, seeming to do a mental count. "This morning you begin building your cabins. You'll find two kits already unpacked—one for each group. The foundations have been poured, so all you have to do is assemble them. The instructions are with the kits, as well as a set of tools for each group. Lunch is at noon, and the dinner horn will call you for the evening meal."

She paused. "Blues, don't forget that tomorrow is your turn for kitchen duty. The metal lockers contain the food—keep them locked when you're not here! There are no bears in the San Jacintos, but raccoons are persistent and wily. The ice will last only another day or two, so I would suggest you fill up on the fresh meat while you can."

That was it. She started to walk away. The sudden conclusion of her abbreviated instructions caught us by surprise, but one man raised his hand and yelled loudly, "Yo!"

She stopped and turned, eyebrows raised at the angry tone. It was the same green who had told her the night before that the uniforms sucked. "What about showers?"

"Next to the kitchen wash basin is a spring. You'll find a crate of soap and a bucket next to it."

She started away again.

"That's *it*? A bucket! What the hell is this? A concentration camp?"

She turned back and studied him. "You were warned ... Ralph, right? You were told that you might find the conditions difficult."

"This isn't difficult—this is inhumane!" He waved his hands around, like he was swatting at invisible bees. "This is nuts! I want outta here!"

Plath just watched him until he stopped his gyrations. "We'll see," she said, then turned and walked briskly back to her cabin.

As we were washing up, Rudy leaned in and whispered, "'We'll see?' I don't want to seem paranoid, but that didn't sound so good."

"Maybe she simply meant that she had to see about getting him a ride back," Ellie offered.

It sounded like Ellie was trying to convince herself.

Chapter 6

I wasn't surprised that Iron Man Jeremy wrested the lead role in our cabin construction. No, "wrested," is too strong. "Assumed by default" is more appropriate, as nobody else stepped up. And after watching and tasting the green's breakfast fiasco, we were ready to trade a little independence for stability—Germany under Hitler, Russia under Putin.

However, no amount of capable leadership was going to change my assessment that Plath had been seriously wrong about the time it would take for construction. She had referred to the kits as pre-fab, and I had envisioned this to mean "previously fabricated," versus what these kits were—essentially just the raw materials, albeit pre-cut and drilled. Okay, the window and door frames were already assembled, but still. I was no carpenter, but I didn't see how the eight of us were going to build one of these in less than four days, versus the two days Plath had predicted.

On the other hand, as Ellie pointed out, Plath had been simply quoting the manufacturer's instructions. It could be that she'd been fooled as well.

The welcomed news was that neither Plath nor Burrows said anything more about Rudy's defection. Apparently Burrows had won that one.

Half of Jeremy's leadership role consisted of condescending explanations that were already obvious, such as that lock washers go under the nut, not the head of the screw, and that there was no need to tire oneself on any particular task, as there were plenty of hands to go around. The other half, the moderately useful half, was to sit on a rock and call out the instructions from the booklet that came with the kit. It was frustrating that he insisted on describing the components rather than simply holding up the page for us to see the picture—presumably that would have demonstrated that his role could have been accomplished by simply nailing the booklet to a tree at eye level.

Jeremy was an annoyance, but the real problem was a lack of tools. Having fourteen hands available (two were holding a booklet and not in commission) did little good when there were four slotted screwdrivers, but only one Phillips-head. And not a single screw in the kit had a slotted head. We spent most of our time sitting around waiting for our turn with the only usable screwdriver or level, or trying to peek over Jeremy's shoulder. That didn't last long, since every time one of us tried, he'd send us off on some fool's mission, like dumping the "stale" water from our drinking jug and tasking us with filtering more from the spring.

Lunch was only a power bar, apple, and peanut butter crackers handed out by the taciturn Harry, so even though I'd spent most of the day on my butt, I was famished by the time the dinner horn bleated us to the kitchen tent. Thankfully, Albert had the green crew better coordinated, and Ellie, Rudy, and I filled our shallow metal bowls with spaghetti and meatballs and sat together away from the kitchen bustle.

"These aren't meatballs," Rudy announced, struggling to cut one of the slippery monsters in half with the edge of his fork, "they're meat-melons."

"I guess the greens took Plath seriously about feasting on the meat before the ice is gone," Ellie said.

"I'm not complaining," he said, cursing when one half went sailing into the dirt. "I just wish they'd given us *more* meatballs instead of *bigger* ones."

"Right," Ellie said dryly, "that's not complaining."

"Okay, I'm complaining. But not bitterly."

"Not like you were earlier," I noted, "about feeling foolish for trading a job and bedroom at your parents for a tent and an opportunity to be Jeremy's lackey."

"For example," he agreed.

"Do you really regret it?" I asked.

He chewed, swallowed, took another bite, and finally answered. "No. Or maybe not yet. The jury's still out. It's hardly been twenty-four hours."

"I know what you're talking about," Ellie agreed, twirling her fork in the pasta strands. "It feels like twenty-six."

She looked up to find us staring at her. "You guys really need to develop your sense of humor."

After we'd cleaned up and tossed our bowls and utensils in our tents, we walked back towards the road, mostly because Jeremy was organizing some sort of planning session—namely a lecture on the benefits of good organization. Harry had returned the bus to the university that morning, and Burrows retrieved him in the Jeep. The empty space where the bus had been was a reminder of how isolated we were.

Rudy bent down and pulled off a stalk of wild flowers, a column of dainty purple trumpets. He handed it to Ellie, but she didn't take it. Instead, she grinned. "Do you know what you have in your hand?" she asked.

He looked at it. "Hmm, I thought a nice gesture, unless one of us is a raging feminist."

"No, no. It *is* a nice gesture, unless you're offering it up as dessert."

His eyes went wide, and he dropped it. "It's toxic?"

"It's called foxglove, and yes it's toxic."

He unconsciously rubbed his hands on his pants.

"It won't penetrate your skin. You'd have to eat it."

"I don't intend to. Geez. If it's not mountain lions, it's poisonous plants. Nature's mean."

"Nature's just defending itself," she said.

Poison or no, I was a little jealous of Rudy's gesture.

The orange sun, exhausted after its day-long struggle through Southern California pollution, hovered low over the ridge to the west. We walked east along the lip of our plateau until we came to an outcropping of granite, a giant fist thrusting outward through the pines, with knuckles the size of sofas. We scrambled up and stood, the tops of pines behind us, and cascades of green falling away before us.

"Hey! Look at that!" Rudy said, and moved off down the other side of the little granite mountain.

I saw what he was talking about. A hundred feet further east was another, smaller outcrop, and from it, a slab of granite extended out, away from the plateau, slanting slightly upwards. It looked like a giant diving board, except that the tip dipped back down a bit. Or maybe—

"That must be the Potato Chip," I said.

"You know about this?" Ellie said. "Hey!" she called to Rudy. "Are you *crazy*? Get off of there—it might break off!"

"Nah!" he yelled back. He jumped up and down on the middle of it. "It's been here for, like, thousands of years!"

"You don't know that!" To me, she said, "Why do I feel like his mother? Anyway, you know about this?"

"Only what I overheard at lunch today. One of the greens apparently was here before. The Boy Scouts have been calling it that for decades."

"Ah, I see. So, maybe it's not going to break off any time soon."

"No, Mother."

She whacked me with the back of her hand.

We joined Rudy at the base of the Potato Chip. "Come on!" he called, and jumped up and down again.

"Rudy! You stop that!" Ellie cried. "If you want me out there, you'll stand very still."

He stopped jumping, and held his arms out in demonstration.

The granite slab was maybe five feet wide, and a rather astonishing fifteen feet or so long, considering that it was at most a few feet thick in the middle, tapering to nearly nothing at the edges. We sat down, Rudy at the dipping tip, and Ellie and I side-by-side behind him. We seemed to float above the pines covering the mountainside before us. I felt slightly dizzy, and I put my hands down against the solid rock, countering the sensation of being suspended in midair.

"Man!" Rudy breathed. "This is what is known in the travel video world as 'a vista.'"

The west ridge cast a shadow across two-thirds of the valley below, and the acute angle of the red sun set every knoll and indentation into stark relief. We sat, silent, as the engulfing, mile-long shadow crept slowly eastward, swallowing one lit knoll after another, until only the peaks of Marion Mountain and Tahquitz were still afire with burnished light. San Jacinto peak was somewhere behind us, keeping watch over it all.

"Beats stuffing boxes for eight hours on end," Rudy finally said.

"The Amazon warehouse?" I asked. He'd mentioned that this was where he'd been working.

"It's officially called a 'fulfillment center.' Sounds like a yoga class, but it's murder. Relentless, tedious human-robot work. It's almost as bad as the UPS package hub I worked at last year."

"The difference is that you got paid to do both of those," Ellie said.

Rudy sighed. "Life's dilemma. You have to work to live, but that doesn't feel like living."

"I guess that's why we go to college. If we have to work, at least it might be something we like," she said.

"I'd be happy just for something I could tolerate. Hey, what do you think those lights are?"

He was gesturing toward a matrix of tiny points in the flat plain far off to the right. They seemed to grow in number and intensity as the dusk settled in. "Hemet," I replied.

"How far off do you think it is?"

"Fifteen, twenty miles I guess. Why?" I asked.

"No reason. How far to that town we came through— Idyllwild?"

"I don't know—maybe six miles as the crow flies, twice that using the road."

"Hmm," he said.

"What 'hmm'?"

"Nothing. I just like to know where I am. When my parents took us to an amusement park, they always identified a particular exit, and made sure we knew where it was in case we got lost. They'd test us—randomly asking us which direction it was. It was probably the responsible thing to do, but I think it made me paranoid about getting lost."

"It's easy here—downhill is eventually a road, uphill nothing but a bunch of mountain peaks."

"That easy, huh?"

"A walk around the block," I said.

"So when the mountain lion attacks, I run downhill, not uphill."

"You don't run from a mountain lion."

"You wait to be eaten?" he asked.

Ellie finally spoke up. "Enough with the mountain lions!"

"Okay, a grizzly bear," Rudy offered.

"There's no bears in these mountains," I reminded him.

"Space aliens, then?"

Ellie stood up. "I think it's time to head back, before we find out that this potato chip-shaped rock is the tip of an ancient spaceship."

"You know," Rudy said, following Ellie and me, "I think it is."

"Of course you do," Ellie agreed.

ж ж ж

The violet evening light faded to near darkness when we entered the bowels of the pine forest. Rudy didn't have to worry about being lost, as the voices of the other blues guided our way. The comforting drone of conversation rose and fell, bursting into sudden laughter now and then. As we got closer, I saw a flickering glow playing across the faces of three of our companions sitting together in the middle of the blue tent farm. They'd started a fire, and we quickened our pace—a campfire in the woods draws people like moths.

Dana was approaching from the direction of the kitchen tent, followed closely by Jeremy. We all converged on the campfire as Dana pointed at the flames and turned her frizzy head to look at Jeremy. "See?" she said.

"Sorry, dudes," Jeremy said. "No campfires allowed."

I bristled. His "dudes" sounded way too affected.

"We cleared away the leaves and pine needles," Tim explained. He was the boy who had donated his rain fly. "See? We made a wall of stones around it too."

"Nice work," Jeremy said. He sounded like he was talking to a first grade class. "But you'll have to put it out."

I knew he was right. I'd heard Plath explain the US Forest Service rules about this wilderness area—no open campfires. I knew the fire was toast, so to speak, but I could take Jeremy only up to a point. It was like the insults of his condescending dominance accumulated as a pressure in my head. They needed to be released now and then. "Wait, Tim," I said. "I'd like to enjoy it for a little while."

It was probably a trick of the flickering light, but Jeremy's eyes seemed to glow with devilish anger. "Put it out, Tim," Jeremy ordered.

"Not yet," I countermanded.

Tim stood up, looking from Jeremy to me, then stepped aside, away from the fire. After a moment, the other two—Viona, the squat woman who had given me the other rain fly, and Dale, a quiet thirtyish man—followed suit.

"Tim!" Jeremy warned, like he was talking to a little kid.

I was relieved when the young man stood his ground, even if it was more civil disobedience than active defiance. I wasn't sure what I would have done otherwise.

I knew what I was prepared to do with Jeremy, though. I had no reservations there. I stepped forward, and Jeremy flinched a little, but I sat down at the fire, ignoring him, pretending to warm my hands over the flames instead.

"Don't be stupid," Jeremy said. He wasn't talking to a first-grader now.

His mouth tightened when Ellie and Rudy sat down next to me.

"Fine," Jeremy said. "Have it your way."

I saw him bend over, and then a hail of dirt rained down on us.

"You son-of-a-bitch!" I yelled, jumping up as he bent over to grab another handful.

"What's going on?" Plath called from the darkness.

Jeremy and I stood facing each other until she appeared beside us. "What's going on?" she asked again.

"They started an illegal fire," Dana whined.

Plath looked at Jeremy and me. "It was us," I said, a little lie, since I hadn't actually started it. "We're going to put it out. He's just being a jerk about it."

Plath looked at Jeremy, and then at me again. "Could you put it out for me now, Cal?" she asked calmly.

It sounded like a genuine question, like I actually had a choice about it. So, of course I said, "Yeah. Sure." I gestured to Ellie and Rudy to help me pour sand on the fire with our bare hands. I made a point to include Tim, Viona, and Dale—all of us gladly doing what we refused to do for Jeremy.

By the time we'd doused the small fire and darkness reigned around us, Jeremy and Dana were gone. "Sleep well," Plath said, and walked off.

I stood in the silence of the dark forest and let my heartbeat relax back to normal.

Later, lying in my sleeping bag, I wondered what I would have done had Plath not shown up. The possible outcomes haunted me well into the night.

I wasn't cut out for conflict.

Chapter 7

The next morning the sound of rustling and low murmuring conversation woke me. Pale light filtered through the fabric—the sun hadn't yet risen above the hills to the east. I remembered that the blues were on the hook for breakfast, and I crawled out of my bag and stuck my head out the tent flaps. Viona was whispering with Tim and Dale, and she saw me. She put her finger to her lips and pointed at Ellie and Rudy's tents. I nodded, and quietly got out and came over to them. "We'll take care of breakfast this morning," she said. "You might as well go back to bed."

I looked at my watch. It was 6:10. I felt ragged. "Where's Jeremy?" I asked.

"He's at the mess tent already."

"Okay, thanks. I'll see you guys later."

I felt my entire body sigh as I crawled back into my sleeping bag. I closed my eyes to get another hour of sleep, but I couldn't get the others—Viona and the rest—out of my head. They'd stood by me last night against Jeremy. After five minutes, I apologized to my body, and crawled back outside. They were gone, so I headed off to the kitchen tent.

They weren't there, but Jeremy was, squatting down doing something I couldn't see. I hesitated, but continued on. We had to talk sometime.

"Morning," I said.

He looked up, but his condescending smile was gone. Without a word, he bent down to continue whatever he was doing.

I surprised myself by feeling bad. I'd humiliated him in front of the whole group. Maybe I'd overreacted, maybe I had been the jerk. "Hey," I said, "I uh, I'm sorry about last night."

He looked up at me. "You should be." He studied me. "Let's hope you got it out of your system. Are you ready to join the group?"

I wanted to take back my apology. I heard voices. Tim, Viona, and Dale were coming from the direction of the cabins, carrying plastic jugs of water. "Come on," I said. "Let's just get on with breakfast."

"No," he insisted. "Are you ready to join the group?"

The other three stopped when they saw us.

"Jeremy," I replied, struggling to keep my temper, "I am already part of the group. See?" I said, holding out my arm and pointing to the blue sleeve. "We don't decide what group we're in." *Other than Rudy.*

"I'm not talking about the color of your uniform. I'm talking about your attitude. Are you mentally ready to join the group?"

I could have just said "Yes, Jeremy, I'm ready." That would have been confirming him as the supreme leader, though, as the one who *defined* the group. I waved to the other three to come forward. "Let's make some breakfast," I said.

They each took a step, but Jeremy held up his hand. "No! You can't ignore the responsibility of group membership, Cal."

"What?" I replied, feigning ignorance. "I'm here to help with breakfast!"

"You know what I mean. Just answer the question."

I knew exactly what would happen when I finally caved—it would open the door to a lecture about group cohesion, and how essentially I was letting everybody down if I didn't follow his wise direction. "Okay, Jeremy. You want an answer? I'll give you an answer—"

"Hey!" Ellie's voice broke in. "Let's get this show on the road! There's going to be some hungry greens arriving soon, and we want to show them what real country cooking is like!"

She'd obviously heard us, but she brilliantly pretended otherwise. She saved me from saying something very nasty, something I would probably lie awake regretting.

Jeremy scowled and mumbled that I'd have to face the music eventually, but we had to hustle to prepare the scrambled eggs and ham before the greens arrived.

ж ж ж

Jeremy continued calling out cabin kit directions, but we'd gotten the hang of it and anticipated the assembly steps before he voiced them. He reprimanded us for not waiting, but we continued on a step ahead of him, thrilled to be making such good progress. He finally gave up and put the instructions down, referring to them only now and then to make sure we weren't going seriously astray.

We couldn't help wondering how much progress the greens were making on theirs. The pre-formed foundations were a good hundred yards apart, equidistant from the ends of the plateau and each other, and the dense stand of pines rendered them invisible. We sent Rudy over to spy, and though they barked at him to stay away, he came back to report that they had fallen behind us.

Later in the afternoon, I collected the packing cardboard from the kit and carried it to the large bin near Plath's cabin. I was about to toss the bundle inside, when I heard Plath and Burrows' voices coming from her open window. I paused. I wasn't exactly eavesdropping, since I had come to that spot on routine business. Okay, I was eavesdropping. I didn't hear every word, but it was clear that they were talking about Albert and Jeremy. I caught the gist: Plath was worried about the two, that they would skew the results, but Burrows downplayed their roles, pointing out that it was inevitable that one of us would end up at the top of each pile. Just then a blue jay began squawking, and I wasn't sure I caught Plath's response, but it sounded like she said she wasn't looking for piles.

Jeremy called to me to hurry up, and although I resented bending to his will, I was afraid that Plath would catch me snooping, so I tossed the cardboard and went back.

Dinner was instant mashed potatoes and patties of ground beef. Jeremy organized us into groups: three cooks—one on each stove—two servers, and three kitchen assistants who made sure the cooks had what they needed. I went along with him. One, it made

47

sense; two, I really didn't like to fight with Jeremy; and three, he seemed to be trying to be less overbearing—he appointed himself as one of the lowly kitchen assistants. It helped that I was a cook.

We cooks were the last to eat. After all the greens were served, we fed our kitchen assistants and servers, and only then made servings for ourselves. By the time I was done and had cleaned up, Ellie and Rudy had returned to the blue group's tents. As I walked back, I saw that they were sitting together talking, so I went for a stroll, repeating the route we'd taken the evening before. I was proud of myself for letting them have together-time, and also a little frustrated. I didn't want them to see, so I sat on the Potato Chip until the sun set and the evening chill drove me back.

I was surprised to find everybody except Dana and Jeremy once again sitting around in a circle with the light of an open flame dancing across their faces. As I came close, I saw Dana approaching. She stopped, stared at the group a moment, and then turned and trotted back the way she'd come.

"Hey!" I called, "You guys are really determined to piss off Jeremy and Plath—oh! I see!"

They didn't have a campfire. Instead, a blue propane flame hissed upwards from a small metal spider. "A camp stove," I remarked.

"Actually, a backpacking stove," Dale said. "It's mine."

"Ah. Why didn't you use it last night?"

"I didn't bring any propane along. I thought we'd be flying somewhere—you know, the passports."

"Right. So, where'd you get the propane?"

"Well …" He glanced at Rudy.

"You stole it from the kitchen?" I asked my friend.

"I borrowed it," Rudy replied. "They've got, like, a year's supply."

"And you're sure we won't need that much?"

I was joking, but Rudy looked at me with alarm, and for reasons I wouldn't have been able to verbalize, my joke unsettled me as well.

Just then we heard footsteps, and a moment later, Jeremy entered the lit area, followed close behind by Dana.

"See?" Dana said.

"Yes," Jeremy said, "I see." Even he seemed a little annoyed at her grade school politics.

"I, uh, it's m-mine ..." Dale stuttered.

"I brought the propane," Rudy said, which was technically the truth.

"Plath told you about fires," Jeremy said.

"We're not allowed to have open campfires," Dale said, not happy that he had to explain. "The Forest Service allows these types of stoves."

"You're sure about that?"

"Oh yes. I, you know, go backpacking."

Jeremy nodded, looking around the group. "Okay. Sounds good."

He was clearly waiting for an invitation to join us. Everybody sat looking up at him.

"They should have asked permission," Dana said softly.

Jeremy sighed. "Maybe next time you should check with me—or Dr. Plath," he said, and then turned and walked away.

"Jeremy!" Dana whined, running after him.

I had the idea that Jeremy wanted to leave before further discussion turned into an argument.

I sat down, and we all watched the tight little circle of blue flames. Rudy was the first to speak. "If I was Dana," he said, "I wouldn't wander away on my own."

"Rudy!" Ellie exclaimed.

He looked at her with pretended surprise. "I was talking about mountain lions—what were *you* thinking?"

She gave him one of her playful backhands. "You know. And you'd better watch yourself."

Conversation picked up, and laughter echoed into the darkness until one by one we yawned and went off to our tents.

ж ж ж

The following days passed in harmony, with the satisfaction of doing work that resulted in visible progress at the end of the day,. At my previous job—the one I'd quit to come west—I would arrive in the morning at a clean desk, and leave in the evening knowing that the fruits of the nine hours I'd spent in the chair consisted of binary bits that had been changed from 1's to 0's or 0's to 1's on other computers somewhere else. Not exactly graphic fulfillment.

By the beginning of the second week, the blues had completed two cabins, and were starting on a third. We were a well-oiled team, as long as Jeremy and Dana kept out of our way. Two of us used the slot-head screw drivers to work screws most of the way into cabin components that two others fed to us. The person wielding the single Phillips head screwdriver was then much more efficient, as they went along tightening behind us. This method was our trade secret, and we guarded it jealously from the greens.

Jeremy tried to maintain his leadership role, but now that we had our routines down, he didn't have a lot to offer. Now and then he would assign roles, and we'd go along—sometimes just until he left, rotating around on our own when we got tired of one task.

The greens, on the other hand, were falling further behind. They were barely half done with their second cabin. We heard a lot of yelling from their end of the camp, arguing that usually died quickly as Albert intervened, but at least once a day a shouting fest would erupt that echoed up and down the slopes, disturbing the eternal quiet of the mountains.

Ellie, Rudy, and I had developed our evening routine to include walking the perimeter of the plateau—a half-hour stroll—always ending at the little granite mountain and the Potato Chip. We occasionally came across lone greens, and we'd exchange greetings, but never struck up a conversation. We had the sense that they just wanted to be left alone. The greens and the blues were different groups, and as time went on, it felt odd to talk in a familiar way to somebody in green clothes. We never ate breakfast or dinner together, since one group was busy feeding the other, who departed soon after. Lunch was carried back to the cabin construction plots. Our interactions were reduced to polite acknowledgements, like two companies sharing the same elevator.

I was surprised at how quickly living in the open, in the woods, became the new normal. In fact, it was hard to imagine the appeal of walls and a roof. Building the cabins had become an abstract project that filled the hours of our days rather than a goal that would ultimately benefit us. We woke each morning to sunshine and song birds, and ended each day in quiet conversation around

Dale's little trail stove, falling asleep to the sound of crickets and owls. I would have preferred more alone time with Ellie, but I was too contented to begrudge falling just short of a perfect existence.

Whereas we embraced the open air, Doctor Plath seemed to hide from it. We rarely saw her anymore, other than for meals, when she would fill her plate along with the off-duty group, and immediately retire to her cabin. Tim heard from a green who had heard from Harry that she was feeling under the weather.

One afternoon I was carrying some packing cardboard to the recycle bin when I again overheard Plath and Burrows. I stood and listened, glancing back at the blue crew to make sure no one was watching me. Burrows' tone was mild and reasonable, gently persuasive. "You've got the results you were looking for," he said.

Plath sounded tired, weak. "You make it sound like I'm just trying to demonstrate my theory."

"Aren't you?"

"There's a difference between proving and demonstrating. One serves science, the other, ego."

"My apologies. I wasn't careful with my wording," Burrows said. "You know what I mean, though. You have the results—just as you predicted. Maybe it's time we moved on to my phase."

There was a pause. Plath might have been considering this thoughtfully, or she might have been glaring at him with clenched fists. "No," she said. "I'm not going to stop the exercise as soon as I see what I've been looking for. Like I said, that's not science. It might evolve yet. The dynamics might swing the other way."

"Sure," he agreed amiably. "I understand." Another pause. "You really should go home, though, where you can get some proper rest, maybe see a doctor. I'll watch over things here."

I heard her sigh. "No. I've got too much invested. It's taken me two years to arrange this. And I'm still worried about Albert and Jeremy."

"Well, you know what I think about that."

"I know," she said with resignation. "You think it's inevitable."

"In any case, suppressing leadership development could be viewed as an artificial manipulation."

Pause. "You might be right. You probably are. Anyway, I still want the experiment to proceed unchecked for now."

"Right," Burrows said. "Very well."

The flavor of his voice indicated that he didn't like it "very well." I sensed that he was going to leave, though, so I dropped my load into the bin and returned to the blue crew.

I didn't talk about what I'd heard. We mice knew we were in a laboratory, but I had peeked over the wall to discover that we were working our way through the maze. In fact, one of our scientist caretakers believed we'd reached the end. I wanted to talk to Ellie and Rudy about it, but felt I'd be betraying Doctor Plath. We weren't supposed to know the layout of the maze, just the route options in front of our noses.

Based on what I'd heard, though, the layout of the maze was configurable, and the endpoint still under debate. That lead this particular experimental subject to the uneasy realization that lab mice are in the hands of experimental destiny.

Chapter 8

By the time we were half done with our third and last cabin, it was clear that Jeremy had abandoned the role of crew boss, and was just trying to be part of the crew. We didn't actively exclude him, but we had our routine down, and were cautious about welcoming him into the ranks. We didn't really trust that he could resist flexing his boss-man muscle. We hadn't discussed any of this, sharing a sort of group awareness. In the beginning, newly immersed in a wilderness environment, we had been accepting of a leader. Situations evolve, however, and the role had become superfluous.

Perhaps to compensate, Jeremy was even more insistent that we perform our daily house duties—cooking, washing, campsite cleanup—as a coordinated group. At first we went along, feeling some compassion for him, but after a couple of days, we abandoned even that. We let him voice his directives, then ignored them. We didn't actively rebel, we just mutinied by disregard.

We'd never had to disregard Dana, since she hadn't shown any interest in joining the cabin-building crew, and that was fine by us. Instead, she played Jeremy's lackey, running errands and providing an affirmative voice to his opinions.

The day after my second eavesdrop, I was coming back from the porta-toilet and noticed Dana standing with Burrows and Jeremy. The three of them were talking, glancing now and then at the blue crew hard at work. When they noticed me walking by, they went quiet until I'd passed. I figured Dana was whining about some injustice she'd imagined, but I didn't care.

A couple of hours later Jeremy came to the cabin site and stood before us, arms crossed. It had been many days since I'd last seen that patronizing smile, and it gave me a sinking feeling.

"Okay, blue crew," he began, "we don't need everybody to finish up our last cabin."

Rudy elbowed me and whispered, "We never *had* everybody."

"So," Jeremy continued, "we'll split into two teams. Ellie, Tim, Viona, and Dale will finish the third cabin. Cal and Rudy can begin assembling the propane heaters. The nights are only going to get colder, and we'll need them soon."

We all stood looking at him. Tim glanced at me and Rudy. "Maybe we could, like, rotate," he suggested.

I was touched. He didn't want us to feel ostracized.

Jeremy shook his head, rejecting the idea outright.

Dale jumped in. "Yeah. I think that's a good idea, Tim," he said, looking stone-faced at Jeremy.

That surprised me. Dale, nearly thirty, was the senior member of the group, and the most reserved. Ever helpful, he never initiated conversations, and only rarely joined in.

Jeremy looked at Dale like he might a child who had pulled candy off the store shelf, knowing it wasn't going into the cart. "This isn't open for discussion," Jeremy declared, never losing the condescending smile.

"Who died and made you the boss?" I challenged, the cliché springing from my mouth.

Jeremy's smile didn't waver, but one eyebrow lifted as he turned to me. "I've been assigned," he said simply.

"By whom?" I asked, but I knew what the answer was going to be, so I jumped ahead. "Has Doctor Plath agreed to this?"

Jeremy didn't answer immediately. He glanced off to the side, and I noticed that Burrows had quietly approached. I didn't see the balding man make a gesture, but I might have missed it. "Yes," Jeremy said.

"Plath has assigned you to be our leader," I repeated carefully.

Jeremy's smile was somewhere between commiserating with my defeat, and a gloat. "Yes," he said.

I looked to Burrows, who shrugged.

I hated to give him any more satisfaction, so I just tossed my screwdriver to the ground and walked toward the road, where the extra supplies were stored.

Rudy caught up with me as I was yanking the tarp off the stacked boxes. "Hey," he said, grabbing the other end of the tarp so I wouldn't topple the whole pile, "I have an idea."

"Murder Jeremy?" I said, finding the first stove box, and rolling it roughly off to the side.

"Uh, maybe something that doesn't involve capital punishment. You go over and talk to him, and I'll sneak up behind him and get down on my hands and knees."

I paused in my attempt to unload my anger onto the innocent boxes and looked at him. "Let me guess. And then I give him a push, and he falls over backwards."

Rudy screwed his mouth. "Kind of childish, right?"

"Yes it is. Let's do it."

He looked alarmed. "You serious?"

"No. Maybe…" I shook my head. "No."

He helped me pull open the box flaps. I paused, and he looked at me. "Burrows must have gotten to Plath," I said.

"What do you mean?"

"I, um, overheard a conversation they had."

Rudy dropped the flap and sat on the box. "Give me the juice," he said eagerly.

I hesitated, but decided that Plath had already betrayed us. "Burrows was trying to convince Plath that she'd already proved her theory. He wanted her to wrap up her experiment so that he could start his."

"An experiment, huh?" He grinned. "I *thought* I saw the sun glinting off some glass high up in the sky. We're trapped inside a giant bottle. I hope they remembered to poke holes in the lid."

"She didn't actually say 'experiment.' She called it the 'exercise,' and he called his the next 'phase.' But that's not what bothers me."

"Being trapped inside a giant bottle doesn't bother you?"

"It would if I was. What bothers me is that Plath was worried about Jeremy and Albert."

"They seem to be taking care of themselves just fine."

"No, it wasn't them that she was worried about, but what they were doing to the 'exercise.' She thought that they were—if I remember—skewing the results."

"Huh. Like, on purpose?"

"No, not that. I think it's just the fact that they've become the leaders."

"She doesn't like leaders?"

"Not when they're skewing her results."

"So why does this bother you … ah, I see. Why would she have gone along with assigning Jeremy as the group leader if she didn't *want* any leaders—right?"

"Yeah. Maybe I heard wrong. I don't know."

"Well, be that as it may," Rudy said, getting up and tapping the top of the box, "we'd better get to this critical job before the winter snows arrive and force us to have a Donner Party." He saw me staring at him. "What!" he asked.

"Nothing," I replied. "Nothing that a strong sedative wouldn't fix."

His eyes popped. "You got some?"

I just looked at him.

ж ж ж

The next day, the reduced blue construction crew finished our last cabin, and we decided to celebrate after dinner. The nearest alcohol was twenty miles away, so "celebrate" was an abstraction. Our three little cabins had no plumbing or electricity, but we mounted battery-powered LED lights on the walls, and went on tours in groups of two or three as dusk settled, admiring the handiwork, even though they were essentially all identical.

Rudy and I had finished the propane heaters the day before, and we fired these up as darkness fell. Dale's little trail stove had been a welcomed glow of companionship in the night, a spark of humanity in the wilderness. A heated cabin was civilization. Comparatively.

Carrying the theme of civilization a next step, Rudy struck up a game of poker with Tim, Dale, and Viona, using leftover cabin screws as poker chips. The four players filled that cabin to capacity, so Ellie and I decided to check out the stars from the Potato Chip. Jeremy and Dana's tents glowed like paper lanterns, illuminated by their LED head-lamps. We hadn't seen either of them since dinner.

The green area was quiet as well. Perhaps they begrudged our celebration, maybe viewing it as a victory lap. There was nothing to indicate this, other than the evening silence, and since their group seemed to operate in just two modes, arguing or sullen quiet, my imagined resentment was possibly just that.

It was dark when we reached the edge of the plateau, and the Potato Chip jutted away from us like a giant tongue, or a plank extended from the side of a pirate ship. I was cautious in the darkness, and although tempted, I sat behind Ellie instead of next to her. The ravens had retired for the night, and the high mountain silence was profound. A slight evening breeze set the pines to whispering urgent secrets. And oh, the stars. The vast expanse of sparkling diamonds gave the sense of floating in space, Ellie and me astride our little stone space rocket.

We talked in hushed voices, not wanting to disturb the conversation between the stars and the pines. I asked if she had any brothers or sisters. Ellie didn't answer at first. "Sort of," she finally said.

"How do you sort of have siblings?" I asked.

"When they're not part of your life anymore."

"I see," I said. I didn't want to press her.

The pines hissed softly and the stars blazed.

"My dad abused my older sister when she was young," she said, seemingly out of nowhere.

"Ah," I said. "Abused, like ..."

"Yeah, like that. A week after she graduated high school, she ran off with a construction guy who was in town on a temporary project. She lived with him in Orlando for awhile, then she sent word that she was going to crew on a sailboat being delivered to the Virgin Islands."

"Sounds adventurous. She was, like, finding herself?"

"No. She was running from herself. The sailing thing fell through, and the last we heard was that she'd hooked up with another guy in Fort Lauderdale. It gets murky here. Her letters and emails stopped, and my dad hired a PI to find out what happened."

I waited. "What happened?"

"Drugs. Crystal."

"Meth?"

"Yeah. That was pretty much the end of the line. My dad offered to pay for treatment, but she wouldn't even take his calls."

"Wow. I'm sorry. Were you, like, close to her?"

In the starlight, I saw her shrug. "She's six years older than me."

"I see. But, I guess, maybe your dad, uh, like learned a lesson?"

I immediately wanted to take the simplistic words back.

"Nope."

"Ah."

"Nope," she repeated.

There was something in her tone, something fateful. "You?" I barely voiced the words.

"I would have been."

"But …?"

"My brother. We were pals. He was two years older."

"'Was'?"

"Well, he still is, but it seems like he's dead. He's in prison."

"I see." I waited, not seeing at all.

"He tried to kill my dad. He stabbed him with a kitchen knife."

"Wow. Protecting you?"

"Yeah. Protecting me."

She said it like it was a mistake that could have been avoided. "Sounds like the wrong man went to jail," I said.

"My dad offered to drop the charges if Rob agreed to get treatment."

"Apparently he didn't?"

"Rob said that agreeing to that would be agreeing that my dad had done nothing wrong."

"Yeah, of course. Still. How long is his sentence?"

"He's been in prison three years, and he's got two more to go."

"Shit. Your brother sounds like a hell of a guy."

Her silence was her agreement.

"I see why you didn't want to follow your father's footsteps in medicine."

"The only way I'd follow his footsteps would be to watch him fall into hell."

"Ow!" I couldn't leave it at that. "If there's a heaven, I guess we need a hell to balance the scales."

Silence.

"That was pretty cheesy," I said.

"Yeah," she agreed, "but true."

She didn't say anything more.

"It can't be easy talking about this," I offered.

"Easier than living with it."

"You feel guilty about your brother," I said. It wasn't even a question.

"Oh, yeah."

"But there was nothing you could have done."

Silence.

"I mean," I continued, "it wasn't like you could have just let your father ..."

Silence.

"Ellie!"

"No," she finally agreed. "I keep thinking, though, that there *was* something I could have done. Maybe I could have, like, called the police instead of telling Rob."

"Rob would still have found out. Do you think that would have made a difference in the end?"

She sighed. "No. Probably not."

I was touched at all she had revealed, and pleased that she trusted me. That was followed by guilt about being pleased, considering the tragic nature. Salvation lay in vulnerability. In offering intimate information in exchange. "I told Kelly that I loved her," I said.

Silence.

"Okay," Ellie finally said.

"I mean, I shouldn't have."

"Hmm. Because now you have a broken heart?"

"No! The opposite. I *didn't* love her. I just told her that."

"To get in her pants."

Maybe I'd picked the wrong piece of vulnerable information. "To put it crudely," I replied.

After a few moments, Ellie asked, "Do you do that often? Lie about your feelings?"

"No! Of course not. I just ..."

"That's why you told me," she offered. "You consider it news since it's an aberration."

"Exactly."

"Really?"

"Yes!"

In the darkness, I felt her warm hand find mine.

We were interrupted by distant shouting coming from the green area. As we walked back to our completed cabins, we could hear that it was Ralph, the complainer, angry about being relegated to "gofer" on the green cabin construction. It sounded like Albert was trying to move the discussion so they wouldn't disturb the entire camp, but Ralph resisted any semblance of control.

"Some people shouldn't be in groups," I said.

"Maybe some groups shouldn't have people," Ellie replied.

I didn't know what she meant, but I didn't want to seem thick, so I didn't ask.

I probably should have.

Chapter 9

We arrived at the cabins to find Jeremy in the midst of a quieter argument, apparently trying to allocate cabin assignments. Rudy was pushing back. "What difference does it make?" he asked.

"Well, to start with," Jeremy replied, "the women clearly have to be together in one cabin."

Rudy may have been arguing, but Jeremy wasn't. It was an explanation, not a negotiation.

"What! Are we back in the Victorian age?" Rudy asked.

"It's not a matter of morals—just common sense."

"If it's not a matter of morals, then it's just arbitrary, like saying we'll share a cabin according to alphabetical order."

"It's not the same. The women will be together."

No negotiation.

"Why don't we ask *them*?"

"Of *course* the women have to be in one cabin," Dana said immediately.

"Yeah," Viona said. "I guess it makes sense."

Rudy looked at Ellie.

"Oh, no," she objected. "You're not putting me in the middle of this one."

Rudy looked like a lost puppy.

Ellie sighed. "It probably does make sense. I'm sorry, Rudy."

"Fine," he said. "At least I can be with Cal."

"I'm afraid not," Jeremy said. "Cabin two will be you, me, and Dale. Cabin three is Caleb and Tim."

"Why?" Rudy demanded, his voice starting to rise.

"Because I said so," Jeremy replied. "Because we need structure," he added.

"Why don't we vote on it?"

"This isn't a democracy."

I would have preferred to be with Ellie and Rudy, but since Plath had agreed to make Jeremy our leader, arguing with him was essentially arguing with her. Also, he had placed himself in the three-man cabin, the analog to assigning himself as a cook's helper. I wanted to despise the guy, but he was making it difficult.

Tim and I moved our stuff from the tents to our respective sides of the cabin, and I sat on my cot, taking in our tiny new home. I had looked forward to sleeping on the cot, but now when I lay back in my sleeping bag, it felt strange. After nearly two weeks on the ground, lying suspended in the air was disconcerting, unnatural. I subconsciously expected to fall back to solid earth at any moment.

I lay in the darkness listening to Tim turning the pages of his paperback book, and replayed what Ellie had told me. Long ago at the bus stop (had it only been two weeks?), she had said that she was joining the study to take time out to assess where she wanted to go with her education and her pseudo-fiancée. Now, it seemed her anger and guilt had driven her from an inarguably safe and secure path. Perhaps each participant had their own troubled history, seventeen distressed vector arrows all converging on this plateau in the San Jacinto Mountains.

I rolled over, away from Tim's light, and waited to fall to the ground. I fell asleep instead.

ж ж ж

I woke the next morning to knocking. It was the blue's turn to make breakfast, and Tim was already up and out. I unzipped my sleeping bag and sat up in my underwear as the door opened to bright sunlight. A silhouette stood in the doorway. "I'm glad I didn't bunk with you after all," Rudy said. "I just hope I can erase this memory."

"You can close the door," I said.

Rudy stepped inside and shut the door, then stood watching as I got dressed. "A glutton for punishment?" I asked.

"Just making sure you don't crawl back into bed. Jeremy sent me to get you. You're late for KP duty."

"It's the cabin's fault. When you're in a tent, you hear everything, and everybody wakes up together."

"I'll suggest that Jeremy punish the cabin."

"Okay, then it's Tim's fault."

"Are you trying to take Ralph's place as chief whiner?"

I chuckled. "You heard him last night? I'll bet Albert wouldn't mind handing off the leader role with that guy under him."

As I was tying my shoes, Rudy sat down on Tim's bunk. "Hey, I overheard Plath and Burrows," he said quietly.

I looked up at him.

"We could hear them arguing until one of them closed the window."

"In Plath's cabin?"

"Where else?"

We hadn't seen Plath in a couple of days. The kitchen crew had taken meals to her cabin the first day, but then it was just tea and crackers. We figured she'd caught the flu, and nobody wanted to make the deliveries for fear of catching it.

"What'd you hear?"

"They were arguing. Mostly it was Plath yelling at Burrows—that he refused to be cooperative. After they closed the window, I made an excuse to get close, and she was saying that she'd had it with Jeremy and Albert—also Ralph. She wants them out of here."

"No kidding," I said. "Well, that makes more sense."

"That she wasn't in fact cool about having Jeremy assigned as leader? Which means that he was—"

"Yeah, lying."

"But what about Burrows? He was standing right there when Jeremy lied."

"Complicit by association, I guess."

"What's with this Burrows' program, though?"

"You know as much as me." I said.

" 'As I,' you mean," Rudy said.

"Okay, Ellie. Speaking of which, we should find out if she's heard anything."

"I think you mean, 'speaking of whom.'"

"Does it boost your ego to correct me?"

"Immensely," he said.

ж ж ж

I took advantage of our turn at kitchen duty to make sure that Ellie gave me Plath's tea and crackers to deliver. When I knocked on the cabin door, I thought I heard her say to come in, but I wasn't sure, so I knocked again. After a minute, she opened it and emerged from the darkness inside. I almost didn't recognize her. The slim woman was now a gaunt skeleton. Her previous tamed hair was flying free, a gray cloud floating listlessly. Her ashen, wrinkled face seemed to have aged a full decade, but looked as though the skin would be solid to the touch, like marble.

She reached out to take the cup of tea, and I said, "Can I talk to you?"

For a brief moment, I saw something like panic in her eyes, but then she gave a short little nod, turned, and disappeared into the darkness.

I hesitated, and then stepped inside. The air smelled of old vomit. As my eyes adjusted to the dim light, I saw that unlike our cots, hers was substantial, with a small mattress. She practically fell back onto it, then arranged her pillow so that her head was raised. "I'm not well," she stated.

"I, um, guessed. Do you think it's, like, the flu?"

"It feels like that. I was hoping I'd be feeling better by now, but it seems to be getting worse."

"Maybe you should …"

"Get help? Perhaps. If it's not improved by tomorrow I'll have Harry drive me home."

Or to the hospital.

"You should wash your hands when you leave," she added, "and don't touch your nose or mouth until then."

"Right. Thanks. I uh, was wondering if you would answer a question—but only if you're, you know, up for it."

"That's fine. It's probably time for questions."

"Right. Um. Did you … did you say that Jeremy should be the leader of the blues?"

Her eyes narrowed. "No! Why would you think that?"

My mind whirled. What to say? What *not* to say? *Oh hell.* "Jeremy said you did."

"He lied," she said simply.

I stood there. There was nothing for her to add. He'd lied. Her simple, direct answer encouraged me to press on. "Your study … it's an experiment, isn't it?"

She took a breath and let it out. "Yes. It is."

"Building the cabins isn't the preparation, it *is* the experiment, isn't it?"

For the first time in some days, she smiled, even if it was tiny and weak. "It is."

"You're comparing how we operate when one group is all together in a communal tent, and the other is separated in individual tents."

"That's right."

"Our group won."

"There's no winner. It's just data."

"But we finished way ahead of them."

"It wasn't a race."

"But they're, like, always arguing. They fight constantly."

"That's true. They do."

"Isn't that, you know, losing?"

She didn't answer at first. "That's one way of looking at it, I guess," she finally replied.

"How can arguing and fighting ever be winning?"

"I don't know. Maybe when fighting is appropriate."

I didn't know what she meant, but another realization was sinking in, distracting me. She wouldn't be telling me all this unless she was giving up. "Is the experiment over?"

"We'll see."

It would depend on whether she went to the hospital, I guessed. *But, if her part of the study is complete …* "Do you know what Burrows has in mind?"

She looked at me. "You've overheard our conversations?"

My face felt hot, and I hoped the dim light hid my blush. "Uh, yeah."

"That's a good question for which I don't have a concrete answer. My illness has thrown us off schedule. He has been waiting to observe the state of the group cohesion at the end of my program before finalizing his own. I only know the large brush strokes. James has a strong interest in evolutionary biology and socio-genetics. He's been developing a theory that includes existing concepts, but pulls together specific emphasis of multiple threads to encompass an operational paradigm that's only been tangentially touched on previously. In general, his theory states that group hierarchy dynamics are more heavily dependent than previously credited on the level of danger perceived by the group."

"Uh, I see."

She smiled her weak little smile again. "Do you? Or are you being polite?"

"A little of both."

From outside, I heard Jeremy calling my name. "My leader is calling. I'd better go. I hope you ... feel better."

She shook her head. I wasn't sure if it was for the probability that she would feel better, or that I had to jump when Jeremy called.

As I stepped outside, I saw movement off to my right. It was Burrows, just entering his cabin. I had the paranoid thought that maybe he'd been listening outside her window.

I started towards the kitchen tent, but paused. Plath wouldn't have told me anything about Burrows' program—wouldn't have even acknowledged that he had a program—if she thought it was actually going to happen.

Maybe we were going home.

As I trotted off to keep Jeremy from calling again, I wished I had a home to go home to.

Chapter 10

"It's hard to believe that it's over already," Ellie said.

The three of us—Ellie, Rudy, and I—had scrambled up the little granite mountain next to the Potato Chip, and were gazing out over the plains of Hemet. This was our first day with no cabin building, and it felt like a holiday.

"She didn't actually say that," I reminded.

"I think you're right, though. She wouldn't have described Burrows' program otherwise."

"Unless that's just part of the game," Rudy said.

"You think it's a smoke screen? Maybe Burrows wants us to make a false guess about part of his experiment?" I asked.

"Plath fooled us about building the cabins, didn't she?"

"Yeah. That's true." I said. "Hmm."

"She never actually lied," Ellie said. "She just let us assume that whatever program she was conducting would begin *after* the cabins were built. She was careful about that."

"About not lying?" I asked.

"Yes."

"You don't think she would lie? About anything?"

Ellie shrugged. "Some people just don't."

"But, how do you know?"

She shrugged again.

ж ж ж

It was the green's day for kitchen duty, but—unlike those that are incapable of lying—I told them that Plath had asked that I bring her tea and crackers. This time, I opened the door myself after knocking and hearing the faint response. Plath was lying on her bunk, and looked at me without lifting her head. The stale, fetid air almost gagged me. I put the tea and crackers on the little table next to her and asked, "Do you want me to open some windows?"

She waved off the idea weakly.

"Are you feeling any better?" I asked, although the answer was obvious.

She blinked, and that seemed to be her answer.

I glanced back at the open door. "Doctor Plath, I'm sorry to bother you, but I was wondering if I could ask just a couple more questions?"

She took a breath and nodded ever so slightly.

"Yesterday, you explained that Doctor Burrows has a theory, but I'm not sure whether he plans to continue the, uh, program."

She just looked at me, as if waiting for the actual question.

"Is he?" I asked.

She raised her eyebrows. A minimalist shrug.

"Right. Well, about what you said yesterday, how his theory is about, uh, group dynamics, and how it's affected by dangers to the group."

She waited a moment, and then said softly, "What about it?"

"Well, um, like, what kind of dangers?"

The pale, marble skin of her face shifted slightly. It might have been a grin. "Mountain lions, for example," she whispered.

"Ah, right. Um, are you joking?"

Her eyebrows shrugged again. "It's one example."

"I was thinking more along the lines of what Burrows might use in his … program … I mean, assuming he, like, uses danger."

This time she mustered the strength to use her shoulders to shrug. "Listen, Cal, whatever James has in mind, it obviously won't present a serious danger to the participants. That would be … ridiculous."

She closed her eyes. It was a day's worth of words for her, and it seemed to deplete whatever energy she'd stored.

I waited, wondering if I should leave, but she eventually opened her eyes and looked at me.

"Should you be telling me this?" I asked. "I mean, won't it affect Doctor Burrows' experiment ... uh, program?"

She bounced her eyebrows. "You asked."

"Right," I said. "Still. Why are you telling me?"

She blinked, and after a while she blinked again. "You helped with the bags."

"The bags?"

"The bus," she said.

I thought back. "At the university? Loading the bags into the bus?"

She blinked her assent.

I jumped—literally jumped up—when a loud voice boomed from behind me, "Doctor Plath is ill!" It was Burrows, standing in the doorway, a silhouette. "She needs rest, and could be contagious. You shouldn't be here."

"Oh ... right," I stammered. "Sorry!" I turned to Plath. "Sorry about that!"

Burrows stepped aside, and I hurried out. My last image of the prone woman, was of an expression of consternation. She was either surprised at or disapproving of his intrusion.

ж ж ж

"It's been days," Ellie insisted.

She, Rudy, and I had gathered in my cabin. "She does seem to be getting worse," I admitted.

"So why hasn't she gone to the hospital?"

"I don't know. I guess people don't go to the hospital for the flu unless it gets really bad."

"Hers isn't really bad?"

"It seems bad, but everybody looks bad when they have the flu. She said that Harry would drive her home if she's not improved."

Rudy broke in. "What if Burrows is holding her hostage?"

Ellie and I looked at him. "Maybe you should cut back on the thriller novels," Ellie suggested.

"No, seriously," he insisted. "Think about it—Cal says that Burrows has a whole program of his own that he wants to kick off after Plath's is done. But maybe he has to make sure that Plath's *gets* done first."

Silence. "Maybe you need more sleep," Ellie offered.

Rudy leaned back with his hands clasped behind his head, and put his feet up on a shelf. "I'm going to relish the 'I told you so,' when the time comes."

"Okay," Ellie said. "But we won't hold our breath." To me, she added, "You need to check in on her later."

"Sure," I replied, agreeably. "I need to take every opportunity to expose myself to a potentially lethal virus."

She gave me the same look that we'd both been giving Rudy.

ж ж ж

I waited until dusk to sneak around to Plath's cabin. Burrows seemed to be hanging around, almost as though keeping an eye on her. I pretended to fiddle with the solar panels we were installing on the roof of the cabin nearest to them until I saw Burrows walking off through the pines, presumably to the porta-toilet. I ran over.

I knocked on Plath's doors and listened. I thought I heard a moan. I knocked again, waited a few seconds, and then opened the door and went in, closing it softly behind me. The air absolutely reeked. "Doctor Plath?" I whispered, waiting for my eyes to adjust to the near total darkness.

I heard a small moan again, and could tell it was coming from her bunk. I stepped closer, and dimly made out her form, her loose hair now lying flat against her head. "Doctor Plath? Are you awake?"

Suddenly, I realized that her eyes were open, and that she was looking right at me. Her mouth fell open, but all that emerged was another moan.

"Doctor Plath! We have to get you to a hospital!"

She moaned again, and I had the impression she was trying to say something. I leaned over, putting my ear close, very aware that we were sharing the same air. She moaned incoherently.

"Doctor Plath, I don't understand," I said.

She took a deep breath and her brow furrowed in concentration. I leaned over again, and this time I heard her whisper, "Reason."

"The reason?" I repeated.

She opened her eyes wide and gave the slightest nod.

I had no idea what she meant. She must be delirious, and I was wasting time trying to find meaning in her fevered ramblings. I sprinted to our cabins and called to Ellie and Rudy, "Come on! We have to get Doctor Plath out of here!"

Darkness was falling quickly. My mind raced, searching for a solution. There was really only one. I ran towards the road, tripping on logs twice. The second time I rolled forward, twisting my shoulder. In the light of the open sky beyond the edge of the plateau, I saw the Jeep. I pulled at the handle, and was relieved when it opened. I yelped with joy when my fingers found the jangle of keys still in the ignition.

I heard Ellie and Rudy calling to me, and I shouted for them to meet me at Plath's cabin. The three of us together should be able to carry her. When I arrived, though, a dark figure was standing in front of her door. It was Burrows. "Calm down, Cal," he said evenly.

"No! You don't understand! Doctor Plath is very sick. She needs help. Now!"

"I know that," he said, in the same measured tone. "Harry and I are taking her to the hospital."

"Oh," I said. I felt like I'd run right off a cliff.

"You shouldn't have gone in, you know. You may be the next one we take to the hospital." Ellie and Rudy arrived, huffing and puffing. "Keep an eye on Cal," he told them. "And make sure he stays outside." Then he walked briskly away.

Harry had been sleeping in the old, original log cabin behind the kitchen tent, and I had plenty of time to relate what I'd seen to my friends before he and Burrows came walking back from that direction. Harry seemed disgruntled, as though he'd been woken from a nap, but he was wearing a slinky silk shirt—unusual for him. "Okay, you three," Burrows said. "We'll take it from here. I'll make sure Doctor Plath knows about your concern and efforts."

He stood and waited until we slowly walked away before opening Plath's door.

We didn't go far, just enough to watch without being obvious. Harry and Burrows emerged with Plath between them, her arms thrown around their necks. They hadn't gone a dozen steps when she must have passed out, slumping so that the two men had to ease her down to the ground.

I started forward, but Burrows saw me and called, "Stay back! We've got this!"

I stood, not sure what to do until Harry and Burrows picked her up by her feet and armpits and staggered away towards the Jeep.

In the darkness we heard the engine turn over and saw headlights blaze forth into the trees. A moment later, the engine sound rose to a whine, and the sound of small stones crunching came to us as the Jeep backed carefully down the steep slope.

"Lucky you brought her condition to his attention," Rudy said.

"Huh?" I said. "No. He said that they were all ready to head off to the hospital anyway."

Ellie and Rudy looked at each other. "You're kidding, right?" Rudy said. "Harry pulled on his pants over his pajamas. He was sleeping!"

That fancy, silky shirt was apparently his pajama top. "Maybe you were right after all about the hostage situation," I said.

We stood in the darkness listening to the Jeep work its way slowly along the rough dirt road.

"What's all the racket?" a voice behind us said.

It was Jeremy. "Burrows and Harry are taking Doctor Plath to the hospital," I replied.

"Damn!" he exclaimed. "Too bad."

He was voicing all of our sentiments, commiserating about Plath's condition.

"That sucks," he said. "And just when we were ready to get rolling."

Maybe not.

I glanced at Ellie, but it was too dark to see her expression. I decided that it didn't matter now anyway, and I was curious what his reaction would be. "Did you know that Burrows was planning his own program to follow?" I asked.

I couldn't see Jeremy's face either, but his tone was genuine surprise. "No! *Really?*"

That answered that.

"How do you know?" he asked.

I hadn't thought this far ahead. "Doctor Plath just told me." This was the truth—she had first talked about it earlier in the day. It was a disingenuous lie, though, since I'd already known about it before that.

"All right!" he exclaimed happily. "Maybe there's hope yet!"

"The real issue is Doctor Plath's health, of course," Ellie said.

"Oh, of course," Jeremy said. "Obviously."

I had the idea that it hadn't been obvious at all.

ж ж ж

Somebody was shaking me, calling my name softly. It was totally dark in the cabin, but I recognized Tim's voice. "Wassa matter?" I mumbled.

"Rudy was knocking at the door," he said. "I thought maybe it was important."

I sat up, rubbing my eyes so that the cabin filled with shooting stars. "What's that?" I asked. There were voices in the near distance—one was unfamiliar, loud and gruff.

"I don't know. Probably why Rudy was knocking."

I pulled on my pants and shoes and went outside. The thin, sharp crescent of the moon had just risen above the hills to the east. I figured that it must be three or four in the morning. From inside the cabin, the faraway voices had sounded ominous, as though imperative orders were being given and received, but now that I could hear them clearly, I could tell that they were talking normally.

I also heard other, closer voices. It was Rudy and Jeremy talking softly. I walked over. "What's going on?" I asked, keeping my voice down.

"Doctor Burrows is back," Jeremy said.

"Who's the other guy?"

Both Burrows' and Plath's cabin doors were open, and soft light leaked out, providing glimpses of both Burrows and a large man with a tight, sculpted beard.

"Dunno," Jeremy replied.

I started off towards them, but Jeremy grabbed my arm. "Burrows told us to stay near our cabins," he said.

"Why?"

"Dunno."

"What's the status with Doctor Plath?"

"Dunno."

"Well, I'm going to find out," I said, trying to shake off his hand, but he gripped harder.

"No!" Jeremy ordered. "Burrows was serious."

"What's going on?"

"I don't know, but I'm sure we'll find out in the morning."

"Well, I'm not waiting 'till morning," I said, prying his fingers up, but he grabbed me with his other hand as well. "Jeremy, do you really want a fist fight?" I asked harshly.

I had gotten loud, and Burrows called over, "Who goes there? Go back to sleep!"

This surprised Jeremy, and he loosened his grip long enough for me to tear free, and I strode away.

"Cal!" Jeremy called, but I just raised a middle finger without looking back. It was too dark for anybody to see what I'd done, but it felt good.

Burrows stood with his hands on his hips waiting for me. The large man came out of Plath's cabin and stood with his arms crossed on his barrel chest.

"Go back to sleep, Caleb," Burrows said when I reached them.

"How's Doctor Plath?" I asked.

"She'll be okay. It's late, and we all need sleep. Now go back to your cabin."

The large man stared at me levelly, eying the obstacle that might need removing.

"Where's Harry?" I asked.

"He stayed behind—with Doctor Plath. Now if you're done with the twenty questions, we'd like to get settled."

"Who's he?" I asked, tilting my thumb at the ogre.

"Caleb, this is your last question, and I mean it. This is Sam. He's going to help out until Harry and Doctor Plath come back."

I glanced inside Plath's cabin and saw a large travel bag, presumably Sam's, on the floor. "Doctor Plath won't be coming back?" I asked.

"Cal! Enough! Go back to your cabin!"

Sam hadn't moved a muscle, clearly waiting for the order to haul me away. I glanced inside Plath's cabin again and my breath caught in my throat. "Right," I said, backing away. "Thanks. See you in the morning."

I turned and hurried back.

"Are you happy, now?" Jeremy asked quietly when I reached the small gathering.

"No," I replied. "Not at all."

"Well, I warned you that Burrows didn't want us to get in the way—"

"Who the hell is that guy?" I asked softly, cutting Jeremy off.

"You heard," Jeremy said. "His name is Sam, and Burrows brought him along to—"

"No, I mean *what* is he?" I peered back in that direction, but he'd disappeared inside what was now his cabin.

"What do you mean, what is he? What kind of stupid question—"

"He brought guns." I said quietly.

That stopped everybody.

"What did you say?" Jeremy asked in a husky whisper.

"There was a rifle, or maybe a shotgun, and a pistol lying on the bed."

"Are you sure?"

It was more an accusation than an actual question.

"No, Jeremy. They might have been stuffed animals. Of *course* I'm sure."

"Well," he said, mulling this. "Maybe he wants to do some hunting."

Rudy chuckled at this.

"What's so funny?" Jeremy asked.

"Well, for one, this is, like, protected US forest, and for another, you don't go hunting with a pistol."

"Yeah?" Jeremy said, challenging. After a few seconds he said, "A pistol would be useful if you came across a mountain lion."

Suddenly Ellie's voice erupted from the cabin just behind us. "I want a pistol!"

Chapter 11

"I hate conflict," I said.

Ellie handed me the bag of powdered eggs. "Then why do you search it out?"

"I don't."

"Then why did you confront Burrows last night?"

"I think I was sleep walking."

I scooped out four cups and added water.

"And I'm a monkey's uncle."

"Wouldn't that be 'aunt'?" I asked, stirring the mixture. "And where did that expression come from, anyway?"

"After the Scopes Trial. People who didn't believe in evolution used it as a joke."

"Which means that you don't believe in evolution."

"The joke itself has evolved," she said, "so now it's actually a joke on the very people who don't believe in evolution."

"You just made that up, didn't you?"

"Prove it."

"Let's cut the chatter!" Jeremy called from behind the tent where he was scraping a pan.

Burrows had informed us earlier that morning that the meal schedules had changed. Instead of taking turns preparing meals for each other, each group would make their own meals, and would alternate going first. The problem was that Burrows scheduled the morning turnover for seven o'clock, which meant that the first group—us that morning—had to get a very early start, and we were all groggy from the middle-of-the-night commotion.

The greens started showing up while I was still eating and talking with Rudy who had finished. "Hey!" one of them called. "This pan is dirty!"

"That's because I haven't cleaned it yet," I said. "Take it easy—it's not seven yet."

I looked at my watch and sighed. It was 6:56.

"I'll clean it," Rudy said. "You finish eating."

"Thanks," I said, but remembered that the mixing bowl was dirty as well. I put down my food and followed Rudy.

We were nearly done when the same complainer called out that our time was up. "Jesus Christ!" I exclaimed. "Take a chill-pill already."

"Hey!" he shouted back. "Wise guy!"

Apparently everybody was short on sleep.

"Look," I said, swishing the rinse water around, "just give us another minute, and we'll be out of here."

"I want an apology," he insisted.

"An apology for what? Holding you up for sixty seconds? You going to be late for an important meeting?"

"For cursing, you asshole!"

He started towards me, and I dropped the bowl and jumped up. "Barry!"

It was Albert, the green leader, trotting over. "Cool it! Just start getting the ingredients ready."

"Thanks," I said to Albert, when Barry had walked away.

He gave me the brusque little Albert head wag. "Next time be done by seven."

He turned and walked away.

"For somebody who hates conflict," Rudy said, "you sure seem to find enough of it."

Once the greens were done with breakfast and cleaned up, Burrows called everybody to the kitchen tent. Standing on a boulder above us, he announced that the blue group—the demonstrated master cabin builders—would finish the last cabin. The greens had lost their chance.

Grumbles rippled through the greens who stood clumped together, like we—the blues—always did.

"But the green group will be busy as well," Burrows went on. "The two porta-toilets are nearly full. The green group will dig four holes—the first two to deposit the existing waste. You'll knock out the bottoms of the toilet holding tanks, and position the toilets over the second two holes. This way, we can continue using the porta-toilets indefinitely."

Silence.

"Holy shit!" Ralph yelled, throwing his arms around.

"I can vouch for the accuracy of only half of that," Burrows quipped.

"No way!" Ralph shouted. "This sucks! I'm not cleaning up their shit!"

He was referring to us, the blues, and for once, I felt bad for Ralph.

Burrows shook his head. "Sorry, Ralph. I'm afraid you have no choice."

"Like hell I don't! I can *leave*!"

Burrows just shook his head, seeming sympathetic.

"God damn it!" Ralph called out. "I'm outta here."

"Ralph!" Burrows shouted.

That gave Ralph a moment's pause.

"Don't be a fool," Burrows said more quietly.

"Are you going to stop me?" Ralph challenged.

"In fact, yes."

"Like hell," Ralph said, stomping off.

"Ralph!" Burrows called again, and the angry man wheeled around. "I'm warning you," Burrows called, "you don't want to push this."

Ralph's mouth was a tight line. He bent down, picked a stone and threw it. He meant to hit Burrows, but it fell short. Tim jumped out of the way, and it hit Dale in the thigh.

"That does it!" Burrows shouted. "Sam! Restrain him before he hurts somebody else. Jeremy, Dana, help Sam."

Jeremy hesitated, but Dana, niece of the same-exclusive-club-uncle, practically sprinted over. Brow furrowed, Jeremy followed.

Sam had started for Ralph who stood with his fists raised, but Albert put his hands out. "Wait! It's not necessary!" He turned to Ralph. "Tell them you'll calm down. Tell them!"

Ralph glanced from Albert to Burrows, his mouth working, as though he was chewing his own teeth.

Burrows didn't wait. "Do it, Sam," he said.

The hulk pushed past Albert. Ralph tried to run, but Dana stopped him. Ralph punched her, but she'd given Sam time to reach them, and he slapped aside Ralph's swinging fists like a couple of pesky flies. With smooth, almost instantaneous movements, he wrapped one arm around Ralph's neck from behind, holding the angry young man's wrist twisted behind his back with the other. Then he swept Ralph's feet out from under him with his giant boot, and carefully lowered him to the ground, face buried in the pine needles. Holding his victim down with a knee on his back, Sam reached around and grabbed one of half a dozen long plastic tie wraps from under his belt, which he used to bind Ralph's wrists. Sam lifted the vanquished man to his feet like a sack of potatoes. Still Ralph resisted, twisting and jerking. The sculpture-bearded peacekeeper smacked Ralph on the head with his palm, and the green troublemaker finally gave in to his fate. He stood, slumped, pine needles and leaves adorning his hair.

"Son-of-a-bitch," Rudy whispered next to me.

I glanced at him, and he shook his head in amazement.

Burrows had climbed down off the boulder, and led Albert away, talking to him quietly with one hand on his shoulder. He turned and gestured to Sam, and the hired hand pushed Ralph roughly down to a sitting position and followed.

Ellie came over. "Where did Burrows find this guy?" she said just loud enough for Rudy and me to hear. People were talking together, but quietly—nobody risked disturbing the peace. "Did he borrow him from a Mexican Cartel?"

"Who carries eighteen-inch tie wraps around?" Rudy asked.

I watched Burrows talking to Albert and Sam. We couldn't hear what they were saying, but Albert just stared at Burrows glumly, now and then looking down at Sam's boots as if the full story might be found there.

"He was just looking for a reason to show how tough Sam can be," I said.

"Burrows, you mean?" Ellie asked.

"Yeah. It was like Sam knew exactly what to do, like it had been rehearsed."

"He couldn't have known how Ralph was going to react," Rudy said.

I replayed the scene in my head. "Maybe not exactly, but any of us could have predicted that Ralph would go berserk over toilet duty."

"And it might have been a general order," Ellie added.

"Like, Burrows might have told Sam to just be on the lookout for an opportunity to slap one of us down?" I said.

"Yeah," Rudy said. "And you never have to wait long for Ralph to provide that opportunity."

Burrows had broken up the pow-wow and they walked back. He clapped to get our attention, as though imitating Plath. "Okay! Let's get the day's program started. Jeremy will lead the blue crew on the cabin, and Albert will engineer the toilet reconfiguring."

Albert stood, stone-faced. He was never easy to read, but now he looked like he was in a trance.

"He's been coerced," Ellie whispered.

"How can you tell?" I asked out of the corner of my mouth.

"He doesn't look at Burrows. At all."

"And you think that means—?"

"Quiet!" Burrows called.

I jerked upright when I realized he was staring at us. Sam was looking at us as well, and that straightened my posture even more.

Burrows finished up by reminding us that the blues had first shift for evening kitchen access, and that the turnover time was 6:00 PM—sharp.

We'd started walking away when somebody in the green group called out, "What's going to happen to Ralph?"

Burrows turned back and scanned the gathering a moment. Sam had started to lead Ralph away, but stopped as well. "Nothing," Burrows said. "We'll give him time to cool down in Sam's cabin."

"The jail," Rudy said, louder than I would have liked.

"Who said that?" Burrows barked, looking across the faces. Nobody spoke up, but his gaze rested on Rudy and me.

When we finally split up and walked away, I whispered to Rudy, "Thanks a lot! I hope you like tie wrap scars."

"Ah," my friend replied, "he's just a big teddy bear."

I shot him a glance.

"With big, sharp claws," he added.

"And guns," I reminded.

"Oh yeah." Rudy said, thoughtfully. "And guns."

ж ж ж

The blue group hadn't lost the cabin-building finesse during our short respite, and once we organized the scattered mess the greens had left behind, we swung into gear, and the progress became visible hour-by-hour.

The greens, in the meantime, had a short, if frustrating, run at digging their four holes. "Digging," consisted of pulling away a foot or so of fresh and decayed pine needles, and then hauling out the rocks and boulders underneath. Although hard work, the process was self-limiting, as only a couple of feet of mountain stone rubble could be removed before striking the bedrock bones of the mountain itself.

If the hole-digging was shorter than expected, "reconfiguring" the toilets was significantly more unappealing than expected, at least as measured by the curses and howls of odorous protest echoing among the pines as the sloshing-full tanks were pierced to let the vile sludge gurgle out. The good news for the greens was that they had the two porta-toilets positioned over the fresh cavities by mid-afternoon, and their ordeal over.

I was taking my turn with the Phillips screwdriver, trying my best to keep up with the slot-heads advancing ahead of me, when Rudy elbowed me. For the last five minutes or so, I had half-consciously noted shouts from the other side of the plateau, but now I saw what Rudy was pointing at. The green team was lined up in two rows of four, with Albert facing them, waving their arms over their heads in unison, swinging down to touch one toe, and then another. All the while, they were chanting.

"What are they saying?" I asked.

Rudy listened a moment. "I think they're saying:
'Greens are lean,
 greens are mean,
 boos to blues,
 loose the blues!'"

"Sure," I said, "sounds good to me."

"What sounds good?"

"That they're giving us their booze."

"No. 'Boos' as in 'Boo! You guys stink!'"

"Really? That's not very nice."

Burrows stood off to the side watching the show, arms crossed on his chest.

"It's a morale builder," Jeremy said. He'd come over and was watching them as well. "Like cheer leaders at a football game. He's countering their shame over toilet duty."

"Albert or Burrows?"

"It was Doctor Burrows' idea. He told the greens that it's to prepare them for the games."

"It was his idea to put 'em on toilet duty—what games?"

"Dunno. Are you guys going to work? Or do you want Doctor Burrows to have *us* move the toilets?"

"Right!" I shouted to the rest of the crew. "Get to work, you lazy slobs!"

ж ж ж

Dinner ended in a mad rush. I wanted to get an early start to avoid a repeat of the green's morning bitching, but Jeremy insisted that we finish the last wall of the cabin. I think he wanted to prove that we were indeed the better builders. That meant, however, that we hurried through preparing the canned hash and canned boiled potatoes, and made enough mess of it that whatever time we saved, we lost in cleanup. As it was, Barry and another green arrived five minutes early, insisting that it was 6:00. This time it was Viona who carried the argument, fruitlessly trying to get them to look at her self-calibrating watch, tuned to the US government's atomic clock. Their tactic was simply not to look, and this frustrated her so much that she finally called them nincompoops. They laughed at this, which made her all the angrier.

Albert showed up, and his comment was that if we could prepare canned foods as efficiently as building cabins, then we'd manage to be done early. I thought he was joking until I remembered he never joked. I looked at Jeremy, but he just called for us to wrap it up already.

As we were walking away, Rudy stopped and made a dramatic gesture of sniffing the air. "Hey! I smell eau de toilette—no, my mistake, it's just plain old toilet."

Barry growled and started towards him, but Albert put his hand out and stopped him.

During all of this, Sam sat on a log eating hash from his bowl. I expected him to play policeman, but he didn't even look over.

ж ж ж

An hour later we sat on the Potato Chip watching the wispy feather clouds turning pink. Surges of shouting and laughter issued from the dark forest behind us. It was the greens, playing charades, a complete turnaround from the usual cantankerous melee that could erupt at the drop of an insult.

"Do you think Plath's gone for good?" Ellie asked.

I sighed. "Good question. We've finished the cabins—or are about to. Even if she comes back, I guess her experiment is finished."

"She told you that the cabin-building was the extent of it?"

"Actually no. I assumed that. But her whole attitude was that she was done. I believe it."

"Huh," she mumbled.

"What're you thinking?"

"Well, you said that she told you that Burrows has his own experiment—"

"Program. Or exercise. He doesn't call it an experiment."

"Whatever. The point is, when is he going to begin his?"

"Another good question," I said. "Doctor Plath talked about his theory."

"That group hierarchies are affected by dangers to the group."

"Yeah. I wish I'd, like, recorded it. I'm not sure I got it all."

"Let's assume you got that much right. What if the experiment—the *program*—has already begun?"

Silence. Rudy had been reclining, listening to us, but now he sat up.

"Uh-oh," Rudy said. "I'll bet it's Sam."

"Sam's the danger?" I said.

"You don't think he's dangerous?" Rudy said. "He has guns. And a rap beard."

"What's a rap beard?"

"Any beard that takes more than three minutes a day to maintain."

"You're insane."

"Guys," Ellie said.

"Right," I said. "Burrows' program. I don't know. Sam was pretty rough with Ralph, but otherwise, he just ignores us."

"Exactly. Does he help us?" She asked.

"No, that would be the opposite of ignoring us—ah, I see. Burrows said he brought Sam to help out until Harry returned."

"Maybe he's just lazy," Rudy said. "Maybe he's, like, a big disappointment to Burrows."

"Sure, Rudy." I said. "And Burrows is going to just go along with that."

"Sam's got the guns," he said.

"You are insane."

"That is possible, I suppose. I'd be the last to know."

We watched the pink bleed from the clouds, leaving behind a charcoal sketch where there had been a watercolor.

"Hey," Rudy said. "Remember what Burrows told us about the toilets? By digging holes, we could continue using them indefinitely." Feigning ignorance, he added, "Indefinitely means no expected end, right?"

Our shared silence was a collective sigh.

Chapter 12

Rudy kept his gaze glued to his watch. "Okay!" he said, "Let's go!"

He jumped up, and I followed.

"You're both insane," Ellie said as we took off for the kitchen tent. "You know that, don't you?"

"It's a matter of blue honor," I replied.

"No," she called, "it's a matter of macho head-butting!"

We waved to Dale and Tim, and they followed along.

"You're all nincompoops!" Viona shouted.

The greens disappointed us. When we arrived at the kitchen tent at precisely 6:59 AM, they had already vacated, and were sitting together on rocks and logs, eating. "See?" Barry shouted. "That's the way it's done, blue-dogs!"

Albert told him to shut up.

"Darn," Rudy said quietly as we started our preparations, "no head-butting today."

"We'll have another chance at dinner," I reminded him.

"Yeah," he agreed, nodding. "In fact, we can stack the deck— hide the pans when we're done this morning."

"You're dangerous, you know."

"Fine. I'll do it myself."

"I didn't say I wouldn't help."

As we were cleaning up later, Dale expressed reservations at the plan, and Tim agreed. He suggested that it might backfire. I caved, and we told Rudy that we'd tell Sam if he did it on his own. He called us a bunch of pansy-asses, but that was the end of it.

After breakfast, Burrows called us together again for another announcement. He told us that it was obvious that we were all getting out of shape, and he had the remedy. "It's a game that's been played in these woods for over six decades," he said brightly.

"Pin the tail on the donkey?" someone called.

Burrows smile disappeared, and he glanced pointedly at Sam who stood off to the side. There were no more interruptions.

Burrows reached into a box and pulled out a pair of green shorts, sturdy twill, the baggy sort worn in junior-high gym classes. He reached into another box and held up an identical blue pair. "These are your game shorts," he explained. "They're one-size-fits-all, no gender."

As we filed past, taking the dreaded ghosts of our pre-teen years, he also handed us two small squares of cloth, also of our group color. We passed around a permanent marker, writing our initials in large letters on our two cloth squares as instructed while Burrows explained the game. "These are your passport tags," he said. "You need one attached to the back of your shorts to stay in the game."

The shorts had a loop sewn on the back of the waist band; each cloth square had a pliable plastic hook that could be hung from the loop. "Each group has a team flag," he continued, holding up green and blue cloths one foot square. "The goal is to hang your flag from the opponent's embassy—a pole."

Does he think we're *third-graders*?" Rudy whispered, and I elbowed him to be quiet, glancing at Sam to see if he was reaching for a tie-wrap.

"You'll start the game," he went on, "wearing one of your passport tags, but you'll want to give your other one to someone you trust. If the opposing team manages to take your first tag, you must sit down and wait until your trusted friend delivers your backup tag. If your opponents capture both your passports, you're out of the game. You also forfeit whatever other tags you may be carrying."

He scanned across his two groups of Olympic hopefuls. "Any questions?"

After a moment, Tim slowly raised his hand.

"Yes?" Burrows asked.

"Are there any, um, rules of engagement?"

"Rules of engagement?" Burrows repeated as though surprised by the question. "It's just a game, Tim. It's not a battle." He chuckled.

I assumed he was laughing at the absurdity of the thought.

ж ж ж

"No way!" Albert insisted. "That's not even ten feet."

"How do you know?" I said. "You haven't measured it."

I was standing on rungs that we'd nailed to the tree trunk—the "embassy tower"—holding on with one hand and poised to drive a nail through the mounting board with the other. Dale, the tallest among the blues, was standing on one of the cabin's packing cases holding the mounting board in place. This board in turn supported the "embassy pole," a one-foot aluminum pipe with a metal ring bolted to the far end.

"Because I can touch it," Albert said, illustrating by reaching up on his toes and resting the tips of his fingers against the bottom. "It's not even ten feet," he repeated.

"Fine," I agreed, despondently. Nailing hardware into a live pine tree was an exercise in spreading resin from your hands to your clothes, and eventually to your face and hair. And pine resin doesn't come off with just soap and water.

"We'll need more rungs to get higher," Dale observed.

I climbed down and Rudy handed me another board that we'd salvaged from the cabin scraps. I was at least thankful that Jeremy wasn't hovering over the construction, doling out obvious advice. He was at the other end of the plateau, policing the green's construction of the embassy tower and pole in our blue territory. Burrows had arranged the construction this way to ensure fairness—each team was building its own embassy destination. If a rung broke off at a critical moment in the game, it would be our own fault.

"Fifteen feet," Dale muttered, gazing up the trunk. "We probably need at least three more rungs."

According to the rules—Burrows' rules—fifteen feet was the minimum height for the embassy pole.

"Do you think the Boy Scouts really played this game?" Rudy asked.

"No idea," I answered. "It sounds a lot like capture-the-flag, but sort of the inverse."

"Why do you think he didn't just have us play capture-the-flag?"

I shrugged.

"It's more team-oriented this way," Ellie said. She and Viona sat nearby, content to let the men show off their masculine talents and cover themselves in pine resin. "One person has to transport your team's flag all the way across the playing field. That's very vulnerable. The whole game can be won by just capturing that one person. In capture-the-flag, anybody who gets close can grab the opponents' flag and tear for home. Also, there's the strategy of who carries who's spare tag. Burrows' game requires coordination and planning. Capture-the-flag is more like a pack of hyenas going after a crippled fawn."

"Nice imagery," Rudy said. "It's nightmares for me tonight."

"You had nightmares from seeing a raven grab a worm," I said.

"I happen to be sensitive. Women like sensitive guys, right, Ellie?"

"Oh yeah. Especially if they're covered in pine sap. So get to work."

Ж Ж Ж

When Burrows called us together to kick off the first rounds of the game, I was still struggling with my dilemma—whom to pick to carry my spare passport tag. Dale was the logical choice, since he was tall and fast, but I hated to lose the opportunity to connect with Ellie. Rudy had already been tapped to carry Viona's, and I was secretly relieved, since I wasn't sure how much I trusted my highly honorable, but hapless friend to carry mine.

Of course, it was just a game. I had no reason to be concerned.

"The game today will be won by the first team to win two rounds," Burrows announced. "Each round begins with my whistle—I'll referee. Each team will have a leader who will decide how the spare passport tags are allocated and who starts off carrying the team flag."

So much for worrying about who will carry mine.

"Note that there are no boundaries," he added. "You can climb San Jacinto Peak if you like. The green team will be led by Albert, and the blue team by Ellie."

Silence.

"Excuse me?" Ellie asked.

"You heard me. You'll be leading the blue team today."

Ellie was stunned, staring at Burrows wide-eyed. I sneaked a look at Jeremy. He too was staring at Burrows, but his fists were clenched.

"You have fifteen minutes to change into your game clothes and gather behind your home line before I blow the whistle to begin," Burrows said, and walked away.

Ellie turned to Jeremy. "Look, forget what Burrows said. What's he going to do? Stop you from talking? What matters is who we *want* as a leader, right?" She looked around at the rest of us blues. "We want Jeremy, right?"

Silence.

"No," Jeremy said, before the silence became too obvious. "It's Burrows' show. You're the leader."

Ellie didn't like it, but we didn't have time to argue. "Let's change and meet at our starting line as soon as possible," she said. It was a suggestion, not an order.

I despised those shorts. On men, the one-gender monstrosities looked like women's shorts, and on women, they looked like men's.

We met at our end of the plateau, and Ellie asked if anybody hadn't yet exchanged passport tags. I was the only one who raised my hand. "I guess you and I will just trade, then," she said, handing me her spare tag.

"Hey!" Dana objected. "I thought you were supposed to allocate them?"

Ellie shrugged. "Looks like we've already worked it out."

"That's not the way a real leader would do it——"

"Seems as good as any other method," Jeremy interrupted, and I was impressed that he stood up for Ellie. "At least, at first," he continued. "It takes experience to assess the capabilities of your people and make informed decisions," he said, deflating my heightened opinion.

"How much time do we have?" Ellie asked.

"Maybe three minutes," Dale replied.

"Crumb! What can we do in three minutes?"

Ellie looked around. "Jeremy, how about you take the team flag?"

He hesitated just a moment before taking it. "What's the plan?" he asked.

I couldn't tell if it was a challenge.

Her mouth puckered sideways in thought. "I guess we'll just have to play it by ear for the first round." Her eyes brightened. "Hey, how about we sort of try a rush—we stay close to Jeremy, and keep all the greens away."

"We'll just get tagged," Dana scoffed.

"That's okay. It's sort of a big sacrifice. The only thing that matters is which team hangs their flag first. In fact, we could do a fake-out—let them think somebody else is the flag carrier. Jeremy will keep it hidden."

She thought a moment. "We'll run in pairs—stay close to your tag partner. If he gets tagged, don't hang around too long—if you can't get him his spare tag right away, just leave him and keep going. We'll let them think that Dale is carrying the flag—keep him surrounded, as though protecting him. Jeremy, you're going to have to be out front. They'll be expecting that. Who's Jeremy's partner?"

Dana's hand shot up, and Ellie hesitated only a moment. "If Jeremy gets tagged, you'll have to stay with him—"

"They'll be expecting that too," Rudy quipped.

"Quiet, Rudy. If Jeremy gets tagged, we'll have to draw the greens away somehow so Dana can get him his spare tag."

Burrows' whistle sounded somewhere off in the thick pines.

"Quick!" Ellie urged. "Gather around close to cover Jeremy so he can hide the embassy flag."

He tried to tie it around his waist under his shirt, but it wasn't long enough. In desperation, he shoved it down under the waistband of his shorts. Perhaps the only positive attribute about the androgynous embarrassments was that there was enough room inside to hide a pillow.

We took off, an uncoordinated stampede with Jeremy vaguely out front, and Dale approximately in the middle. Something seemed wrong, but in the rush, I couldn't place it. We passed Burrows. He was striding purposefully towards our home end.

We met the line of greens just our side of the kitchen tent. They had chosen a different strategy. Instead of a confused gaggle, they were advancing in a line. Their tallest runner, dead ahead of us, was carrying their flag openly, balled up in one hand. When he saw our mob advancing, he sprinted off to our right, and the three greens on that side followed. The greens on our left began converging towards us.

The hole in our plan became immediately obvious, and it was large enough to drive a Jeep Wrangler through. We were all offense.

"Rudy! Viona!" I shouted. "Go back and guard our tower!"

Rudy spun and took off. "You mean their embassy!" he called. Viona followed him.

The four greens attacking us were calling to each other, trying to figure out who was carrying our flag. Ellie ran towards them, heading them off. "Protect Dale!" she yelled, and it took me a second to remember that she was playing them up. I took off after her, but she was too far ahead. Two greens came in on each side of her, and before I could reach her, one of them grabbed her, while the other reached down and tore away her tag, holding it up triumphantly as they ran on. They eyed me, but ran past, deciding that I wasn't the flag bearer.

I ran to Ellie. "Here," I said, panting, handing her the spare tag.

She didn't take it, turning her back to me instead, saying, "You weren't supposed to hang around."

"I ... I didn't."

I was flustered, wondering why in the world she'd turned her back on me.

She glanced back. "Well?" she said.

"Oh!"

I attached the tag to her hook, and we ran off to catch up with the rest.

I saw Jeremy running ahead of the pack, and I pointed, but Ellie was already angling in that direction. Out of nowhere a green woman was upon us. I jumped in front of Ellie and held out my hands defensively, and the woman came right up and wrapped her arms around me, as though meeting a long-lost lover. This was so unusual in my experience that I was momentarily stunned. I felt something tug at my shorts and an instant later she backed away holding my tag.

She tried to step around me to get at Ellie, but I blocked her. "Sorry, Cal!" Ellie shouted, and I heard her footsteps pounding away. The green woman gave up and ran off towards the blue mob. "Not even a kiss goodbye?" I yelled to her, but she ignored me.

I was tagless, and was supposed to sit and wait. I rebelled and stood and waited. Jeremy was standing still, fifty feet away. A green man faced away from him, holding a blue tag. The green guy had already tagged Jeremy, and was vying for Dana, who hovered waiting to get to her mentor.

That's when I saw Ellie being really stupid. She was limping slowly back to me, holding out my spare tag, not twenty feet from the green man.

I was confused. "You have no spare tag!" I yelled. "He's going to get you!"

She wagged her head. "It doesn't matter! You still have it, right?"

She gave me a look like I was dumber than a doorknob.

Her ploy finally seeped through my thick skull. I reached into my empty pocket and balled my fist, hoping it looked like I was clutching a balled-up flag. "Yeah! Come on, girl!" I shouted, reaching out hungrily with my other hand.

The green took the bait. He abandoned Dana and sprinted for me. I held up my hand to him. "You need both my tags first!"

It just might work.

Cursing, he turned to run back to Ellie, who started to limp away, but then he stopped and came back. "That's not in the rules!"

"You sure?" I asked, but the ruse was over.

"Come on," he demanded. "Hand it over."

I stared at him until he reached forward to take it himself. I held up my free hand to stop him, and slowly pulled my other hand from my pocket, grabbing the bottom first. He watched expectantly until the pocket emerged inside-out.

"What the hell?" he said, then realized the scam and turned away.

It was too late. Jeremy was a small figure, racing away to our embassy at the far end of green territory.

A minute later, an air horn sounded from that direction, announcing we'd won the round.

I trotted over to Ellie. "What happened?" I asked.

"What do you mean? We won!"

"No. I mean your foot—you hurt it."

In answer, she jumped up and down and ran around in a quick little circle.

"Remind me to never play poker with you," I said.

Chapter 13

"I'm thinking the same configuration," Ellie announced, "but this time, Jeremy's in the middle, and Tim is out front."

Burrows had given us precisely ten minutes to catch our breath and regroup before the second round. If his goal was to get us into shape, he was either going to achieve it quickly or kill us.

"That's stupid," Dana said. "They'll know now that Tim will be carrying the flag."

"I didn't say that Tim would be carrying it."

"Me again?" Jeremy asked, skeptical about the simple switch ploy.

"You're both assuming that it will either be the guy out front, or in the middle, and I'm hoping they'll assume the same thing."

Jeremy nodded appreciatively. "They'll be trying to guess whether it's Tim or me with the flag, when in fact it's neither of us."

"Yep," Ellie said, eyeing the rest of us, and finally handing the flag to Rudy. "Protect it well, sir knight," she said.

He held it between the tips of his forefinger and thumb. "Did you put this inside your undershorts?" he asked Jeremy.

"Can it, Rudy, and stash the flag already," she said.

"So much for fealty to knights," he muttered as he folded the cloth before tucking it under his waistband.

"It's knights that swear fealty to the queen," she corrected. "Dale and Cal, maybe you two could stay and guard the post."

This required exchanging some spare flags, and Burrows' whistle sounded just as we were done. The six of them trotted off, and I shouted, "God-speed! Blues uber alles!"

The greens came into view running at top speed well before our pack reached the cabins, and I watched as the battle unfolded. Ralph and Barry—the complainer and the troublemaker—went immediately for Tim, who tried to avoid them, but they blocked him on both sides. Behind Tim, the rest of the blue herd angled off to the left, leaving him as a sacrifice. Instead of pulling off Tim's tag, though, Ralph wrapped his arms around him, pinning him, while Barry yanked his shorts down to his ankles. Only then did Barry snatch the tag away and, having found no hidden flag, took off. Before following him, Ralph gave Tim a push, and, his legs hobbled, the boy fell hard, out of my view behind a log. I held my breath a few seconds until he got up on his hands and knees, and then sat back, rubbing his shoulder.

Viona was standing by herself as the rest of the blues ran on. Her tag was gone—she'd obviously been caught. The two green strippers ran to her, and I caught enough words to gather that they were demanding she lower her shorts. I saw her shake her head, and Ralph stepped in to restrain her, but she flailed her arms. He grabbed one wrist, and wrapped his other arm around her neck. She twisted and kicked, but Barry managed to grab her waistband, and with one yank, the loose garment came down revealing white, heavy legs and panties.

Ralph let her go, and they both turned to meet an angry Ellie who was sprinting towards them.

Dale was shouting protests next to me, and I told him to wait there, and I took off. Ellie was screaming with rage, and Barry circled around, so that her torrent of curses was divided. Ralph stepped in to grab her, and she pulled a fist back to swing, but Barry caught her wrist. This threw her off balance, and she fell back, into his arms. Ralph hung on as Barry went in for the yank. Ellie waited for the right moment, then kicked, catching Barry in the chin, knocking him down. He was up in an instant, rubbing his cheek. He kicked her leg, then slapped her across the face. Hard. Her head twisted sideways, and she slumped in Ralph's arms.

I heard myself spitting foul curses as I ran towards them, seemingly in slow motion. Rudy was closer, and he reached them as Barry struggled to hold up the dazed woman so that Ralph could do the yank.

"I've got it!" Rudy shouted, and the two bullies paused. As he ran the final ten yards, Rudy reached inside his shorts and pulled out the folded flag. "Here, you sons-of-bitches!" he shouted, and threw it at them.

Ralph let Ellie slide to the ground while Barry picked up the flag.

I finally reached them. Rudy was kneeling beside Ellie, and I could see that she was conscious, rubbing her face. "What the hell?" I screamed.

Barry shoved the flag at my face. "You lose, sucker!" he crowed.

"Are you a complete psychopath?" I shouted. "Are you insane or just a total idiot?"

That got to him. Evidently Barry did *not* like having his intelligence questioned. He handed the flag to Ralph, and rushed me, but, heart pounding, I stood my ground, waiting for a fist to slam me. Barry's nose was nearly touching mine when he growled, "What did you say?" I could smell that'd he had peanut butter crackers with lunch.

"I said you're a psychopath—tearing clothes off women!"

Okay, I did chicken out. I guessed he didn't care about being accused of assault.

"You're just jealous," he said, stepping back.

I realized I'd been holding my breath.

"Hey!"

It was Jeremy, walking over to us. Albert was coming from the opposite direction.

"What's going on?" Jeremy asked. Rudy had helped Ellie to her feet. "Are you okay?" Jeremy asked her.

"I'm fine," she said, giving her head a little shake, as though waking up. "These imbeciles decided it's okay to disrobe women to find the flag."

Our group leader looked around at us, then stepped back, saying nothing more. He'd been replaced as leader for the game, and was making a show of the fact.

Albert arrived. "You hurt?" he asked Ellie.

"I'm okay, but your goons—"

"He punched her," I said, pointing at Barry.

"I didn't punch her, you stupid fu—"

"Wait!" Albert said, cutting him off. "Why'd you hit her?" he asked Barry.

"She kicked me first!"

"That true?" he asked Ellie.

"Probably, but it was self-defense, and in any case, who hit who is not the point. The point is that your monkeys think it's okay to rip clothes off women!"

I wasn't sure Albert had heard her. He looked around, sizing up the group. "Looks like you guys got a little rough," he said to Barry and Ralph.

"Damn right—!" I started.

He held his hand up to stop me.

"What did you expect us to do?" Albert asked Ellie.

"What do you mean?" Her eyes got big. "You told them it was *okay* to pull our clothes off?" she squeaked, flabbergasted.

"I didn't tell them to get rough," he reasoned. "You chose to hide your flag that way."

Burrows called to us, making his way through the maze of tree trunks. "What's the problem?"

"Blues are unhappy with the way we play," Albert said.

Burrows looked at the blue flag in Ralph's hand. "Greens win?" he asked.

"Yeah," Albert replied.

"Very good. Looks like the next round will decide the game."

"Wait one goddamn minute!" Ellie shouted. "Do you know what they *did* to win?"

Burrows looked at Ralph and then at her. "Seems like they captured your embassy flag."

"They're pulling our *pants* off!" she screeched.

Burrows looked at Albert, who shrugged. "They were hiding their flag," the green leader said.

Burrows turned to Ellie.

"That's no excuse!" she exclaimed. "It's a game! There's absolutely no excuse—"

Burrows put his hand up to her. "I have an answer."

She stood, waiting.

"Don't hide your flag down your pants," he said. Then, he clapped his hands, calling loudly, "Ten minutes 'till the next round!" and Ralph and Barry sped off.

"Now wait a minute!" Ellie objected, but he walked away. "No! You can't just …"

She gave up. She knew it was no use.

Albert started walking away. "Wait!" she called, and ran over to him. I couldn't hear what she said, but the two of them walked slowly away, talking and gesturing with their hands.

Viona came over. "You gave up the flag," she said to Rudy.

"Yeah," he said, surprised at the challenge.

She smiled. "Thanks."

Rudy smiled back and raised his eyebrows. "Nice panties, by the way."

She lowered her head and glowered at him from under her eyebrows.

"Sorry!" he said, holding up his hands to thwart her charge. "Boy," he said to me, "try to give a gal a compliment!"

We waited as the minutes ticked by, then gave up and ambled back to our home line. "How long's it been?" I asked Dale.

He looked at his watch. "At least fifteen minutes."

"I wonder what's going on?" I said, but the answer was walking towards us, crunching twigs and swiping stray branches out of the way.

Sam didn't say anything until he stopped in front of our group. "Burrows wants everybody at the mess tent," he announced, then turned, and crunched his way back in the direction he'd come.

"What's going on?" Tim asked.

"As Burrows himself would say," Rudy responded, 'I have an answer.'"

Rudy's answer was to sprint away towards the kitchen tent.

When we arrived, the greens were all there, including Albert, but I didn't see Ellie. Rudy nudged me, and I saw her coming from the direction of her cabin. She looked even angrier, if that was possible.

We didn't have a chance to talk to her, as Burrows called us to attention with a sharp clap from what had become his podium boulder. He didn't look happy, either.

"I'm afraid we've had a bit of cheating!" he announced.

Ellie looked like she was going to explode, and Sam stood casually next to her, and I guessed that this was not coincidence.

"Jeremy will be the leader for the blues team, now," Burrows went on, paused, then lifted his head and smiled. "Let's have some fun for the last round today! Ten minutes to the whistle!"

He clapped his hands again, and the greens and blues walked off in different directions.

"What happened?" I asked Ellie.

"That son-of-a-bitch," she muttered, barely able to contain herself.

"Who, Albert?"

"No! That bastard, Burrows."

"What'd he do?"

She just shook her head, as if she couldn't believe it. "I was talking with Albert about setting some ground rules, like no physical contact, no hiding the flag."

"Yeah? Sounds good."

"Burrows didn't think so. He saw us talking and asked what was going on. When I told him, he looked at Albert and asked him if this was his idea. He said no, which was true, and Burrows got angry and accused me of sabotaging the program. Now, how could I be sabotaging his program when we were just playing a game? When I challenged him about that, he got even angrier and corrected himself—I was sabotaging the game, not the program. And then when I asked him how it was sabotage when Albert and I were going to agree on everything, he just cut me off and said I was done. I was so mad, I had to walk away before I spit in his face."

Rudy, Ellie, and I walked on in silence. "Spitting in someone's face is a misdemeanor, you know," Rudy finally said. "Can I watch if you do?"

Ж Ж Ж

Jeremy had only a couple of minutes to formulate a strategy, and nobody had their hearts in it. Not even him. We lost the round in record time, and the greens were the game winners that day.

We waited until 6:10 before heading over to the kitchen tent. It gave the greens plenty of time to vacate before we arrived.

Chapter 14

The faerie lights of Hemet twinkled in the distance. The Potato Chip beneath my legs and hands was still toasty from the warm day, the warmth welcomed as the mountain temperature fell steadily towards chilly.

"Why do you think he did it?" Ellie asked.

"Burrows?" I said.

"Yeah. Why make me team leader for the game, when it was obviously a slap in the face for Jeremy?"

"I've been wondering about that. Let me ask you this—why did Burrows agree to let me come along in the first place?"

"Back at the bus stop?"

"Yeah. Remember? He was adamant that he didn't want me."

She lifted her shoulders. "We convinced him, I guess."

"No, you extorted him. You threatened to drop out if he didn't take me—thanks, by the way."

"It wasn't just me. It was Rudy as well."

"But it was you he wanted badly enough to cave in about me."

"How do you know that?"

"Okay, I don't know, but my intuition tells me it's a sure bet. It was the way he looked at you. He seemed happy—no, intrigued—about having you join."

"Why, for God's sake?"

"Besides the obvious?"

"What's the obvious?"

"Oh, come on. A vivacious young woman, along on an extended group encounter in the wilderness?"

She gave me a little shove. "You're more insane than Rudy. He hasn't made the slightest—not the tiniest—move towards me."

"Maybe he's gay. But your female appeal would be just the obvious reason to maybe want you along. I think—I intuit—he had other motives."

"Like what? He likes people with names that contain a lot of vowels?"

"What was your original question?"

She had to think a moment. "Why he picked me to be the game team leader. I still don't get it."

"You just *said* it. Because he thought you might make a good leader. He saw a strength in you. After all, you stood up to him over me."

A cricket fired up nearby. "Maybe," she conceded. "If so, I certainly disappointed him. I still don't understand his objections. His reaction was way over the top."

"Like you said, you disappointed him. I think that he wants to keep the two groups completely separate, and you were trying to build a bridge."

"Huh," she muttered, contemplating this.

The sound of footsteps announced Rudy's return. He'd gone back to the cabins to get our jackets. "Jeremy's putting together a schedule for meal duties," he said. "He wanted to know where you two were. I told him you were with the greens, trading tomorrow's blue game plans for their dessert."

"He didn't believe you," I predicted.

"He has no sense of humor whatsoever. By the way, Burrows has announced new time windows for meals and now for baths as well."

He handed me and Ellie each a sheet of paper. In the dim light, I made out:

<u>AM</u>
6:00-6:30 bath, blue
6:30-7:00 meal, green

7:00-7:30 meal, blue
7:30-8:00 bath, green

<u>PM</u>
5:00-5:30 bath, blue
5:30-6:00 meal, green
6:00-6:30 meal, blue
6:30-7:00 bath, green

"You've got to be kidding," Ellie said after reading it. "We're going to be stepping all over each other. What if we just ignore it? Take a bath whenever we like? Is Burrows going to, like, stop us?"

"I don't think it would be Burrows who would be stopping you," Rudy said.

"Sam," she guessed.

"If you're lucky, he won't shoot you—just pick you up and throw you."

She looked at the sheet again. "He has the two groups switching between baths and meals with no breaks. It's like he's going out of his way to induce contention."

I looked at her. "I think you've got it exactly."

"He wants us to fight?" Rudy asked.

"He wants to make sure we remain two distinct groups. Contention seems a viable method. We were talking about that when you came back. Think about it—Plath's experiment had a natural separation between the groups, but it was only temporary until the cabins were completed. Once that was done, Burrows had to come up with ways to keep the two groups from mingling together."

"Why?" Rudy asked.

"For *his* experiment, I guess … whatever that is."

"When do you think it will start?"

"Good question. I don't think we can just ask him. Whatever it is, I guess we're still assuming it somehow involves a danger to the groups."

"You said she mentioned mountain lions," Rudy said.

"No mountain lions!" Ellie objected.

"She just used that as an example," I said. "There's always Sam."

"And Sam has guns," Rudy said. "Sam with guns—that could be a very effective danger."

"Better than mountain lions," Ellie said.

"Speaking of mountain lions," Rudy said, "the Potato Chip is essentially a dinner plate for them, so I'm heading back."

"Dale's got a game of poker starting, doesn't he?" I guessed.

"Coincidentally, as it happens, yes."

After Rudy left, Ellie said, "Remember when Sam had to restrain Ralph?"

"I'm still not sure he had to, but yeah, I remember."

"Well, remember how Burrows told Jeremy and Dana to help him?"

I had to think a moment. "Yeah, he did … ah, I see. Even then, Burrows was driving the wedge between the groups. What the greens saw were blues putting down one of their guys. Ha! And if I were them, I'd definitely have been on Ralph's side about not wanting to clean up our crap."

The evening breeze was picking up, and even with our fleece jackets, we were getting cold, so we decided to head back. As the darkness of the forest enveloped us, Ellie said, "I was so angry today that it didn't register at the time, but now as I think back, it seems pretty strange."

"What?" I asked.

"When Burrows sent Sam to get you guys, the hulk was occupied at the spring—I think he was maybe shaving or something. Anyway, Burrows called him over, but Sam didn't seem to hear. I mean I know he *heard* him—Burrows was only, like, twenty feet away—but it didn't register. Burrows had to call him a second time, with emphasis."

I stopped, and Ellie walked a few steps before turning around.

"His name isn't really Sam, is that what you're thinking?" I said.

"I don't know. What do you think?"

I started walking again. "I think I agree with Rudy—Sam with guns could be a very effective danger."

We didn't talk any more until we reached the comfort of propane-heated cabins.

Ж Ж Ж

Tim was in his cot reading and I was puttering around, procrastinating going out into the cold night for one last pee, when we heard shouting. I was curious, and grabbed my jacket. As I stepped out, I saw my breath in the light of the open door. Winter arrived early in the mountains.

The shouting was clearer now, and I could hear that it was Ralph. I wasn't surprised. He was near the kitchen tent and spring—I could see a light waving and flashing there. As I got nearer I saw that there were actually two lights. One was steady, illuminating Ralph. The dancing light was his headlamp, bouncing about in rhythm with his gesticulating arms, Ralph's anger dance. I heard a second voice, the one holding the light on him. It was Sam. "Rules is rules," Sam was saying.

"What is this!" Ralph yelled. "A concentration camp?"

"You saw Mr. Burrows' paper. You can take a bath in the morning."

"I don't want to wait 'till morning. You don't own this water!"

"You're not taking a bath," Sam stated simply.

I saw that Ralph was wearing only his bathing suit, and I shivered just thinking about dumping a bucket of cold spring water over my head now. Tim had mentioned that Ralph always took his baths after dark, and he wondered if the guy hadn't perhaps been given a hard time in the shower after gym class. That might explain both his fetish to bathe in privacy, and his angry core.

"Screw you!" Ralph screamed. "You can't stop me!"

In answer, Sam lifted Ralph off the ground and carried him away. Ralph's torrent of curses became suddenly muffled as Sam wrapped his ham-sized hand around his mouth.

Sam even without guns was apparently an effective danger.

Ж Ж Ж

I woke the next morning to the sound of Tim rushing to leave. It was still dark. I looked at my watch, and saw that it was only 5:30. "Kind of early, isn't it?" I grumbled.

"Sorry," Tim said. "I think somebody's missing."

I sat up, blinking away sleep. "What? How do you know?"

"I overheard people talking—near the greens' cabins. I think Burrows sent Sam to find them."

"'Them?' More than one?"

"I don't know. I'm going to find out."

I was out the door just seconds behind him. By this time, lights were on in all the cabins. Ellie, her sleeping bag wrapped around her shoulders, joined our little group as we made our way to the greens area. Most of them were outside, milling about. Our groups merged and we found out that it was Ralph. "A mountain lion got him," Ellie declared.

"How do you know?" asked one of the greens.

"It was bound to happen eventually," she said.

Blues and greens were talking together, sharing ideas and concerns. Whatever animosities from the day before were temporarily set aside in the face of a possible common danger.

One of the greens finally announced that Ralph had apparently left on his own in the night. He'd taken most of his belongings.

"What's going on!"

It was Burrows.

"Ralph's left," the same green said. "It's okay—he left on his own."

"It is most definitely *not* okay," Burrows corrected, and strode away.

Minutes later, we heard the Jeep fire up and tires slipping and spitting pebbles as it trundled away. I was surprised to see Burrows come back. It must have been Sam who had left. "Blues!" he called. "Back to your cabins—now!" He looked at us, all mixed up, blue and green uniforms talking together. His jaw clenched. "The games start early today!" he announced. "Eight-thirty sharp! Assemble at your home base. Be on time, or else!"

Somebody muttered, "Or else what?"

It looked like Burrows was going to respond, but he held out his arm and pointed. "Blues! To your cabins! Now!"

We hustled away. It didn't seem like a good time to cross the professor.

ж ж ж

We were waiting for the greens to finish their breakfast slot when we heard the Jeep returning. We all—blues and greens—started off to meet it, but found Burrows standing with his fists on his hips. "Everybody back to their breakfasts!" he shouted. "You'll find out soon enough about Ralph!"

We stood, torn between curiosity and the familiar voice of authority. Burrows clapped his hands sharply, and we turned and walked away.

Tentative bridges had been built between the two groups, and news filtered across that Sam had locked Ralph away in Harry's cabin—the old log cabin behind the kitchen tent. He'd apparently made it almost to the highway before Sam caught him. At 8:00 Burrows called us to his podium boulder with his whistle. He waited until we gathered, and then said, "You're probably wondering about Ralph. He's back, safe and sound, but will be doing a few days of detention for his little stunt. He's promised to behave himself, and I have no reason to doubt him."

"I feel like I'm in kindergarten," Rudy whispered.

"I indicated earlier that the game would begin at 8:30," Burrows continued, "but that has changed. You'll meet back here at 9:00 for an update. Are there any questions?"

My body reacted before my brain could intercede. I raised my hand. "Why don't you just let Ralph leave? He obviously doesn't want to be here."

I cringed, expecting a burst of anger. Burrows must have been expecting the question, though, for he answered calmly. "This is a scientific study, and it wouldn't serve the process if we allowed ourselves to pick and choose the participants. We have to run with what we've got."

My reflexes were sharp, and my brain still too slow. "What about me?"

"What *about* you?"

"I was a pick-and-choose."

Burrows apparently hadn't prepared himself for this angle, for his eyes flashed and he retorted, "I didn't realize you held a doctorate in the human sciences. Do you have any other criticisms of my work?" He seemed to immediately regret his outburst, and took a deep breath. "Sorry, it's been a trying morning for us all."

He clapped his hands, the usual carriage return/line feed announcing a new paragraph. "See you at 9:00 sharp!"

As we were breaking into two groups again, Burrows called to Albert, and the two of them walked away together. Jeremy watched them until they disappeared into Burrows' cabin, then turned and followed us.

Ж Ж Ж

I was sitting with Rudy, soaking up the warm morning sun outside his cabin when Burrows came by and asked, "Is Jeremy around?"

Our game leader practically shot out of his cabin. "Here I am," he said.

Burrows waved for him to follow, and Jeremy fell in, practically stepping on Burrows' heels.

"Albert walked away from Burrows' cabin just a few minutes ago," Rudy noted. "He looked thoughtful."

"Albert always looks thoughtful," I said.

"Okay, he looked positively pensive."

"No need to get smart."

"That's what I tried to tell my teachers."

When Jeremy returned twenty minutes later, he seemed distracted. He glanced at the rest of us blues lounging around our cabins, and then turned and walked away into the maze of the forest without a word of explanation. Rudy decided that he seemed positively pensive as well. At 8:55 Jeremy returned, and called to us, "Time to head over to the kitchen."

"He's not pensive anymore," Rudy observed. "He seems high."

Jeremy did seem all smiles. "We'll follow him next time and see what he's smoking," I said.

Burrows was already perched on his boulder when we gathered around. "The game will begin soon, but first we have a little chore to take care of. I want the members of the green group to pull all the boxes of desserts from the kitchen tent and take them to Plath's cabin—stack them against the wall opposite the bunk. Blue group—you'll do the same for the stores located under the tarps near the road. When you're done, meet back here."

"Sam's got one hell of a sweet tooth," Rudy observed as we headed off for the road. "Now we know why he brought the guns."

"To protect the desserts?" I asked.

"He'll shoot one of us at random, and then hang our body above his door as a warning."

Ellie had caught up with us. "Rudy, have you ever considered writing horror novels."

"No. They scare me."

"You'd be writing it."

"So, I'd scare myself. Then I'd have a hard time trusting myself."

"You are insane."

"Thank you."

I was surprised at how much dessert we had in reserve. It took two trips for the blues to carry it all. It gave me a sense of security, knowing that we had enough treats to last the whole winter—obviously way more than we'd ever need. When we returned to the kitchen tent, Burrows addressed us. "Okay, the game will begin in fifteen minutes. A reminder that the only rules are those related to winning the game. Ellie's mistake was well intentioned, but a mistake nevertheless." He looked at us and smiled. "Today we're adding a reward for the winner—dessert after the evening meal!"

Silence.

"You mean, extra dessert?" Viona asked.

"No, dessert."

Silence.

"The loser doesn't get dessert?" Rudy asked.

"That's correct."

Silence.

"That's not adding a reward, it's introducing punishment," Rudy said.

"If that's how you choose to look at it," Burrows said. "Okay! Let's have some fun!"

As we trotted back to our cabins to change, Rudy remarked, "I have a feeling that 'fun' is something I'm going to remember with nostalgic longing."

Chapter 15

It may have been simply the fact that Jeremy had time to think and prepare, but he seemed to approach the first round with real gusto. Maybe it was the dessert. He had a strategy, but he impressed on us that it wasn't strategy that would win the game, but our commitment, and to that end, he encouraged us to defend against green attacks with everything we had, and apply equal determination to our own attacks.

"You make it sound like a battle," Tim said.

"They're metaphors," Dana sniped, and I thought it was magnanimous that he didn't punch her.

"But metaphors that are not far off the mark," Jeremy added. "*Think* of it as a battle, not a game."

"Um," Ellie said, "but it *is* a game."

"Of course. I mean," he said, showing a little irritation, "for Christ's sake, I'm just asking you to try your best!"

Silence.

"I will. I promise," Ellie said.

The strategy—that couldn't by itself win the game—did not involve hiding the flag. This time, the flag would be carried prominently—proudly—by Dale. Tim and I would be rear guard. We would start out along with the pack, but would hang back and peel off after any greens that tried to get past us and make for our tower. The rest—Ellie, Rudy, Viona, Dana, and Jeremy—would guard Dale. But they wouldn't just defend him, they were to aggressively go after any green that came within striking distance (that was Jeremy's term). Offense was the new defense.

"How aggressive is 'aggressive?'" Rudy asked.

"Aggressive," Jeremy repeated, as though it was a dumb question. "Whatever it takes."

"That includes a lot," Rudy observed.

Burrows distant whistle announced the beginning of the first round.

The blue pack took off, a gaggle of billowy blue clown pants with Dale's head bobbing above the rest. Tim and I waited until they'd gone a hundred feet, then took off as well. We had to hold back, as the pack was being cautious, going slower than our natural gait.

We scanned through the trunks around us for the enemy. Tim and I would stop near the cabins, if we got that far. We hadn't even gone half that distance, though, when Jeremy began shouting angrily and pointing off to our left. Fifty yards away, I saw movement here and there through gaps between the trunks. They were making progress towards our home base.

"Oh shit!" I called, turning one-eighty and sprinting back. We should have just stayed at home. As I ran for home base, I heard Tim's feet pounding the pine needles behind me. I hurdled a log, and heard Tim grunt and a simultaneous thump. I glanced back, but he was already getting back up, so I kept running.

We were converging with the enemy, and I now saw that it was Barry and Sheryl, the nice women we first met at the bus stop. I expected them to race for our tower, and was surprised when Barry turned and came for me. We stopped, facing each other over a large, moss-encrusted log. I envisioned wrestling opponents, gauging their first strike. Who would make the first move?

Neither, as it turned out. Tim shouted a warning and a moment later I felt a tug on my waistband. "Got it!" Sheryl shouted.

She'd came around me, waving my tag. I had subconsciously discounted the woman as the more serious threat.

"Stay!" she shouted at me, like I was a dog, and went after Tim, who'd started again for the tower. Barry, though, raced around the log and cut him off. Tim had seen how they'd gotten me, and he stood sideways between them, whipping his head back and forth, trying to keep an eye on both of them as they slowly approached. I didn't understand why he kept his hand in his pocket. Barry lunged, but it was a fake, and Sheryl reached in and grabbed his tag.

That's when I saw why Tim had kept his hand in his pocket. He pulled out a blue ball that opened and fluttered as he threw it at me. It rolled and stopped close enough that, by lying down and stretching my hand out from my "stay" spot, I was able to grab it.

It was my spare tag! He'd used the plastic hooks to attach it to a small rock, and then wrapped it like a pigs-in-the-blanket. *How ingenious*, I thought. I wondered why he hadn't shared the idea. I knew. He was too shy, concerned he'd be seen as bragging.

I quickly pulled the cloth tag off the rock, but had trouble reaching behind to attach it to my loop. Instead, I found that there was enough play in the loose shorts to twist the whole band around so the loop was at my side, and I was able to re-activate myself back into the game.

Oops! Sheryl was already at the tower, and she was holding their embassy tag in one hand. I sprinted for her as she started climbing, and reached the tree before she made it to the embassy pole—the metal pipe. Her knee was at eye level, and I grabbed it with both hands. She looked down at me, and the kind, peaceful woman I had first met at the bus stop was gone. The face above me was anger and fierce determination. It occurred to me that a knee was not the best place to grapple with someone, and she proved it by giving a sharp kick backwards. I saw the heel of her shoe arc up towards me, and then my chin exploded in pain and a burst of stars filled my view.

I was lying on my back. My vision cleared just in time to see Sheryl, the enemy, attach their flag. She reached up and sounded the air-horn, the signal of victory, that hung from a limb above.

As I lay there, Barry stepped over me and handed another blue flag to Sheryl, who draped it over the pole as well. I saw that this flag had a waistband.

I sighed.

I rolled over and looked back. Tim was getting up. He was wearing just his underwear and shoes, and the poor kid had a red scrape on his forehead, another battle wound joining the bruised shoulder Barry had delivered the day before.

Whatever inter-group goodwill had begun to develop when Ralph disappeared had evaporated, and the cross-group bridges lay in ruins.

This was war.

ж ж ж

"They obviously cheated," Rudy said.

"Can you prove it?" Jeremy asked. "If not, we have to just let it go. Look forward, not back."

"If they started after Burrows' whistle, there's no possible way that Barry and Sheryl could have made it to our tower when they did."

"You want to take them to court? Maybe hike down to Idyllwild and call the police? Forget it, already."

"They hurt Tim," I reminded him.

"I *know*!" Jeremy said, frustrated. "And I'm sorry, Tim. But the best way to get even is to win this next round. And the whistle is going to blow any second."

"Okay," I said, caving. "What's the plan?"

Jeremy looked at me levelly, evilly. I don't think he was really seeing me. He took our embassy flag from Viona and hid it behind a rock. "The plan is that we're going to get even."

The second-round whistle echoed along the mountain slope.

Jeremy held up his hand for us to wait. "There's two ways to win a round—hang your flag from their pole, or—"

"Capture their flag!" Rudy finished.

"Right. That's what we're focusing on this round. We're not even going to try to hang our flag. Tim, Ellie, you start ahead and intercept them. Do what you can, and don't worry if you get tagged. Everybody else, find places to hide between here and the cabins. Once you see their flag, wait until the right moment, and then shout the warning. Then everybody attack the flag bearer at once."

"And we do it aggressively—whatever it takes," Rudy said, parroting Jeremy from the previous round.

Jeremy gave him a hard look, but realized that he wasn't being sarcastic. "Whatever it takes. Yeah. Now, let's go!"

Everybody started off. "Wait!" I called. "You're leading off with the same two people who got their pants pulled off. What are they? Sacrifices?"

Jeremy turned and nodded. "Yeah," he said and ran on.

Tim and Ellie looked at me and she shrugged. "Whatever it takes," she said. "It's okay." She turned and ran off, and Tim followed.

I hid behind a large trunk with a boulder next to it and waited, peering out expectantly. Shouts came from near the cabins, then laughter. That didn't sound good.

I waited.

Motion. Yes, here they came—neither an advancing line, nor a tight pack, but just a jumble of greens running along, looking to each side. I wondered what strategy they were trying. More importantly, where was their flag? Were *they* now hiding it?

I heard soft thumping behind me. A lone green was running along, obviously trying to be quiet, attempting a sneak run-around. One of his pockets bulged.

"Here!" I cried, jumping up and pointing, and took off after him. I had the advantage, and easily cut him off. I grabbed him around the waist, and he tried to push me away, and when that didn't work, he punched me in the face.

Once again I saw stars and went down. When my vision cleared, I saw the green hadn't gotten very far. He was also down with Dale's arms wrapped around his feet. He was trying to kick and punch Dale. The tall man hung on tight, though, until Rudy arrived and put his foot on the green's chest. Still he wouldn't give up, punching Rudy's leg without much effect. Rudy bent down and grabbed a double handful of pine needles, which he began sprinkling onto the man's face. Cursing profusely, the green finally put his arms out in defeat, and Rudy reached into his pocket and pulled out the green embassy flag.

I got up and turned to shout our victory to the others, and was surprised to find the three of them occupied, fighting with the greens that had been advancing.

Rudy had to stand on a boulder waving the flag and shout at the top of his lungs before the message got through and the fighting ceased.

ж ж ж

Burrows called an ad hoc meeting right there where the second-round battle had ended—the Gettysburg of San Jacinto. Everybody except Rudy was bruised and on edge. Ellie's arm was red, smeared with blood, and Tim's back was scratched. When cornered, the kid had pulled down his own pants to avoid man-handling, but a green had drug him around by his feet anyway.

I fully expected Burrows to either call the game off, or at least reprimand us for the rough play, and I waited in vain as he climbed a boulder and congratulated the blues on our victorious round. "I expect it will take a few minutes to get all the passport tags back to their owners," he said, "so I'm giving you an extra five minutes—the third round whistle will blow in fifteen minutes." He checked his watch and climbed down.

"Hey!" I called. "Wait a sec—"

Jeremy caught my arm and gave me a serious glare.

Burrows looked at us, and walked away with the greens.

"This is getting out of hand!" I protested to Jeremy. The other blues were gathering around, waiting to see the outcome.

Jeremy glanced at them. "No time to argue. Get your tags back and meet at home base—now!"

As I joined up with Ellie, I noticed Tim heading in the other direction, following behind a green, pleading. "Son-of-a-bitch," I muttered and ran back. "What's the problem?" I asked.

"He's got my tag," Tim said.

The green didn't even slow down.

I ran up and grabbed him by the arm, and he spun around and knocked my hand off.

"Give it back," I said.

He looked at me, then past me. He reached into his pocket, pulled out Tim's tag, and dropped it to the ground, then trotted off, accelerating to a sprint.

I looked behind me to find Dale standing with his arms crossed on his chest. I would have sprinted away as well.

ж ж ж

The third round would have been even more bruising than the second, except that we—the blues—had lost the gumption to fight. Dessert just wasn't enough incentive against the pain. A lot of the greens seemed spent as well, but there were enough of them—Barry, Sheryl, and Albert—with sufficient determination to push their way past our half-hearted defense and plant their flag in what was probably a new record time.

Later, lounging in front of our cabins, licking our wounds, we complained to Jeremy, but he just shrugged it off.

"Games are supposed to be fun," I protested.

"Who says?" he asked.

"That's why they're called games," I said.

"I doubt war games are very fun."

"This isn't a war."

"Of course not." He stared at me. "It's not a war," he confirmed.

"I don't need to be convinced," I said. "It was my point."

His brow contracted as though deep in thought, but I'd come to recognize that this indicated he was irritated. He addressed all of us. "The trick is to be the better player, and that means getting the better of them before they get to you."

"We need some ground rules," Rudy insisted.

Jeremy shook his head. "Not going to happen."

"Why not? Without rules, it's not a game—it's a free-for-all."

Jeremy looked at Rudy a moment, and shook his head again. "Burrows has his reasons, I'm sure."

"Do you know what they are?" Rudy asked.

I thought Jeremy was going to say something, but he just shook his head and shrugged. "Look, guys," he said, addressing us all now, "we're in this together, and the truth is, we don't know for how long. So we need to make the best of it, and that means working together, watching each others' backs."

"Everybody?" Viona said.

Jeremy blinked, the word slowly seeping in. "No! I'm talking about us—our team. The blues."

We didn't say anything, twirling the pine needles around with our toes.

"It's just a game," Viona said, so quietly I almost didn't catch it.

Tim stood up. "Tell them that," he said, pointing east, and walked away.

Chapter 16

Even though the green's meal time-slot came first that evening, Burrows made them wait until we were done before allowing them their victory delicacies. As we began cleaning up, they scampered off to Sam's cabin. Sam didn't bother to accompany them, lounging instead on a hammock outside Harry's log cabin. The greens meandered back, munching and smacking away on candy bars and cellophane-wrapped cupcakes. Rudy elbowed me as he handed me a greasy pan and gestured with his chin. One of the greens stood there watching us, making a point to hold up the Almond Joy for us to see before shoving the rest of it in his mouth.

I had guessed that Burrows wanted us to feel penalized, punished with deprivation. I wasn't expecting, though, to feel jealous, almost outraged with envy. I hadn't wanted a treat this badly since I was a kid.

"I'm going to save my desserts," Rudy said, loud enough for our antagonist to hear, "until I have enough to shove them down his throat and choke him."

The man shook his finger in reprimand and ambled away.

"I hate the color green," Rudy proclaimed.

Sam got off his hammock, and Rudy cringed, backing away behind me, but the mountain of a man lumbered off to his cabin to lock it again now that the greens had been provided their rewards, and we our punishment.

ж ж ж

"You're wearing two shirts," I said.

"No, I'm not," Rudy objected, as we left the kitchen tent for the game the next day. He glanced around, making sure no greens were nearby, then leaned in and whispered, "Icks-nay with the irt-shay."

"I wonder sometimes if you believe in your own sanity."

When we assembled at our home base Rudy stripped off the top layer and, looking to make sure there were no green spies, held the blue shirt aloft triumphantly.

"It's a shirt, Rudy," Ellie said dryly.

He smiled and cocked his head knowingly at her.

"It's a red herring," Tim suggested.

"That will be its new title," Rudy agreed, "the Blue Herring."

"Rudy," I said, "you're insane, but every now and then you slip across the line into genius."

He bowed dramatically. "Thank you, thank you, thank you."

Jeremy nodded reluctantly, abandoning the plan he'd been describing.

Five minutes later, the whistle blew, and Dale took off holding Rudy's balled-up blue shirt in his fist, while Jeremy, with the real flag folded in his pocket, pretended to be one of his guards. The ploy worked perfectly. I lay on the ground where I'd fallen after a green yanked off my tag and then gave me a hard shove with his forearm across my chest, and listened to the sweet sound of the air horn in the direction of the green's tower.

I sat up and watched Sheryl railing at Albert while gesturing at Dale who sat at their feet calmly listening. Albert held up his hands in defeat, but she continued to demand a hearing with Burrows.

"No ground rules!" I called. "Remember?"

The angry woman lifted a finger at me.

Shouts of continued arguments moved off towards the green side as we limped back to our home base for round two.

ж ж ж

"They have my shirt," Rudy said.

"I know," Jeremy concurred impatiently. It was the second time Rudy had interrupted him, preventing him from explaining the next plan.

"They won't give it back."

"I *know*, Rudy! That's why they have it—they won't give it back. I'll talk to Albert later. Forget it for now."

Rudy pouted, but let Jeremy begin.

But then Ellie interrupted him. "I have an idea."

Jeremy rolled his eyes. "You have five seconds."

"Hide somebody up in the tower, and then the rest of us hide near home base and trap their flag carrier. That was four seconds. Now five."

Jeremy's brow wrinkled, then relaxed. "Hide where in the tower?"

"One person climbs up, and—see that limb? The one that sticks out the back? If they stand on that, they can hide behind the trunk. Then when the flag carrier tries to climb, they come out and stop them. With their feet. You know, by kicking."

"That sounds … underhanded," Jeremy cautioned.

"And brilliant," Rudy said. "My knee hurts so bad, I can hardly walk. Those bastards have abandoned fair play."

Jeremy grinned. "Who wants to climb the tree and kick a green?"

Seven hands went up.

ж ж ж

I was lying on the ground again, in what was becoming my standard position at the end of a round, waiting for the pain in my back to subside. Dale had run off, waving the green embassy flag, on his way to sound the triumphant air horn. We'd won the game. Just like that. Two rounds, and it was over. Winners. By golly, we'd outsmarted them. I could hear the green who'd Ellie had the honor of kicking off the tower screaming foul, and the arguments of other greens as they walked away, waving their arms at their beleaguered leader.

"We won!" Ellie said, sitting down next to me. "You okay?"

"I can wiggle my toes."

"That's the best you can do?"

I raised my arm, then a leg. "I'll walk to fight again."

She snorted.

I raised my head to see why.

She looked at me and sighed. "That's what I'm afraid of."

"That I'll walk?"

"The fighting. It only seems to get worse."

"It was your idea to position yourself so you could kick a green in the face."

"Yeah, it was. Am I happy about it?" She sighed again. "Yeah, I am, and that's exactly what I'm afraid of."

"You have a fear of happiness?"

"You know what I mean. Winning a round justifies any means."

I lay there, feeling the pine needle tips poking at me in a hundred places. "In boxing, they also use the term 'a round.'"

"Indeed," she said, standing up and extending a helping hand, "except that they wear gloves."

Ж Ж Ж

"Here," Jeremy said, tossing Rudy his shirt. "I had to trade Albert tomorrow afternoon's bath slot. Don't blame me if our women tear your eyes out."

"Hey!" Rudy exclaimed in shock, holding the shirt up. Swaths of dark brown were smeared across the front.

"Don't worry," Jeremy said. "He assured me that it was just mud."

Rudy carefully put his nose near the shirt and sniffed. "I don't know. Doesn't smell like mud to me."

"It probably smells like Rudy," Ellie offered, "which would be bad enough."

We were sitting around in front of our cabins glancing at our watches, counting the minutes. Burrows had told us we could—we should—take our dessert rewards before we ate. The reason was obvious—this way the greens would still be around to watch us gloat.

Rudy laid the sullied shirt off to the side, careful not to let the rest of it touch him. "You should be appreciative of my sacrifice for the team."

Ellie reached out and grabbed it. "Oh, all right, you baby. I'll wash it for you."

"While you're at it, could you do the rest of my laundry?"

"You'd have to sacrifice your pants as well for that."

"Okay."

"Never mind. I forgot you have no shame."

"Hey!" Dale called. "It's time!"

It was a mad scramble to Sam's cabin.

Sam was gone, and his cabin door ajar, so we crammed in—or tried to—jostling each other before Jeremy arrived and brought order, making us form a line outside to enter one at a time. I went to the back of the line so I could be with Ellie, and Rudy came out holding a small pack of donuts and looking perplexed. "That's odd," he said, cradling his donuts like they were a tiny newborn baby. "I could have sworn there was a whole box of Ding Dongs."

"Maybe the greens ate them all last night," Ellie suggested.

Rudy raised one eyebrow. "A box holds sixteen packs of Ding Dongs. There are eight greens."

She shrugged, and it was our turn to enter the candy store.

It was a difficult choice, as multiple boxes lay open, their sugary, fat-laden goodies beckoning seductively. I decided on one of the coffee cake packs, mostly based on the fact that they held the greatest quantity of goodie, but I couldn't find the box. That was odd. Pondering, I took Rudy's lead and picked up a pack of six mini-donuts.

Outside, Rudy had opened his donuts and was chewing.

"Are you thinking what I'm thinking?" I asked.

"That this is going to ruin my appetite? It's not possible, and I wouldn't care anyway."

"That the greens have stolen some desserts."

He shoved a whole donut in his mouth and nodded vigorously.

"The bastards," I said.

"It just means that their teeth will fall out sooner than yours," Ellie said. "If we don't hustle over to the kitchen, we'll miss dinner."

"Mchmfd an tchkl," Rudy mumbled, the half-chewed food visible as he attempted to talk.

"Your donut has ruined *my* appetite," Ellie said.

ж ж ж

The greens disappointed us again. They rushed through cleanup so they wouldn't have to be there when we arrived with our dessert rewards. "Jesus Christ!" Jeremy yelled. "They've left the boiling pot filthy!"

"Just leave it," Dana said. "They'll be sorry tomorrow night when they need it."

"Oh no," Viona said, taking the pot from Jeremy. "I'll clean it. Flag wars are one thing, but I'm not going to risk botulism poisoning over food fights."

"Sam!" I called, "Go rip their heads off!"

The hammock seemed to have become the giant's permanent roost. He was reading a comic book and didn't even look up. He never responded to us—he acted as though he didn't even know we were there—and we'd gotten into the habit of calling out to him, beseeching him to bring retribution down on the green's much-deserving heads, like he was a pagan god of punishment.

We began the evening meal preparation, and after a few minutes Silent Sam rolled off his hammock and left to lock his cabin.

We had the ramen noodles cooked, and I was opening cans of albacore tuna when Ellie asked where Rudy was.

"Maybe he choked on his last donut," I said.

Ellie ignored me, peering among the sea of tree trunks.

"What trouble could he have gotten himself into?" I asked.

Now that I was taking her seriously, she replied. "You never know."

"That's pretty ambiguous—wait, you don't seriously think that a mountain lion got him."

She looked at me. "I hadn't thought of that one."

"What were *you* thinking?"

She shook her head slowly. "It *was* his shirt," she reminded me.

I let that sink in. "Oh, wait a minute, you don't actually think that the greens have done something. They wouldn't hurt him."

Her look admonished me to not be so naive.

Her eyes suddenly lit up and she smiled. "There he is!" she said, pointing.

Rudy came trotting over from the direction of our cabins.

"Where you been, boy?" I asked, affecting a redneck accent. "Shirking your kitchen duties?"

"Tit," he said, grabbing bowls to begin serving out the noodles.

"What?" I asked, dropping the accent.

"For tat," he replied, and that's all he would say.

Ellie's worry had been silly, but I found myself happy that he'd arrived.

I just wished Ellie wasn't quite so happy.

Ж Ж Ж

Ellie, Rudy, and I took our usual evening stroll around the plateau to the Potato Chip, and the whole time, Rudy seemed fidgety, like he was on the verge of telling us something stupendous. As the night sky deepened to complete black, he finally broke. "Hey, you guys wanna see something?"

"It's about time," Ellie replied.

"You sensed it too?" I asked.

"He's like a five year-old with a secret."

"If you guys knew, why didn't you say something?" Rudy said.

"And spoil your fun?" Ellie replied. "So, show us your secret."

He practically pulled us through the woods to our cabins. "Guess," he said, standing in front of my door.

"If there's a mountain lion in there," I said, "Ellie will never forgive you."

"No mountain lion, just this!" he announced, opening the door to—nothing.

I stuck my head inside, cautiously. I pulled back and turned to Ellie. "The boy has lost his marbles." I turned to Rudy. "Is that the surprise? You've lost your mind completely?"

He stepped inside and beckoned us to follow. He held out his hand, and then slowly lifted it until he was gesturing up.

I looked up. "What the ..."

"The bastards got my Ding Dongs," he said, "but they're not getting my raspberry Zingers."

Above our heads, tucked up against the roof on makeshift shelves, were three cardboard boxes. They sported various snack food company logos.

"This is why you were late to dinner," Ellie surmised.

"You know," I said, "once the greens discover you've dipped into the dessert pile, they're going to take even more next time."

"It's going to snowball," Ellie agreed.

"You're right," Rudy said. "We need to sneak over tonight and get all the rest."

"That's not what I was thinking," I said.

I looked at Ellie. "But maybe we should at least get *some* more. I'd hate to spend the winter here living on just ramen noodles.

We found that Sam's light was on, and the door closed.

"I guess we'll just have to make sure we win the game tomorrow," I said as we walked back to our cabins.

"Sure," Ellie said. "We'll outsmart them again."

"Sure," I agreed. "We're smarter than them."

"I think you mean, 'than they,'" she corrected me.

Silence.

Chapter 17

"Isn't it kind of, you know, cheesy?" I asked.

Jeremy had decided that our team needed some theme music. "One person's cheese is another person's nectar," Jeremy replied as he slipped the CD into the boom box. Burrows had given him the music-making dinosaur that morning, a further reward for our victory the day before.

"That doesn't really make sense, you know," I said. "Cheese and nectar are, like, two different food types."

He patted my shoulder. "That's okay. You'll understand after a while."

This would have irritated me a few weeks before, but I'd come to accept Jeremy's patronizing as a fender dent in an otherwise reliable car. It bothers you at first, but after a while you learn to ignore it, since it doesn't affect the overall performance.

The guy tried hard.

Billy Idol's "White Wedding" suddenly blared from the speakers. "Talk about cheese!" I shouted.

Jeremy turned the volume down and ejected the CD. "Sorry— wrong one." He shuffled through a small stack and slid in another. This time the evocative percussive piano of Bruce Hornsby's "Mandolin Rain" kicked in.

"This is supposed to be *less* cheesy?" Rudy said.

I happened to like Bruce Hornsby. As a musician. I didn't say anything, however, since I thought the whole idea of team theme music was fatuous, almost insulting in its blatant attempt to inspire emotional bonding.

Jeremy turned the volume down, but let the music play in the background as we discussed the upcoming day's game. He thought we'd exhausted the ploys of hiding and faking our embassy flag. Half the group agreed, and half thought that there was still traction to be found. We tossed ideas around, and Jeremy let us run open-loop for a while before calling for order. I had the impression that he was intrigued by the whole brains-over-brawn approach.

"Why don't we try the trick of misdirection?" he said.

Shrugs rippled through the gathering. "Like what?" Dale asked.

"*The Purloined Letter*," Jeremy responded.

I was impressed. I hadn't taken him for a fan of Edgar Allen Poe.

"I saw it on TV," he explained, "Mystery Theatre, I think."

At least it wasn't reality television.

"I don't get it," Dana objected. She seemed annoyed that everybody else apparently understood.

"I think he means that we'll—somehow—hide the flag in full view," Tim explained.

"I *know* that," Dana retorted. "I mean, like, where?"

I would have bet Dana had not known that.

"Misdirection with the obvious," Jeremy said. "We'll carry the flag—the real flag—right out in the open, like an actual flag."

"I don't get it," Rudy said. "How's that hiding it?"

It wasn't exactly like *The Purloined Letter*, since we were inviting the enemy to see the actual flag, but I liked it. "We've thrown so many tricks at them," I said, "they'll be trying to figure out what we've got up our sleeve."

"And the trick is that there *is* no trick?" Rudy asked skeptically.

"Exactly," Jeremy said. "It'll confuse them. Maybe they won't believe that it's the actual flag."

"'Maybe.'"

"There's never any guarantees."

Rudy still wasn't buying in, which was a twist, since normally he'd be the one initiating the hair-brained schemes. "Sure," he said sarcastically, "and we can confuse them even more by running around flapping our arms and clucking like chickens."

"Oh, come on, Rudy—"

"Okay," Ellie said, cutting Jeremy off.

"O-*kay*?" Rudy squawked.

"Sure," Ellie said. "the more confusion the better. Hit them with the inexplicable."

"*Et tu, Brutus?*" Rudy said. He sat back, folding his arms across his chest. "I predict it's going to fail miserably, but at least it should be fun."

"It would be nice to have some fun again," Viona said.

We contemplated the scheme as Jeremy assigned us, one by one, our parts to play.

"Who's going to carry the flag?" Dale asked.

Jeremy surveyed the group. "Viona."

"Oh, sure," she said. "pick the weakest."

"It's your chance to get revenge," Jeremy replied diplomatically.

"I don't think this is going to be fun," she said, taking the stick from Jeremy.

Jeremy tied two corners of our embassy flat to a stick so that Viona could carry it like a battle flag. I would run alongside, her only guard. Bruce Hornsby's "The Valley Road" was playing in the background.

Jeremy checked his watch. "Okay! Listen up! Just a few minutes before the whistle. Remember, Chicken Guard—don't stop until you hear me yell. Runners, make sure you stay ahead of everybody. Any questions?"

Rudy raised his hand.

"Yeah?" Jeremy asked regretfully.

"Is it okay to throw stones at them?"

"No, Rudy," Jeremy replied tiredly. "Not yet. Not unless they throw first."

The whistle sounded.

"Runners, go!" Jeremy called.

Rudy and Dale took off, angling away to each side. They would stay in front of us, to the left and to the right. Jeremy and Dana lined up on our left, and Ellie and Tim on the right—our Chicken Guard.

"Okay!" Jeremy yelled, "now us!"

The Chicken Guard started forward, watching each other to make sure they formed an advancing line. I counted to five and said, "Okay," and Viona and I fell in behind them.

We made the cabins without sighting any greens, and I was nervous—maybe they'd hatched some masterful plan of their own. They began appearing, though, a seemingly unorganized pack of determined hunters slipping forward between the trunks.

Closer and closer they came, calling to each other and pointing. I made out details of their faces, and then the whites of their eyes, and I began to question whether Jeremy was miscalculating. I was about to shout the order myself when Jeremy finally called, "Chicken Soup!"

The Chicken Guard stopped short and stood straight, their arms folded across their chests, and Rudy and Dale tore off on each side as fast as they could run. An instant later, Viona, carrying the flag high, and I, as close as I could get without tripping her, continued on all alone, facing the greens who had taken up howling like wolves.

The ploy seemed to be working! The howling modulated, and then fell silent as one by one the enemy hoard faltered, looking right and left at the Runners. Albert called out commands—names to go after Dale and Rudy, the Chicken Guard, and the flag. Two of the greens split off, angling to catch Viona and me, but one of them shouted, "It's a trick!" and took off after Rudy.

That left one green, and worst case, I could sacrifice myself if need be. But the need wasn't to be. The woman tried to push me out of the way as she went straight for Viona's tag, but I caught her wrist and pulled, and she tripped and went down. Viona ran on as I stood over the green woman. She lay on her back, glaring at me. "Come on," I said, "roll over."

"Fuck you!" she growled.

Taking a cue from Rudy, I picked up a big handful of pine needles, which I sprinkled onto her head. She howled, and cursed, and covered her face with her hands, which allowed me to reach under and pull away her tag.

I sprinted to catch up with Viona, and didn't reach her until nearly the other side of the plateau. The tower came into sight. I was surprised that Albert was so lax as to leave it unguarded, but then I saw that he hadn't at all. In fact, he'd stolen our idea. A green stood perched on a limb above the steps we'd made. I stopped short thirty feet away.

"Ralph!" Viona exclaimed, stopping short as well.

"You had another day of detention!" I protested. "You escaped?"

"Nope, sucker!" he called. "Released for good behavior!"

Burrows hadn't said anything, had left it as a little surprise. Somehow, I wasn't surprised at the surprise.

"Give me the flag," I said to Viona.

"You sure?" she asked, but handed it to me.

"I don't think you want your face kicked in."

"And you do?"

"Not particularly, but you're ... you know."

"I'm a girl."

I held out the flag, but she stepped away. "I'm a fan of chivalry," she said, "at the right moment."

I stepped forward towards my face-kicking.

My dream was to catch Ralph's foot, give him a yank, and watch him fall heavily to the ground. Pay-back for the vicious things he and Barry had done to Tim, Viona, and Ellie. I took the flag off the stick, jammed one corner under my waistband, and started up. Above me, the foreshortened image of Ralph followed my progress hungrily, waiting expectantly with one boot raised.

I paused. What I was doing was suicide. I had no chance of getting past that boot. I heard a little squeal from Viona. I looked down to see Barry walking towards her. He must have been hiding. I should have known that the Damnable Duo would be together.

"So, Fatty," Barry said to her, "we meet again."

Viona was backing away, but reached behind and pulled off her own tag and held it out to him.

"Nuh-uh," he said, shaking his head. "Not that easy—I'll come and get it."

She dropped it and ran, and he took off after her.

"No!" I shouted, jumping down. Miscalculating the distance, I stumbled before sprinting after them. "You coward!" I screamed.

That did it. Barry hated having his courage questioned as much as his intelligence. He stopped and turned to face me. "It's *you*," he said. "We have a score to settle."

Viona was making good progress back towards the cabins. Now I just had to extricate myself. "It's a game," I said, "a goddamn game. Why do you guys take it so seriously?"

His eyes narrowed, and he held his fists in front of his chest as he took a step towards me, and I took an equal step back. "Who's the coward now?" he jeered.

"What? You want to have a fist fight? Is that all you think of? Fighting?"

He pushed my chest, forcing me back farther.

I knew then that I wasn't going to talk him out of this. I could give up and run away—and, believe me, I was considering it—but we shared the same four isolated acres in the mountains. I could run, but I'd never escape him. And running would only encourage him to come back for more.

I had seen the move a hundred times in films. The top of a human's skull is relatively hard and thick compared to the face. You can use your head as a club. It's the sort of thing that looks easy, but in fact requires practice. I jumped at him, bringing my head down, aimed at his face. In retrospect, the people in the movies are inches apart, but we were a couple of feet. Barry easily leaned back so that I fell into his chest, as though I had suddenly fainted.

I wished I'd had.

A bomb exploded in my gut as he brought his knee up. Punches followed, and I was chewing dirt, but the pain smeared everything together so that I lost track of the specifics. After a few seconds the blows stopped, and I rolled over and got up on my hands and knees. Barry and Ralph were trotting away, waving our embassy flag.

My gut recovered enough to heave, and I spewed lunch onto the forest floor.

ж ж ж

The spirit was knocked out of the blues—and the spit and blood particularly out of me—and we lost the second round without hardly trying.

Afterwards, as we limped back to the cabins, Rudy said, "Maybe it's time to start throwing stones."

Nobody objected.

Chapter 18

That night, Barry stood holding a Mounds bar in one hand, and a Snickers in the other, alternating bites as he smirked at us while we prepared our dinner. Silent Sam had returned from locking his cabin and had eased himself back into the hammock. He surely saw the display, as did Burrows, but neither said a word.

Thus, we had incentive and justification to throw stones at the greens during the next day's game. But we didn't. We were tired and dispirited, and provoking our adversaries was the last thing we wanted to do. Jeremy formulated plans for each round, but the greens bowled us over with all the energy we seemed to have lost. We were Custard's troops to the green's massed Indian nation coalition. For all we know, Brevet Major General Custard had a fine plan as well.

It was brawn-over-brains again that day.

Back at our cabins, Rudy convinced us blues that we needed another plan, for a much more serious issue. We batted around a variety of ideas, from stealing Sam's keys, to having someone hide inside his cabin, but in the end, settled on the simple, tried-and-true distraction.

At 5:50, ten minutes before the end of the green's meal slot, Dale and I took a stroll towards the Potato Chip. Once out of sight of the cabins, we changed course, and stealthily made our way back, slipping from behind one tree trunk to another, until we had clear visibility of Sam's cabin.

And then we waited.

Off towards the kitchen tent, we heard the rattle of pans as the greens cleaned up, and soon after, they arrived, talking and laughing. They filed through Sam's front door, exiting with treats in their hands and pockets to make their way back to the kitchen tent to gloat. The last person emerged and left, but we waited. We knew. As predicted, a few minutes later, a green stuck his head out the cabin door, glanced around, and then disappeared inside again. Seconds later, he emerged carrying two boxes, another green following behind him. We waited until they disappeared in the direction of their own cabins, and then sprinted forward.

We didn't know how long Ellie would be able to distract Sam, and we had to work fast. It was nearly dark inside Sam's cabin, and we saw that our task was going to be a whole lot easier than we'd thought. Over the last two victories, the greens had practically cleaned out all the desserts. A whole winter's supply. Only three boxes remained, one of them open and half emptied. And these were the dregs of the treats—Circus Peanuts and Mary Janes.

We grabbed them and made for the door. As soon as we stepped out, a shout went up. The two greens had come back for the last boxes—the greedy bastards!

"What the hell d'ya think you're doing?" one of them called, running towards us.

Dale and I took off for our cabins. "Same thing as you! You cheats!" I yelled over my shoulder.

"You lost the game!" he screamed in rage.

I didn't bother to point out that Burrows had never indicated that the reward for winning was a whole cabin full of candy. On the other hand, I realized that Burrows had never actually said just how much dessert the winner could take.

The greens easily outran us, since we refused to give up the boxes. These were the dregs of the treats, but, dammit, it was now about the principle. I heard the thumping footsteps getting closer, and then I hurtled forward, tumbling to the ground, as hands shoved my back. I still clutched my box, and a green was struggling to pull it away from me. I could hear Dale fighting his own battle nearby. My green had the advantage since he was standing, and as I tried to secure my grip, my hand slipped, but caught the edge of one of the flaps. The green braced himself and gave an extra strong tug, and the box slipped from my hands. But my fingers pulled away the flap, and one side of the box ripped open, spilling little cellophane packets of artificially flavored foam peanuts onto the ground.

"Son-of-a-bitch," the green muttered and started gathering them back into the torn box. I crawled over on my hands and knees and grabbed the spongy monstrosities by the handful, stuffing them into my pockets. He pushed me away with his foot, saying, "Go away, scavenger," but I grabbed his shoe and pulled. It came off, and I threw it away. "You son-of-a-bitch," he growled and tried to kick my head with his sock.

"You already said that," I pointed out, and tried to grab his foot again, but the sock provided no purchase, and he managed to kick me in the face.

That stunned me. I fell back tasting blood. And that made me mad. I stood up and charged. A moment later, we were rolling around, punching, kicking, and biting, but mostly ramming into fallen logs, which hurt more than the intended damage.

Suddenly my green flew away. Dale had grabbed him by the collar and tossed him aside. I sat up. The other green lay in a fetal position, covering his head with scratched and dirty hands. My green got up and stood looking at us, but he glanced at his colleague and kept his distance. Keeping an eye on them, we quickly gathered what factory-stamped candy was at hand and made our retreat.

I saw Sam walking away as well, towards his cabin. "Where'd he come from?" I asked, rubbing the back of my hand across my nose and seeing it come away covered in blood.

"He watched us," Dale replied.

"He didn't *do* anything?"

"No. Just watched. I think he smiled."

ж ж ж

When we got back to our cabins, I realized that I didn't feel well, like I was catching the flu, so Dale went off to the kitchen tent without me. I lay down on my bunk, but got up and turned on the boom box that Jeremy had left just outside. I lay back down, closed my eyes, and let Hornsby's "The Way It Is" sooth me. The lyrics— how the affluent in society often justify their favored lot by convincing themselves that the less fortunate are just lazy—struck a chord. I was homeless, bereft, and my nose was bleeding from a kick from somebody's smelly sock. In another place or time, or given a chance to start over, it could have turned out completely different. I could have been the guy in the expensive suit and hot car.

I turned over, burying my face in the pillow, probably getting blood all over my only pillow case.

I didn't care.

ж ж ж

I must have dozed off, because the sound of my fellow blues returning woke me. I sat up, blinking.

Ellie stuck her head in. "We brought you dinner, if you think you can eat."

I rubbed my eyes. "Yeah, that'd be great." I felt better, hungry.

"Dale says you're a hero," she said, handing me my bowl.

"For stealing peanut-shaped styrofoam?"

"Is that what you fought over?"

"No," I said. She waited. "I fought for the honor of the group."

"Ah," she said, pretending deep appreciation. "Well, that deserves recognition." She came over and knelt in front of me, took my head in her hands and kissed my forehead. As she leaned back, she paused. Our eyes met for what seemed minutes, but was probably a couple of seconds. She leaned forward again and kissed my lips, softly, tenderly. I opened my eyes, feeling I was floating, but I was still sitting on my bunk. She had sat back to look at me, gauging my reaction to her impulse action.

"Thanks," I said.

She smiled.

"I mean," I stammered. "That was nice—*really* nice."

"I'm glad," she said and stood up just as Rudy came in.

"She tell you how I got beat up too?" he asked.

Ellie rolled her eyes.

"What!" Rudy protested. "It's true! Sam nearly killed me."

"I was trying to distract the Mafioso," she explained, "but the guy's not as dumb as his vocabulary would lead you to believe. I was playing around with him—you know, joking, and trying to get him to talk—and he just gets up off the hammock, walks over to Rudy who was there with me, and—"

"Slugs me a good one," Rudy said.

"No," Ellie said. "He gives Rudy a thump on the side of his head with the palm of his hand, then walks off towards his cabin."

"Thump? *Thump?*" Rudy exclaimed. "He nearly knocked my teeth out."

"Why'd he do that?" I asked. "Hit Rudy, I mean, when you were the one obviously trying to delay him."

She shrugged. "Mafia honor—you never hit a woman."

"Unless you intend to murder her, I guess." I said. "Do you actually know that he's with the Mafia?"

"No. I don't *know* he is, but it's obvious. Have you *seen* his shoes? They're Gucci!"

I looked at her a moment, then at Rudy.

He shrugged. "And she calls me insane."

ж ж ж

I woke the next morning to the sound of the Jeep whining and bumping away down the mountain. As usual, Tim was already up and out. I stepped out into the brisk morning air rubbing my eyes and almost ran into Dana. "Wha's up?" I mumbled.

"Nothing," she said, continuing on.

"Why's the Jeep leaving?" I asked.

"How should I know?" She snapped. "I'm not Burrows' secretary."

But you'd love to be.

I glanced at my watch. I had just enough time for a bath before the greens showed up for their breakfast slot. I'd missed the blue bath slot the night before, and blood was still dried on my face.

Ellie was just finishing, and even though she shivered and her teeth chattered, her two-piece bathing suit offered a lot of goose bumps to admire.

"D-d-d-ump m-m-m-me," she said, handing me the bucket full of near-freezing spring water and turning away. I lifted it and poured slowly over her head, letting the shampoo wash down her shoulders and back as she smothered a squeal. I filled the bucket and she turned around, shivering a little dance. Facing me, she closed her eyes and said, "D-d-d-o i-i-it," as though I was about to dig my hunting knife into her wound to extract a bullet.

"Any idea where Burrows was going?" I asked while torturing the woman I admired with an icy wash.

"T-t-t-o I-i-i-dlwild f-f-f-r m-m-m-ml," she chattered.

I put down the bucket and wrapped her towel around her shoulders. "I got the 'To Idyllwild' part."

She sat on a rock to put on her sandals. "F-f-f-for m-m-m-mail," she repeated.

"Ah," I said.

Burrows went into the small town about once a week. He hadn't given any of us the luxury of a forwarding address, but on the other hand, none of us would probably have needed or wanted one.

"Y-y-ou want m-m-e to d-d-ouse you?" she asked.

"And make me responsible for your pneumonia? No way. Skedaddle, girl."

She danced a shiver shuffle back to her cabin, and I was left alone to yelp at the expected, but nonetheless shocking, electric shock of freezing water.

Burrows usually returned from town within an hour or two, so we were puzzled when lunch came and went, and game time approached with no sign of him. We weren't sure if we should proceed with round one, particularly since the desserts were now all gone, or at least not available for reward. We'd just convinced Jeremy to cross over into green territory to talk it over with Albert, when we heard the distant, struggling whinny of the Jeep climbing the dirt road.

Life on the mountain was routine and completely devoid of news from the outside world, and Burrows' late return had generated curiosity, if not downright excitement. All except for Sam, who required an unambiguous need to get down off his hammock.

We migrated slowly to the road, the greens gathering together on their side, and we on ours. We saw each other every day at the kitchen tent, and had grown accustomed to mostly ignoring each other, much as birds might ignore a cat they've come to understand can't get through the glass of the window. The contact during the games occurred within a completely different frame. Physical contention was—had become—the operating mode, and once a round was over, you high-tailed it back to your home base as quickly as possible.

This was a third frame. For the first time in a long time we stood looking warily at each other across a divide no greater than a stone's throw. It was difficult remembering when these greens, watching us cautiously, were not adversaries. I was waiting for one of them to shout, launching the mass of them at us with rocks and clubs.

"Should we send someone to guard the cabins?" I heard Dale ask Jeremy.

"They're all here," he said. "I counted. It's a good idea to keep an eye on them, though. Make sure nobody sneaks away."

The sound of the Jeep grew louder as it rounded the last turn, and appeared, struggling up the last steep slope, fish-tailing and throwing dirt like a bull pawing the ground.

The Jeep topped the slope and stopped between our groups, a cloud of dust following. Burrows got out, his face, serious concern cut in stone. He didn't say anything until he'd walked around to the front and climbed up on the hood. He stood there surveying us, Moses returned from the Mount. "I have some terrible news!" he shouted.

Silence.

"Somebody—presumably terrorists—has set off a dirty bomb in Idyllwild."

A muted rumble quickly swelled to a roar.

"Quiet!" Burrows shouted. "You're in no danger at present. The wind is blowing the radioactive material past us. They've evacuated the town, and are starting to evacuate Palm Springs."

"We have to leave!" Dana shouted, almost a scream. "Now!"

Burrows face turned darker. "I'm afraid that's not possible. At least for awhile. The radioactive cloud is blocking our exit."

"Holy Shit! Look!" a green shouted, pointing.

There, below us, an ugly black billow of smoke rose and slanted off sideways in the wind, like a malformed tornado stuck to one spot.

Chapter 19

"They have their hands full, obviously, but will do everything humanly possible to get us out of here," Burrows assured us. "We have to stay calm until they do."

"When they tell you to stay calm," Rudy said quietly, "you know the shit's about to hit the fan."

"How did *you* get through?" another green asked.

"I didn't," Burrows said. "I met up with some local police who'd gotten trapped on our side of the cloud. The authorities had just dropped radiation suits for them to escape."

"Dropped?" the green said.

"By helicopter, of course."

"Why don't they lift us out of here?" Dana asked. Her voice was brittle, ready to escape into hysterics.

"There's nowhere to land. They'd have to lift us out one-by-one in baskets, with very long lines. They'll get to us eventually, but right now they have a bigger problem on their hands."

I heard the distant chatter of a helicopter, then saw it, sweeping back and forth around the cloud.

Burrows held his hand up to make sure he had our attention. "The police gave me more than just advice." He surveyed us, gazing at each group in turn. "It may be possible for some of you to escape."

Dana's voice screeched. "How!"

Sam had walked up, and Burrows motioned him to the rear of the Jeep. "The police had hazmat suits with them, but the air filters weren't activated—that's why they dropped new suits to them. They gave the old ones to me."

Sam had taken a large box from the rear, and he set it on the hood next to Burrows. "We have six suits." He reached in and lifted one up—slick yellow material, ending in elastic bands at the wrists. A plastic view window and two round air filters were part of the headpiece, giving the appearance of a giant, desiccated insect.

"What good are they without filters?" Albert asked.

"A US Forest Service engineer as there with the police officers, and he told me that manzanita plants contain an enzyme that can be used to activate the filters. Manzanita grows around here."

Silence.

"I'm asking for six volunteers," Burrows continued, "to use the suits to get out to the authorities and convince them that we need to be evacuated. Do I have any volunteers?"

Every single hand except Sam's reached towards the white puffy clouds above us.

"I see," Burrows said, rubbing his chin. "Well, the first step is collecting manzanita. The engineer told me we'd need to boil down at least twenty pounds of the leaves and twigs." He looked from one group to the next again. "Why don't we have each team see what they can find?" He grinned. "We've about exhausted the embassy flag game. Let's make a little game of this."

"Of course," he added, "if we want a reward for the winners, we'll have to find something other than desserts, since they're all gone."

Before we could raise any more questions, he clapped his hands to dismiss the troops. "Sam and I will go back down to see what the situation is. I hope to find two big piles of manzanita when we return."

The buzz of excited chatter swelled as we broke up and walked back to our respective cabin areas. "How dangerous do you think a dirty bomb is?" Rudy wondered.

"Not as bad as the media generally makes them out to be," Ellie said.

"So, like, how dangerous, then?"

"Oh, dangerous enough," she said. "You definitely don't want to get caught in the path of that smoke. The real danger is breathing the radioactive dust. That stuff gets lodged in your lungs, and then you're just waiting around for lung cancer to develop."

"So those hazmat suits could really help?" he asked.

"Definitely. They're not ideal—better to have your own oxygen supply—but the filters should get you through the cloud if you don't dilly-dally."

Rudy nodded. "Okay, Miss Biology Major, what about this manzanita magic stuff?"

She shrugged. "My classes didn't cover filtration techniques. I always had the idea that the filters in these suits were just the kind of paper that blocks particles above a certain size. But that's just my notion."

I looked over at the greens who were slowly diverging towards their own cabins. Several of them glanced our way.

"It sounds like Burrows intends to use the suits as the reward for gathering the most manzanita," I said.

Rudy watched the greens watching us. "An Easter egg hunt with deadly consequences for the losers."

"But only if the wind shifts suddenly," Ellie reasoned.

"Sure," Rudy agreed.

We walked along in silence.

"And only if they take too long to rescue us," she added.

"Right," Rudy said. "Nothing to worry about."

"Of course. Panic serves no purpose." She glanced over at the greens. "But we're going to kick ass finding manzanita."

"Oh, yeah," Rudy and I said together.

We hurried our pace as panic nibbled at us.

ж ж ж

"You've never seen one?" I said to Viona.

"Not that I'm aware of," she answered.

"They don't grow very high—maybe five feet. At least the ones I've seen. The leaves are oval, but it's the bark that's distinctive. It's smooth and bronze, almost reddish. You can't miss them after you've seen one."

"Which I haven't."

"Well, let's find one for you."

We had split into three groups. Dale wanted to send everybody out solo to cover the most area, but Jeremy told us to stay as close together as possible. When Ellie asked whether this was because of mountain lions, Jeremy had replied, "Sure, Ellie—mountain lions." Rudy suggested that the "mountain lions" probably wore green shirts.

Both Dale and I remembered seeing manzanita at lower elevations, so three pairs of us had spread out below the plateau, leaving Jeremy and Dale to guard our cabins from "mountain lions."

I paused and looked back up the mountainside. "The trickiest part may be finding our way back." We'd been gone only about twenty minutes, but the slope above us looked like an awfully long slog, like gazing up a fifty-story stairwell. "Twenty minutes down could mean an hour back up."

"Does a manzanita look like that?" Viona asked.

She was pointing at a small shrub fifty feet away.

"Holy shit," I breathed.

We ran over, and I caressed the smooth bark, our possible salvation. I looked around, but this one manzanita stood all by itself, perhaps a seed that had been dropped by a bird years ago.

"What do we do now?" she asked.

We hadn't thought past finding the plant. "I guess we could just pull off the leaves."

"We have nothing to carry them in, and didn't Burrows say that we could use both the leaves and the twigs?"

"Right. Sorry little buddy," I said to the miniature tree. It was barely a foot high. It would be like pulling a large weed. I squatted down, grasped the trunk in both hands, and heaved. And heaved. And grunted. And heaved. And then I sat back, huffing and puffing.

I looked back up at that slog and sighed. "Okay. You stay here and I'll go get something to cut it down. Listen for me coming back, though. I may have to call to find you."

The climb was slow. My calves burned from the exertion. Something caught my eye, and I stopped. Two greens were coming down, a hundred yards off. I stepped behind a tree. Two of them, and just one of me. I didn't want to get caught out of hailing distance of my tribe. When they were out of sight, I continued up the never-ending incline.

The farther I ascended, the more often I had to stop to catch my breath. Going down had been so easy. As I crunched through some dry oak leaves, I heard a shrill squeal. I wondered if there were eagles in the San Jacintos. I heard it again, coming from directly downslope. I stopped to listen, but all I heard was the echoed caw-caw of a raven.

I continued working my way up, but stopped again. The greens had been angling away. If they'd continued their track, they would have passed by hundreds of yards from Viona.

I started again, but immediately stopped, turning to look downslope. What if they'd changed their track? What if they'd seen me and guessed what was up?

"Shit," I said to myself. It was like walking from New York City to Boston, but upon reaching Hartford, remembering that you forgot your wallet.

At least it was easy going down.

I tried to follow my tracks, but it was impossible to spot in pine needles. I'd thought that I'd gone straight upslope, so I expected to come back to her going directly down. After I'd gone what I thought should be at least half the distance, I stopped. *Damn.* I couldn't call for her—the greens would hear me for sure.

I hear voices. Coming up. I froze. *There!* The two greens, and one was carrying … a *manzanita bush!* What were the chances? "Hey!" I shouted, before thinking it through.

They stopped and looked at me. One of them cursed and ran towards me carrying one of the small trim saws we'd used on the cabins. I turned to run, but tripped on a root and tumbled to the ground. I started to get up, but it was clear I wasn't going to get away, so I crabbed backwards on hands and feet until my back was braced against a tree trunk. It was instinct, protection from a rear attack. All I could grab in the way of a weapon was a flimsy stick before the green was standing right above me, brandishing the saw. "It's ours!" he shouted, holding the saw up like a battle ax.

"Okay!" I shouted back. "It's yours! Geez! Don't have a cow!"

He just stared down at me, and I held my breath. The guy was clearly deciding what to do—and that scared the crap out of me.

The other green called to him, and my assailant kicked pine needles at me and ran off.

I sat back against the tree and inhaled a deep lung-full. That had been close. What the hell? I hadn't done anything! It was like the guy had been pre-loaded with adrenaline.

Oh shit! Viona!

I jumped up and ran down the hill, calling. I thought I heard something, and I stopped. There it was again, a hiss. No, a sniffle. I heard her crying. I found her sitting on a log, head buried in her hands. "Viona!" I called, running to her. "Are you okay?"

She lifted her head, and her face was wet with tears. The front of her shirt flopped open, missing several buttons, revealing her bra. "They took it!" she wailed.

"It doesn't matter," I assured, squatting down in front of her. "Viona," I asked softly, "Did they ..."

She saw me looking at her torn shirt. "No! *No!* I tried to stop them from taking it ..."

"And they got rough," I finished.

She nodded vigorously. "I called them parasites."

I smiled. "Good."

A nasty scratch ran at an angle down the fleshy upper part of her arm. She touched her wound gingerly. "That's when they hit me with the saw."

I helped her up. "Let's go get you cleaned up," I said.

I was going to add "and call the police," but remembered that we might as well have been at the south pole.

ж ж ж

It was a long, long haul back up to the plateau. I was exhausted from climbing twice, and Viona was still recovering from her emotional slap. We intended to come back via the road, but ended up off course, finally stumbling onto the plateau at the far end, near the blues' retired embassy tower. I found this disconcerting, and told myself that we'd all have to hone our mountain navigation skills before striking out too far in search of manzanita. The only place to go when lost would be down, where lethal radiation lurked.

Even more disconcerting was that Jeremy and Dale had abandoned their guard posts at our cabins. I poked my head inside each one in turn. "They're all over there," Viona said, pointing towards the road. She went to her cabin to change shirts, and I walked over to see what all the fuss was about.

As I got close, I saw that the fuss looked more like a funeral. Everybody stood around talking quietly, the greens on their side, and we on ours. Ellie saw me and ran over. "Oh, Cal! It's just awful!"

I hadn't seen her this upset before. This was beyond fear—more like horror.

"What happened?" I asked.

"It's Harry."

"What about him?"

"Cal, he's dead."

I blinked. I heard the word, but it was like it didn't pertain to this universe. "Dead?" I said.

"He was coming back, and got caught in the cloud."

I shook my head, trying to understand, but a clear picture wasn't coalescing.

"Burrows and Sam found him staggering up the road."

"Why was he walking?"

"They don't know. He was incoherent. He died before they got him here."

"But … but how do they know it was the dirty bomb?"

Her answer was a deadly serious look.

"Is that the only possible explanation?" I offered.

She shook her head, and motioned for me to follow her. We walked over to where people were crowded around the other side of the Jeep. People parted to let me through, and I saw that they had laid Harry on the ground.

I gasped. It *was* horrible, as though sections of his skin had melted, oozing clear liquid. I turned and ran away, fighting a gag reflex. I stood, bent over, hands on knees, and managed to hold down my lunch until the waves of nausea passed.

I felt a gentle hand on my shoulder. It was Ellie.

"That's no ordinary dirty bomb," I gasped.

"No, it's not," she agreed.

I looked up at her. "Holy hell! We're screwed!"

"Yes," she agreed, "we are. If we stay here."

Chapter 20

"Wood's getting low," Jeremy observed. "Ellie, Rudy, I think it's your turn."

We'd all agreed that from now on, nobody would leave the cabins alone. The sun still hovered on the horizon, but it was already getting cold. Winter was upon us. Dale and Tim had built a fire pit, lined with stones, and encircled by logs to sit on. Concern about Forest Service rules was a memory from a long time ago, a happier time, when we still had the possibility of contact with the rest of the world.

"I'll help," I said. Ellie's sweet kiss still seemed fresh, and as much as I liked Rudy—he was basically my best friend now—I wasn't about to let her slip away. Ellie was not a gift to be shared.

The dead wood, mostly fallen branches, was plentiful, and for now we didn't have to go far from the cabins to collect it. We'd only begun gathering the fuel when Ellie glanced in the direction of the cabins and motioned for us to come closer. "I've been thinking about Harry," she whispered.

"So have I," I whispered back, wondering why we were whispering. "It's horrible."

"No," she said, "I mean his skin."

"I know, it's *really* horrible."

"Of *course* it is. But I don't understand how the radiation would act so quickly."

"I've seen pictures of Japanese taken after Hiroshima ..." I said. "Ah, yeah—that damage would have been from the heat flash. You're right. I remember reading that most radiation damage becomes visible, like, days after exposure."

"At least skin blistering. Nausea can happen in a few hours."

"That wasn't blistering," Rudy reminded. "That was creamed corn." He saw our faces. "Well, it *was*!"

"You're right, Rudy," Ellie conceded. "It sounds insensitive, though."

"Don't worry, I wouldn't say that to, like, his wife."

"I'm glad," she said.

I wondered why I'd been concerned about them being alone together.

"But Rudy's right," she went on. "That was beyond blistering."

"What kind of radiation could cause that so quickly?"

She shrugged. "Really—*really*—intense radiation, I guess."

"Would you expect that kind from a dirty bomb?"

She shook her head, not in denial, but in doubt. "I'm not qualified to know *what* to expect. It does seem incredible, but ..."

"What?"

She took a breath and sighed. "If radiation at the bottom of the mountain could do that to Harry, then ..."

"We're already dead, aren't we?" I asked.

"I don't *know*!" She wanted to deny that herself.

"Those hazmat suits are made to protect against airborne alpha particles," she added. "There's one thing for sure—with radiation like that, those hazmat suits are going to be useless."

For once, Rudy had no comment.

Ж Ж Ж

When we got back to the fire, Jeremy was gone. Sam had come to fetch him. Burrows wanted to talk with him and Albert. We had agreed not to upset the others with our fears and doubts about the dirty bomb, so we just dumped our wood, sat down at the fire, and listened to the music. Bruce Hornsby had become "our" music. We had two of his CDs, and listened to them exclusively. I didn't get tired of it, though—just the opposite. I equated it with the safety of our cabins, and felt more at ease when Bruce was banging out his piano riffs. If music could tame the savage breast, then that savage was now me.

When Jeremy finally returned it was obvious he was upset. He wasn't one to complain, or be negative in general, actually, so we'd learned to read his face. Now it said, "I've really been raked over the coals on this one."

He just stood there, staring at the fire until Dana finally spoke up. "Well?"

He looked at her like he'd forgotten she was still with us. He sighed. "Burrows is sticking with the manzanita contest—whichever group gathers the most gets to use the suits."

I saw Ellie put her hand on Rudy's wrist. She was afraid he'd say something about our conversation.

I had a good guess that this wasn't the only subject Burrows had discussed, but I knew Jeremy wouldn't talk if Burrows had told him not to.

"I'll be back," he suddenly said, and walked off towards the toilets.

Ellie looked at Dale, and he got up and followed Jeremy. It was a rule, now.

"Oh, my!" Viona gasped.

We looked and saw Burrows standing in the shadows.

"Oh, lord!" she said, putting her hand over her heart. "You gave me a scare."

He stepped forward, into the light. "How's everybody doing?" he asked.

Burrows never came by to ask how we were doing. It was obvious that he was checking up on Jeremy—probably making sure he kept quiet about … something.

"Not so good, actually," Ellie said.

Burrows studied her. "I would imagine. It's a terrible situation. Everybody's feeling a lot of stress."

"It doesn't have to be like this," she said, whacking a stick against the fire pit wall, avoiding his eyes.

"Really?" is all he said, watching her closely.

"Yes. This whole manzanita contest is counterproductive."

He raised an eyebrow. "I think it's pretty effective."

"At what?" she challenged, finally looking up at him.

He looked her in the eye, a tiger watching a rival approach. "Collecting the manzanita needed for the filters, of course."

"It doesn't have to be a competition."

"It's effective," he reiterated. "And besides, it provides a diversion from our troubles."

"No! It's *causing* the troubles—it's setting us against each other! We should cooperate instead of competing. We could draw straws, or—"

"Ellie!"

It was Jeremy, storming into the light of the campfire. "That's enough!"

She was shocked into silence. Jeremy, normally Mister Cool, prided himself on not getting riled up. We had never seen him display anger like this.

"I—I was just explaining that—"

"I don't care!" Jeremy shouted, cutting her off.

Silence.

"Jeremy," I finally said, "what's wrong?"

He looked from Burrows to me. He seemed scared. *Of what?* I wondered.

When he replied, he was calmer. "We have enough problems already. We don't need Ellie stirring the pot, trying to change Professor Burrows' program."

"A Manzanita contest?" I asked. I didn't mean for it to sound so sarcastic.

"Yes! And whatever else he comes up with."

"Because he's the boss," I suggested.

I looked at Burrows, who was watching me benignly.

"Because we need him," Jeremy said. "We need someone in charge. A leader."

"More like a god," Rudy whispered, and I nudged him to be quiet.

"Good night," Burrows suddenly said and turned to walk away. "Sleep well," he called back.

Jeremy watched him as he disappeared into the darkness, and continued watching as though expecting him to suddenly come back.

"Well!" Rudy announced, "that certainly relieved my stress!"

ж ж ж

I woke to utter darkness. I'd heard something, a scream.

"You hear that?" Tim asked.

"What was it?"

"Dunno. Maybe an owl?"

"Maybe."

The sound replayed over and over in my head. I couldn't tell how much of it was real, and how much a remnant of a dream. I tried to go back to sleep, but it bothered me. It seemed familiar. Then it came to me—dream or not, it had sounded exactly like Viona's shrill scream when the greens had stolen our manzanita.

I decided that I was going to have to go and make sure Viona was okay. Then I changed my mind. That would actually be selfish, to wake her so that I could go back to sleep.

My dilemma was solved when more screams—sustained screams—split the night. I was struggling to get my shoes on when footsteps pounded by outside, and shouts from across the plateau amplified the urgent sense of a call to action.

Outside was a shock of bitter cold winter wind. Flashlights weaved and blinked off towards the kitchen tent and toilets, and I ran, stumbling on stones and nearly breaking my leg on a log. As I got near, I saw blues clustered together, all intent on something lying on the ground. A scattering of greens stood nearby, onlookers keeping their distance, but fascinated and curious.

"What happened?" I called.

Rudy turned and put his hand up for me to avoid coming closer, but that was not going to happen. Peering between the arms and torsos of my blue companions, I saw that it was Viona lying on her back. There was a lot of blood.

Suddenly Ellie was in my arms, sobbing on my shoulder.

"What's going on?" It was Burrows, with Sam behind him.

Multiple blues started babbling together until Burrows put up his hand. "Move aside," he said, and stepped up to look. He knelt down beside Viona's body, and then stood up.

"Is she ..." Dale asked. "Is she dead?"

"Of course, she's dead," Burrows replied. "Her jugular has been opened. Did anybody see what happened?" he asked.

Silence.

"I—I found her ..." Ellie sobbed, unable to say more.

"She got up to use the toilet," Dana explained.

"Viona or Ellie?" Burrows asked.

Dana looked at him and blinked. "Viona! She went out to the bathroom. I was only half awake, but when she screamed, Ellie and I went and—and—"

"Found her lying here," Burrows finished for her.

"Yeah," Dana said, staring at Viona.

Burrows knelt down again. He stood up. He looked at us, the blues, then looked over at the greens, who backed away a step or two, then back at us. "Maybe ..." he started. He looked down at the bloody mess, then at us again. "Maybe it was a mountain lion."

"A mountain lion?" Rudy asked, incredulous, or maybe frightened.

"They go for the throat," Burrows reminded.

Dale stepped forward and, taking a deep breath, bent over. He shook his head, and looked up at us knowingly. "It was no mountain lion," he declared.

"How do you know?" Dana challenged. She *wanted* it to be a mountain lion.

"A mountain lion would bite the throat. This was a cut—there's no teeth marks. If a lion slashed her throat, it would be ripped, torn by fangs."

I was surprised at his surgical precision, his confidence. Jeremy stood staring at the body, offering no comment.

Burrows shrugged and nodded. He seemed to accept Dale's conclusion.

"It was them!" Dana cried, pointing at the greens, who backed away a couple more steps.

Several greens protested, but I noticed that Albert said nothing. He looked on, serious, silent, morose. It was the same stoic Albert I'd met on the bus, the same Albert I'd seen direct the greens cabin building, toilet digging, and game direction, except that every few seconds he would glance down at the corpse and wince ever so slightly, as though between each glance, he'd forgotten she lay there.

"Let's cover her until it gets light," Burrows said. "You can use one of the tarps. You'll need to bury her," he added matter of factly.

Silence.

"What did you say?" Rudy asked.

"I said you'll need to bury her once it's light."

"She's been murdered! We can't just bury her! We shouldn't even touch her!"

Burrows looked at Rudy, waiting for him to come to his senses. "You'd like to leave her lying here in the warmth of the afternoon sun, then leave her here at night for the animals to get at?" he finally asked.

Rudy was stuck. He didn't have an answer for that.

"We need the police," Ellie said, still crying.

"Of course, we do," Burrows said. "Unfortunately, that's not possible. Unless you're volunteering to go for help. You can take the Jeep. Take a hazmat suit as well, if you like, but it's useless without the filter."

She glared at him, then looked around, but everybody avoided her eyes. "Well, we can't bury her. That just seems wrong."

"Maybe somebody would like to volunteer their cabin?" Burrows asked.

Tim looked at me, took a breath, and nodded.

"Okay," I said, shivering in the freezing cold wind. "Tim and I can move into the other cabins."

I was assuming that Tim wouldn't want to sleep in the same room with a corpse. I certainly didn't.

Nobody said anything. Before, nobody could take their eyes off Viona's body, now they avoided looking.

"It's going to smell," Dale finally said quietly.

"She'll be inside the cabin—" Rudy started.

"Bad," Dale said, cutting him off. "Really bad."

"I'm afraid there's only one option," Burrows concluded.

Dana wiped her face with her shirt. Crying time was over. "We'll do it!" she declared.

"We will?" Rudy asked. "Who's 'we'?"

"Blues!" she retorted. "We take care of our own."

I glanced in the direction of the greens. They were gone.

Chapter 21

Despite the horror during the night, I slept late the next morning, emotionally wrung out. I woke to find that the cabin was filled with a strange, translucent glow, as though we'd been lifted above the clouds. When I stepped outside, I saw why—the cold wind had left a dusting of snow, transforming the forest into a winter fairy land. This was an ephemeral state, though, since the sun was shining, and the trees' needles were already dripping with melting snow.

I heard activity, people talking and calling to each other, and an occasional bang off towards our embassy tower. I needed coffee, and I grabbed my cup and shuffled over to Rudy's cabin, where I nearly collided with Tim, who was coming out. "Any left?" I asked.

"Some," he replied.

"Thanks. What's going on?" I asked, pointing towards the voices in the distance.

He just looked at me.

"Ah," I said. "They're, uh … Viona."

"Yeah," he said. "I'm heading over."

Inside, I found barely twelve ounces of lukewarm coffee left. They'd left me cold breakfast sausages and a hash-brown as well, and I devoured them without sitting down. Meal and shower time slots had broken down, and we used the kitchen tent and spring whenever we could get access. Never alone.

I headed towards my group. The activity was beyond the embassy tower, up the slope a ways. I saw Ellie and Dana carrying a small boulder between them, and then Rudy with one as well. As I got closer, I saw that Dale was digging—actually, mostly striking buried stone with the shovel, which he used to try to pry out the offenders.

Rudy handed me his boulder. "About time, sleepy head."

I took it and nodded towards Dale. I found it hard to say the words.

He understood. "It's impossible to dig a proper grave," he explained. "I don't think there's six feet of dirt within fifty miles. Dale's going to get down as far as he can, but it's mostly going to be a pile of rocks on top."

"A cairn," I suggested.

"I guess."

"How's everybody holding up?" I asked.

He shrugged. "Ellie's taking it pretty hard. Everybody's mostly still in shock. Except Dana. She picked up the bullhorn and whip, and for once nobody's bothered to tell her to shut up."

"Maybe that's just what we need right now. What about Jeremy?"

Rudy looked puzzled, thinking. "He's not saying much. Probably in shock, like everybody."

"Maybe he feels responsible, somehow."

"Yeah, I didn't think of that."

"Any news? You know, anything coming from the other side?"

He shook his head. "It's almost like they're avoiding us. When Jeremy and Dale went to start breakfast, a couple of greens took off, like they didn't want to face them."

"Huh. Sounds kind of guilty."

"Or afraid."

"True."

Rudy glanced around, then leaned in. "Tim suggested that maybe it was Sam."

I nodded slowly. "He is an unknown factor. His past—hell, his occupation—is a complete blank."

"Jeremy cut him off."

"Tim's idea? Why?"

Rudy glanced around again. "Jeremy says he saw Sam just about the time that Viona was ... murdered."

I shrugged. "So it was the greens after all."

He thought a moment, then nodded. "Yeah. Probably."

"What? What're you thinking?"

He sighed, then leaned in even closer. "If Jeremy was up when Viona was ... killed, you'd think he'd be the first one on the scene after she screamed."

"He wasn't?" The whole thing was a blur in my head.

"He was practically the last to show up."

"Huh. That doesn't necessarily prove anything."

"It's not a trial, here. I just think it's odd, that's all."

Our little conspiracy was cut short when Dana shouted a rhetorical question as to whether we ever intended to bring our boulder.

ж ж ж

We finished before lunch. The pile of rocks stood nearly five feet high, a crude little pyramid in the middle of nowhere. The worst part had been laying Viona in the shallow hole that Dale had managed to scrape out. We'd left the tarp wrapped around her, but it was impossible not to visualize her in there, all alone. Ellie broke down, and stumbled a short distance away. Rudy and I went and sat with her until she recovered enough to go on.

Jeremy tried to say a few words over Viona's primitive grave, but he struggled. I could have done no better. We'd become a tight group—our team, our tribe—and felt a deep loyalty to each other, but the truth was that we'd known Viona barely a month. I suspect that, like myself, the only thing that came to mind was to curse the greens, and swear revenge. And we weren't ready to voice that out loud.

Not yet.

On the slow, sad walk back to our cabins, Jeremy suggested that we should come up with strategies to protect ourselves.

"From mountain lions," Rudy confirmed with mock seriousness.

"You know what I mean," Jeremy said.

"Strategies?" Dana asked. "Like keeping guards at night?"

"Sure," Jeremy said. He frowned. "For a start."

"What else?" Dana asked.

His frown deepened. "You know, like, insurance."

"Insurance?" Rudy said. He chuckled. "Like kidnapping one of the greens?"

Jeremy didn't reply. In fact, he carefully watched the ground as we walked.

"Hold it!" Ellie exclaimed, stopping, and causing everybody else to stop and turn to her. "You're serious, aren't you?"

Jeremy looked beat upon. "I'm just saying," was his response.

"I know exactly what you're saying," Ellie persisted. "You want to kidnap one of the greens and hold them hostage—as protection."

Jeremy stared at her.

"We should consider it," Dana said, reasonably.

"No," Ellie corrected, "we should *not* consider it. We're not some criminal gang."

"No, we're not," Jeremy agreed, starting forward again. "But maybe the greens are."

ж ж ж

We were filthy from grave digging, but the greens had the kitchen tent, and we had to wait until they left before washing up. Lunches—and dinners—were tense affairs, hurrying through preparations while keeping an eye out for greens. Simple, quick fare was the rule. For this lunch, we merely boiled water and opened cans. As we made our way back to our cabins with styrofoam cups of ramen noodles and cold tuna, Rudy said, "Shouldn't there have been more cans of tuna?"

I thought about it. "Yeah. Wasn't there, like, three boxes just a couple of days ago?"

"Now there's just the one that's already open."

Jeremy was nodding, like it made sense.

"You were expecting this?" I asked him.

He looked at me in surprise. "Weren't you?" he asked.

I nodded as well. "I should have. Maybe the tuna boxes just got moved. We'll have to keep an eye on the stores."

Rudy stopped and glanced around at our group. "Hey, where's Tim?"

"Last I saw him, he was going into one of the toilets," Ellie said.

"How long ago?"

"Gosh, maybe ten minutes."

"Anybody see him come out?" Jeremy asked, taking charge.

We all shook our heads.

"Dammit!" Jeremy spat, and turned and ran back.

I set my cup and bowl on a log, and the styrofoam cup immediately tilted and fell off. No time for recovery, I sprinted off after Jeremy.

We reached the toilets just ahead of the rest, and found both doors open. "Tim!" Jeremy called. I joined in, and soon the whole group was calling his name.

"Son-of-a-bitch," Jeremy muttered, roiling with frustration.

"They beat us to it, didn't they?" I asked.

Jeremy glanced at me but didn't respond.

Ellie's face was white. She stared at nothing with wide eyes.

Jeremy looked at her. "So, what were you saying about criminal gangs?"

She took a deep breath and let it out slowly. "They want insurance as badly as we do."

"Protection from retribution," I said. "For Viona."

Dana's face was a visible growl. "They *should* be scared. They're gonna pay."

Jeremy shook his head. "If they have Tim, we have to be careful."

Rudy had taken a few steps in the direction of the greens' cabins and was peering into the impenetrable maze of tree trunks. "We're wasting time!" he called to us.

Jeremy seemed to wake up. "Let's go!" he shouted and ran off towards the greens' area.

We didn't get far before running into the enemy, lined up wielding limbs that they'd fashioned into clubs.

"Let him go!" Jeremy shouted.

Albert came forward. "We won't hurt him," he said.

Jeremy stepped forward. "Why don't we just—"

Albert cut him off. "Unless."

Jeremy looked at him with a clenched jaw. "Don't worry," he said. "We'll keep our distance, if you will."

Albert didn't agree or disagree. He turned and walked back to his territory.

ж ж ж

That night we sat around our fire talking in short sentences, quietly, as though Tim was just inside the cabin asleep. We missed him. We missed Viona as well, but that loss was different—permanent, relegated to grieving. Tim, a fellow tribe member possibly within our power to save, was therefore at the front of our minds.

"Shhh!" Rudy hissed. "You hear that?"

It was muffled and some distance away, but unmistakable.

Dale jumped up. "Those animals!"

Jeremy caught his arm. "Wait!"

We listened, holding our breath for many heartbeats, but Tim's one, short, piercing cry was not repeated.

"So much for Albert's word," Dana snarled.

"Maybe Tim stubbed his toe," Rudy said.

"And maybe I can fly away for help," Dale retorted.

We sat listening to the wind whoosh through the tops of the pines above us. The cold winter nights had driven the crickets into hibernation.

Jeremy finally broke the spell. "Maybe it's time we buy some insurance."

Only the wind in the pines responded. We agreed by abstention.

ж ж ж

An opportunity fell into our laps the next morning. The laps were figurative, but the falling was literal, thanks to Jeremy's caution.

Our leader decided that patrols were a necessary precaution. In addition to a guard posted outside our cabins through the night, two of us would take patrol duty while the rest were out searching for manzanita. A patrol consisted of scouting around our territory in irregular patterns. Our territory was the entire eastern half of the plateau, from our embassy tower and Viona's grave to the no-man's zone—a boundary down the middle of the plateau from the kitchen tent, through Burrows and Sam's cabins, to the road.

Rudy and I left on patrol right after breakfast, made our way along the plateau edge, and were coming up on the Potato Chip, when we heard voices. We'd been as quiet as possible and abstained from talking, as instructed by Jeremy, and we both stopped at the same time and looked at each other. The voices were obviously greens, talking quietly, trying to whisper, but breaking into irritated complaints. I recognized Ralph—I could visualize his arms flying around in protest.

I motioned for Rudy to sneak ahead wide to the right, and I started off to the left, practically tip-toeing. Following the voices of the intruders, I found Barry standing beneath one of the few deciduous trees on the plateau—what Ellie had said was a hackberry tree. The green bully was looking up, obviously at Ralph who'd climbed the tree. Barry was occupied with his intractable partner, and didn't notice as I crept closer. I finally stepped out from behind a pine trunk and said loudly, "What's going on!"

Rudy stepped out at the same time. Blues coming from multiple directions completely spooked Barry, and he yelped and sprinted off a short distance before catching himself and turning back, only to find Rudy charging, waving a rock above his head. Whatever thoughts Barry had about helping his fellow green vanished, and he tore away like a rabbit before a coyote.

I heard scraping and scrambling above, then a grunt, a branch breaking, and Ralph fell from the sky. He landed on his back on the blanket of pine needles, knocking the wind out of him. He lay, breathing in little, ineffectual gasps. I took the opportunity to roll him over on his stomach, sit on his rear, and pull one arm back and up towards his neck. I didn't even know that I knew that move.

Rudy returned just as Ralph's stunned diaphragm muscles relaxed, and he sucked in a lungful of air, then turned his head to find Rudy holding the rock over his head. "Shit!" he gasped, still breathless, "what're you *doing?*"

"This is for Viona," Rudy said, calmly.

"*I* didn't do it! I swear! Dear God, *don't!*"

"Maybe not you personally."

"No! No! I had nothing to do with it!"

"Who, then?"

"I don't *know!* I swear to *God!*"

"Too bad, then," Rudy said, and lifted the rock high.

Ralph squeaked and closed his eyes, and I gasped and held mine open wide while Rudy held the rock poised a second, then tossed it aside. "If he moves a muscle, kill him," Rudy said and sprinted off.

"Don't move," I warned, giving his wrist a little shake.

If he did, I wasn't sure how I would kill him. Maybe stuff a pine cone down his throat.

Ralph was making a soft snuffling sound. I realized he was crying, and for a half second I felt sorry for him.

Then I remembered Viona.

Chapter 22

"I don't know," Rudy said. He was skeptical. "What if the cabin, you know, catches on fire? I'll bet it's illegal."

"So," Dana sniped, "killing Viona *wasn't?*"

"He claims he had nothing to do with it. And besides two illegal acts don't, like, cancel each other out."

"Why would Professor Burrows have had Sam hand out the padlocks if he didn't want us to lock the cabins?"

"He didn't say to lock up hostages," Rudy said.

"Ralph's a prisoner," she corrected.

"The fact that we've locked him up *makes* him a prisoner, but the *reason* he's locked up is because he's a hostage. Let's not hide from the facts here."

"You want to just let him go? You getting all traitor on us?"

"Hey! I'm the one who captured him!" He glanced at me. "Uh, Cal and me, that is. I *want* him as a hostage. I just don't want to pretend."

"That's enough!" Jeremy cut in. "He can crawl out a window if the cabin catches on fire. Why was he up the tree?"

"He claims they were collecting berries," Rudy said.

"They're edible," Ellie explained. "They taste okay, actually."

Ralph had been listening from inside his jail. "We didn't know they were edible!" he called through the door.

"Why were you stealing the berries, then?" Jeremy asked.

"We thought it was a manzanita tree!"

"Where did you get that idea?"

"Burrows told us!"

We all looked at each other in surprise. "They must have misunderstood him," Ellie suggested.

"Maybe Professor Burrows was evening the score," Dana said, "punishing them for stealing our tree from Cal and Viona."

Our looks of surprise turned to skepticism.

"Well, in any case, it's our tree," Dana proclaimed. "They were stealing, and deserve to be locked up."

"We would have locked him up even if he wasn't stealing from our tree," Jeremy reminded. "He's a hostage."

"Stealing is stealing," Dana insisted. "If they steal—"

"Quiet!" Jeremy exclaimed. "He's a hostage. He's the insurance we were looking for."

"Hey, Dale's back," Rudy said.

He was watching for the greens to be done with the kitchen tent.

"They gone?" Jeremy asked.

Dale looked concerned. "Yeah, they're gone, but they're up to something."

"We heard banging," Jeremy said. "What was that about?"

"Couldn't tell. They had a guard—wouldn't let me get any closer."

"Well, we'd better go see what they're up to now. Uh, Cal and Dana—you stay here and guard Ralph." He considered that a moment. "Ellie, you stay as well. Rudy, Dale, let's go."

They picked up their clubs, fashioned from leftover two-by-fours, and headed out.

Dana waited until they were out of sight, then walked over to where Ralph was locked up, in my cabin—with Tim gone, it was the obvious choice. She rapped on the door. "You ready to tell us?" she called.

From inside, Ralph's tired voice said, "I've told you, I don't know who did it."

Dana threw Ellie and me a conspiratorial glance. "Ellie," she said loudly, "hand me the lighter. Let's see if a little fire helps him remember."

Ellie rolled her eyes. From inside the cabin, Ralph said, "Look, I know you're bluffing. I can see the other two sitting over there."

Dana's face contorted in fury. She'd forgotten about the small windows on each side. "Have a good laugh while you can, green scum!" she yelled through the door. "We'll see how funny you think it is when we torture you, like you did Tim."

Silence.

"What are you talking about?" Ralph's muffled voice came.

"Don't play any stupider than you are." Dana said. "We heard him scream last night."

"That wasn't us. That was Sam."

"Sure it was— and I can talk with ghosts."

"No! It was! Sam said he wanted to go in and make sure Tim was alright. He came out and said that Tim tried to hit him, and he'd had to restrain him."

"You're lying! That doesn't make sense. Besides, why would Sam let you keep him locked up?"

"I don't know. He minds his own business. You know that."

"Then it makes even less sense. Why would he care if Tim was okay?"

"I don't *know*, dammit!" Ralph yelled. "Let me out of here, and I'll go ask!"

Just then Dale came running up. "Cal!" he called. "Come with me. Ellie, Jeremy wants you to stay near the cabins. Dana, you stand halfway to the kitchen tent. If anybody shows up, you guys start hollering, and we'll come running."

"What's going on?" Ellie asked.

"No time. Later. Come on," he called gesturing to me, and ran off.

I shrugged to Ellie and ran after him.

When we arrived at the kitchen, Rudy was leaning over the stove, prying away with a knife. When I got closer, I saw that Jeremy was on his back on the ground, working from below.

Then I noticed that the other two burners were missing.

Dale saw where I was looking. "The bastards stole them," he explained.

From under the stove, Jeremy called, "Dale! Is that Cal?"

"Yeah."

"You two, grab the tanks."

The propane tanks were ten gallon, and required two of us to carry when full. The greens had taken four and left us just two. Dale picked up his end, and I lifted mine, grunting. It was even heavier than I'd expected. We staggered off. Halfway to our cabins, I called for a break. My arms burned, and my fingers were numb. "Shit," I said, sweating, despite the cold evening air blowing through the pines. "I don't know if I can make it. Maybe we can leave it here, and come back later?"

"Visualize munching on uncooked ramen noodles." Dale said.

"Right," I said. "Okay, let's go."

We dumped the tank between two cabins, and ran back for the second one. Jeremy and Rudy had the burner free, and were being careful to make sure they had all the connecting pieces. "Jeremy," Dale said, "maybe you can help me with the second tank. Rudy and Cal can carry the burner."

Jeremy looked at Dale a moment, but didn't question his suggestion. Dale so rarely voiced a preference, we all took it for granted that when he did, there was a good reason.

I could have resented Dale's implication, but I was relieved and grateful.

The burner wasn't heavy at all, at least compared to the eighty pounds or more of the propane tank, but my arms and hands were already blown out, and I still struggled. I filled Rudy in on what Ralph had said through the door. "That doesn't sound like Tim," Rudy said.

"Trying to hit Sam?"

"Yeah. You think Ralph's lying?"

"I don't know. The guy's a jerk, and I wouldn't trust him as far as I could throw him, but ... I don't know."

"What?" Rudy asked.

"He sounded ... earnest, I guess. Either he was telling the truth, or he's a really good actor."

"A good actor, huh? Yeah, he could play Michael in The Godfather."

"Al Pacino was actually really good in that part," I said.

"Okay, then how about Godzilla?"

"He's a little short."

"He'd be the voice actor."

"He'd roar for two hours?"

"It's a character matching thing. You wouldn't understand."

"Because you had an introduction to the theatre class?"

"Indeed."

"You never say 'indeed.'"

"I'm practicing."

ж ж ж

Rudy and Jeremy re-assembled the burner next to our fire pit on a crude frame we built using a couple of two-by-fours laid across piles of rocks, while Dale and I returned to the kitchen tent for food. We were only thinking of the canned salmon and instant mashed potatoes that we'd planned for the evening meal, but when we threw back the tarp, we just stood, staring.

"I guess this should be no surprise," Dale said.

The greens had stolen a large portion of the boxes. They'd left mostly canned vegetables and soups. All the canned meat was gone, except for one box of sardines.

I took a deep breath, imagining the hungry, cold winter nights ahead. "Let's grab the sardines and some soup," I said. "we can bring Ellie and Dana back to help with the rest." An urge had been building for the last half hour. "I'll be just a minute, I need to use the toilet."

Dale was pulling out the first boxes as I walked off. A minute turned into five, as I sat in the near-complete darkness of the porta-toilet. With the kitchen tent de-commissioned, the toilets would now be the only reason to come to this part of no-man's land. It would be the last intersection between the blues and the ghouls, and it couldn't last very long. We'd have to come en masse to avoid ambushes. I wondered whether we could move one of the toilets to the far end of our territory, but visualizing this, I decided that I'd rather use an open ditch as a latrine.

My contemplations were interrupted by voices. For a moment, I thought it was maybe Rudy and Jeremy, but the tone was harsh, belligerent. I hastily finished, and when I came out, Dale was standing between two greens, his arms out, as though he would hold each of them off with just his palms. One of the greens held a pipe in both hands, and he swung—not a warning swing, but aimed directly at Dale's torso, and he jumped back just in time to avoid serious injury. This threw him off balance, and he stumbled back into the arms of the second green, who wrapped an arm around his neck.

The first green stepped forward with another swing as I shouted and ran towards them. Both greens jumped in surprise, and this gave Dale the chance to jab an elbow into his captor's side and twist free, but the pipe caught him square in the back, and he fell to his knees in agony.

I threw a stone, and implemented a ruse that was in fact my dearest wish at the moment. "Rudy! Jeremy!" I called to my fantasy companions. "Over here!"

I threw another stone, and the green with the pipe jumped out of the way. I had no idea what I was going to do against two greens and a metal club, and I was relieved beyond imagining when my ad hoc ploy worked and the greens ran off. I heard feet pounding behind me, and spun around in shock, only to find Rudy, the real reason they'd run off.

"Where'd you come from?" I asked, astounded that he'd arrived so quickly—that he'd even heard my call.

"I was coming to use the toilet."

Dale groaned. He laid back and spread his arms out.

"The bastards tried to kill him," I said and knelt down beside our stricken comrade. "Are you okay?" I asked. It was stupid, a reflexive question.

"I'm fine," Dale said without moving. "Just in a whole lot of pain."

I didn't know what to do. It had been drilled into me not to move back injury victims until professional help arrived. That could be months.

Dale ended my dilemma and rolled over on his side, then sat up, wincing.

"Move your toes," Rudy urged him.

"I have shoes on," Dale said.

"I know."

Dale looked at him curiously.

"It's what they always say," Rudy said. "I figured it's supposed to help somehow."

"How 'bout you help for real and take his other arm," I said.

ж ж ж

Dale recovered enough to hobble back. The pipe had bruised a muscle, but apparently hadn't broken vertebrae or damaged nerves. After resting for a while in his bed, he even wanted to help us bring back the last of the food boxes, and we had to lie and tell him that there were none left.

We were relieved to finish the task with no more incidents. After a dinner of sardines, canned green beans, and stale crackers, we sat around the fire listening to our tribal music. We left Dale's cabin door open so he could hear Bruce Hornesby as well. Between songs, the ever-present drone of distant helicopters reminded us that the deadly conflagration still raged below. Ralph had complained about the unappetizing dinner fare, which provided an opportunity for us to let off some steam at him, since it was his very own tribe that deprived him.

Jeremy was quiet, absorbed in thought. Ellie finally asked what was on his mind. "Our safety," he replied.

"Anything in particular?" she asked.

"Well, toilet trips, for one," he said. "I don't think we should go even in pairs anymore—groups of three from now on."

Ellie grinned. "That's going to require a lot of bladder coordination."

Jeremy shrugged.

I told them about my idea to build open latrines at the far end of the plateau.

Jeremy nodded. "Wind blows usually from the west, so at least we won't be downwind. We'd still have to go in pairs in case they send a sneak patrol around."

Ellie looked at Dana. "You and me, baby. Unless we want to build privacy screens."

Dana stared at the fire and scowled, what seemed to have become her permanent expression. "We need a pro-active defense," she declared, looking up at us.

Nobody said anything. We'd learned that Dana needed no encouragement.

"We have to teach the greens not to come into our territory—ever."

Silence.

"We attack any greens on our side," she said, "no mercy." As demonstration she held up a spare cabin brace that she'd sharpened to form a crude, but wicked, knife.

Nobody spoke in agreement, but nobody objected, either. It was tacit approval, like a racial epithet that draws no protests because it strikes a tiny core of shared bigotry.

That night, Jeremy changed the evening guard routine—from now on, two blues at all times.

ж ж ж

I woke in confusion, trying to sort out dream from reality. I was on the floor again, and for a brief moment thought I was back in the Pod, but then remembered that I'd moved in with Jeremy, Rudy, and Dale. It wasn't time for my guard duty shift, and I deeply resented that my precious sleep was being wasted.

It took only a second to realize that there was trouble. I ran out into the freezing air in just my shorts and LED headlamp. Rocks and pine needles jabbed the soles of my feet, but I ran on, towards Rudy and Dana's shouts. The swinging beams of their lights led me to where they were struggling with a green—*Barry*! Rudy was trying to hold him from behind, while Dana swung her homemade knife at him. Her small arms delivered little force, and Barry was able to swat away her attempts.

Barry managed to break free from Rudy, and I tackled him. A moment later, Rudy helped me hold him down, one of us on each of his arms. Barry was a solid, stout man, and it was all we could do to just hold him against his squirming and kicking.

Suddenly Ellie yelled "*No!*" The next instant something flashed past my face and landed on Barry with a solid thump, like a screw driver swung hard into a ripe melon.

Barry gave one last convulsive heave and fell limp. In the light of my headlamp, I saw Dana's knife protruding from his chest, exactly above his heart. The slight, angry woman knelt over him panting, growling deep in her throat like a cornered dog.

Ellie turned away, breaking into hysterical sobbing. I stared at the dead man, barely believing what had happened. He had died under my hand. I had felt his last moment of life.

Jeremy extended a hand and helped me up. Dale had arrived, and we all stood looking down at the murdered man as Ellie trailed off into a private, sorrowful weeping.

"Blood for blood," Jeremy said simply.

I was horrified that I had held Barry as my fellow blue killed him. I had never intended that. I chastised myself for not seeing it coming, for not stopping it.

But a part of me, deep inside knew that a line had been crossed. The game had turned irretrievably deadly.

Chapter 23

"What'll we do?" Dale asked.

Jeremy didn't answer. We stood staring down at the horror before us. A man had been killed, right there, before us. His life was gone, and along with it his ability to speak, but the dead body itself screamed *murder!*

Dale picked up a pair of bolt cutters. "He was coming to spring Ralph," he said.

"We have to get a message to the police somehow," Ellie said. Her voice had a nasal twang from crying.

Silence.

"What are you talking about!" Dana exclaimed. "It was self defense!"

Nobody said anything. None of us had the heart to say that it was not self defense at all, at least not in an immediate danger sense.

"There are no police," Jeremy stated woodenly. "We're on our own."

"So that means there's no law?" Ellie challenged. "We can just do whatever we want?"

Jeremy looked at her and scowled, kneeling down to feel for a pulse in Barry that we all knew he wouldn't find. "No," he said. "We have law—the law of the tribe."

"What does that mean?" she asked, blowing her nose into a paper towel.

"It means we are now responsible for each other."

"Where 'each other' includes blues only," she surmised.

"Of course."

She pointed at Barry's body. "So this is okay? Because he's a green?"

Jeremy sighed. "They started it."

Ellie's eyes went wide, and she stepped forward. "You're *serious*? You think it's okay that she murdered him?"

"I did *not* murder him—" Dana started, but stopped when Jeremy held up his hand.

"She shouldn't have killed him. We all know that. Dana knows that—"

"I *had* to do it—" Dana started loudly.

Again Jeremy cut her off. "Shut up! Just listen to me. What's done is done, and we have to deal with the consequences."

"Consequences?" Ellie asked.

"We have to get rid of the body," Dale said quietly.

"Arrggh," Ellie groaned, and walked off, back to the fire pit.

"Any ideas?" Jeremy asked.

"We either bury him," Dale said, pausing to look at us, "or dump him back in their laps."

"Like they did with Viona," Rudy concluded.

We fell silent at the memory of that other horror.

Nobody spoke up for burial, so we carried him away. The propane tank had weighed eighty pounds, and Barry's mass of flesh and bone was more like one-seventy. I could barely lift my eighty-five pound half, let alone walk with him. Carrying a dead-weight body is made difficult by the lack of solid hand-holds—everything is soft and round. Rudy, Jeremy, and I struggled, taking turns, until Dale came back with rope, which he tied between the dead man's armpits and another section across his calves. This provided handles, easing the transport.

To her credit, Dana helped, or at least tried. Jeremy sent her and Dale ahead to scout out our path. We'd made it about half way to the kitchen tent, when they came back and gave us the news that a couple of greens were posted at the no-man's zone near Burrows cabin, obviously waiting for the return of their fellow green. I groaned when Jeremy announced that we'd have to make a wide arc to the kitchen tent, lengthening the trip. But I understood that we had to avoid green contact at all costs.

We lay Barry's body in front of the toilets where the greens would be sure to find him. We talked quietly, almost a whisper. "Should we, like, say a few words?" Rudy wondered.

"Go ahead," Jeremy said. "But be quick."

"Right," Rudy began. "Uh. We didn't know him very well—actually, hardly at all, other than his bullying." He looked up at us, seeming alarmed by what he'd just said. "Oh, hell, sorry, dude." He gestured towards our territory. "Let's get out of here."

We started away, but Dale knelt beside the body. I watched as he removed the rope and curled it into neat loops, then I winced as he grasped Dana's homemade knife and yanked it free. He wiped it with a handful of pine needles, then stood up. When he saw me watching, he shrugged, and we followed the others.

As we were walking back, I sidled up next to him. "Were you in the Army?"

He glanced at me, and I wasn't sure if he was going to answer, but he said, "Afghanistan."

He didn't volunteer any more, and I sensed he didn't want to.

I was thrilled. I couldn't wait to tell Rudy and Ellie—well, at least Rudy—the good news.

We had a bona fide warrior in our tribe.

ж ж ж

I heard the yelling long before we reached our cabins. Ralph was cursing and pounding on the door. When we arrived, Jeremy sighed, and pounded back from the outside. "Keep it down!" he called.

"What's going on!" the prisoner yelled back. "What the hell's happening!"

"Nothing that concerns you!"

"Bullshit!" Ralph screamed. "I saw you guys through the window. You carried somebody away. *Who was that?*"

Jeremy glanced at us, not sure what to say.

"Barry!" Dana shouted, going to the door and putting her mouth against it. "Your beloved comrade," she added sarcastically.

"What did you *do* to him!"

Jeremy put his hand on her arm, but she shook it off. "He's dead! You hear? *Dead!* And you're next if you don't shut up!"

Jeremy took her by the shoulders and pulled her away.

Ralph went silent, but his outbursts were replaced by others in the distance, in the direction of the kitchen tent.

"They found him," Rudy said.

We listened as the shouts moved slowly from the toilets across the plateau to the greens' cabins, where they were joined by a chorus of howls and screams.

We looked to Jeremy, and he gazed off towards the riled greens beehive. He looked back at us. "Rudy, Cal, come with me."

"What about me?" Dale asked.

"You can barely walk. Stay here with Ellie and Dana. If you see any greens, shout."

We picked up our two-by-four clubs. We'd sanded one end of each to make a round handle. Ellie said, "I'm coming with you."

"I thought you abhorred violence," Jeremy replied, hefting his club over his shoulder.

"Don't be ridiculous," she snapped. "Don't make *me* sound ridiculous. I understand perfectly well that we'll have to defend ourselves—now that Dana has necessitated it."

Dana stepped close, face-to-face with Ellie. "Whose side are you on, anyway?"

Jeremy pulled her away. "It's true. You have necessitated it. But that's behind us," he said, throwing a knowing glance at Ellie. "Now we move on."

We started off towards the no-man's zone.

"We have a plan?" I asked.

Jeremy took a moment to answer. "We're not looking for a fight, but they have to know we're willing if necessary."

"We have to hold the border," I said.

"Yeah. We stand our ground, and let them know it won't be easy for them."

There were four of us, and one of us a woman. We could be facing seven of them. There were nine greens before we'd captured Ralph, and killed Barry.

Rudy suddenly stopped. "I'll catch up with you," he said, and sprinted off, back towards the cabins.

Now there was just three of us.

The greens' shouts and curses had gone silent, and we knew that was bad. Jeremy motioned for us to spread out and proceed quietly. The half moon was low on the horizon, but provided enough light for us to see each other. Before we'd even reached the no-man's zone, Jeremy held up his hand and we stopped. I heard rustling, but it could have been a small night creature.

Jeremy waved for us to continue, and I only took a few steps when something light and gauzy wrapped around my face and neck. I knew instantly what it was, and gave a little involuntary cry, intuiting that a web as large at this meant an equally oversized spider. I danced a little jig, swiping my hand along my hair and clothes.

"Good one," Ellie whispered when I finished, panting a little from my struggle.

Jeremy motioned for us to get low, to lie down, but it was too late. The rustling ahead and to the sides swelled to a scramble as frantic whispers were exchanged in the gloom ahead of us. I lay behind a log, my two-by-four next to me, trying to not even breathe. Ellie lay twenty feet away, and Jeremy another thirty feet farther.

The greens appeared, seemingly out of thin air, spread apart in a line as they advanced, clubs poised. It looked like they might walk right by us. One was passing midway between Ellie and Jeremy, and the next in line was coming close, but might not see me. My luck failed. My green moved aside to avoid a sapling, putting him directly in my path. He was stepping up, over my hiding log, and it was obvious that he was going to come down right on me. My only defense was surprise, so I let out what I hoped was a blood-curdling cry.

I rolled away, and a thump announced the green's club slamming the ground where my chest had been. I jumped to my feet, and retreated. Without planning it, the three of us were soon huddled together, backs to backs, facing the squad of greens who cautiously moved to surround us. I saw with alarm that their clubs now sprouted half-inserted screws crowning the ends, handy if you wanted to tear someone's face off.

Albert stepped forward. He held one end of his club in each hand, his thumb caressing the sharp edges of the screws. "You probably think you've evened the score," he said flatly, circling us and gazing into our eyes, each in turn.

"We're not keeping score," Jeremy replied. "Barry attacked us— we had no choice."

It was more lie than truth, but a fabrication I was happy with at the moment.

Albert glanced at his followers. "If there's no score, we might as well take all three of you down."

"And then the others," one of the greens said, "take them all down."

I recognized the voice. It was Sheryl. She'd cropped her hair short, and it looked like she'd painted three parallel lines on each cheek, like cat's whiskers.

Albert put his hand up for quiet. "We'll see. We won't kill them," he said, glancing at the rest of the greens to make sure they understood. "We're not like that. But it's going to be a lesson they won't soon forget."

He stepped back. "Drop them," he ordered, indicating our clubs.

Neither Ellie nor I moved, waiting for Jeremy.

"If we have to knock them out of your hands," Albert said, "things will get very nasty."

I remembered what Jeremy had said, that we had to let them know we'd be willing to fight if necessary. It had come to that.

"Drop them," Jeremy said.

I let mine fall, and Ellie's bumped to the ground as well. I didn't hear a third.

Jeremy stepped forward, "You and me," he said to Albert, cocking his club like a bat.

If Albert had the ability to smile, he would have. "Now why would I agree to that?" he asked. "Some archaic code of honor? Chivalry served the purposes of the lords, not the knights."

"To prove you have guts," Jeremy replied.

Albert eyed him a moment and nodded, and then cocked his own face-tearing weapon and took a step forward.

"Not with that," Jeremy objected, using his club to point at the bristling ring of screws.

"Who's lacking guts now?"

Jeremy clenched his jaw and hunkered down, ready for blood to flow.

I heard the thumping of footsteps, but ignored them like everybody else, waiting for the first swing, until Rudy's voice called out, "Hold it!"

I looked and saw that he was holding a pistol in both hands, pointed at Albert. The two leaders threw quick, shocked glances at him, but kept their attention on each other, lest the opponent take the advantage.

"Drop it," Rudy insisted, "or I'll shoot. I swear."

Ellie offered a solution. "Why don't you both lift your clubs together."

Jeremy was the first, and then Albert threw another quick glance at Rudy before lifting his to point at the sky as well.

"Now step apart," Ellie instructed.

This they did with no hesitation. Keeping his face towards Albert, Jeremy continued backing away, motioning for us to come along. Ellie and I picked up our clubs, and we trotted back until we were behind Rudy, who began backing away with us as well. "Now, get out of here!" he yelled. "If I see any of you on our side, you'll get a bullet right between the eyes."

They didn't get out of there, but they also didn't follow us as we made our retreat.

Once out of sight, we stopped. "Where in God's name did you get that?" Jeremy asked.

As an answer, Rudy tossed the pistol to him, and Jeremy gave a little cry of shock and scrambled to catch it before it fell, maybe going off. He caught it easily and stared at it a moment in confusion, then looked at Rudy with what seemed to be admiration. "It's a toy!" he exclaimed.

"You wouldn't trust Rudy with the real thing, would you?" Ellie said, smiling.

Chapter 24

"Sorry it took so long," Rudy said as we walked back to our cabins, stopping now and then to make sure the greens weren't following. "I had to clean it up—it was still caked with dirt."

"I found it the first night," I told Jeremy. "One of the Boy Scouts must have lost it."

"I hope they heed the warning," Jeremy said, examining the plastic gun. "It won't fool them in daylight. The paint's coming off."

When we got back to the cabins, Dana and Dale were discussing the manzanita situation—or lack of, in our case. "The greens have been purposefully distracting us so they can get it all," she claimed.

"What," Dale countered, "Barry sacrificed himself?"

She didn't like that subject. "That's why they were up that tree."

"Burrows told them it was manzanita," I reminded as we came around the corner. "And, trust me, Ralph wasn't expecting us to find him."

I glanced at the cabin that was his jail cell.

"We heard him moving around," Dale said softly. "But he hasn't spoken." He gestured towards the toy gun. "Did it actually work?"

"The greens backed off when Rudy arrived," I replied. "I don't think it was his muscles that scared them."

Jeremy glanced at his watch. "Four hours till daylight." He looked around at his tribe. "Rudy and Dana took the first guard shift—you guys try to get some sleep. Dale, you need rest. Cal, Ellie, and I will stand guard 'till dawn."

There were no arguments. I didn't think I could sleep, and I was actually more at ease outside, where I could know there were no greens sneaking up for a surprise attack.

Our leader eyed the make-shift stove we'd assembled next to the fire pit. "Help me here," he told me. I held the propane burners as Jeremy wrestled one of the side brackets off, and then we rotated so he could remove the other side. He handed me a two-foot length of angle iron.

"My new club?" I guessed, swinging it experimentally. The end terminated with a nasty four-inch piece attached at right angles, making for an effective battle mace.

Ellie scowled, looking down at the remnants. "You've ruined our stove," she said.

"It won't do us any good if we're dead," Jeremy replied. "We'll split up. They could work around and come in from any direction. I'll cover the north side—that's from Burrows' cabin around past the toilets. Cal, you take the south. Ellie, you watch the rear. Stay quiet and listen, but don't stick to one spot all night. The hard part may be just staying awake. If you see anything—if you even *think* you see anything—call out."

I couldn't even imagine falling asleep. It was freezing, and my brain spun with the violence of the last couple of hours. But it was lonely. I picked a spot forty-five degrees off the imaginary line leading to Burrows' cabin and sat on a log, trying to become all ears. All I heard were helicopters. I felt naked and vulnerable without my fellow blues around. Even Dana would have been welcomed.

After a while, I moved locations just for the opportunity to move. Soon after I settled in, a scraping sound made me jump, jamming my heart into my throat.

The sound had come from *behind* me, though. I quietly stood up, lifting my weapon, ready. Silence. Then another soft rustle, and movement. I discerned the form of a lone person walking stealthily past me. I was about to shout a warning, but I could tell that the interloper was small, unthreatening. The slight form was obviously a woman. "Ellie!" I whispered in a hiss.

She jerked and gave a little squeak, then stood frozen, peering into the gloom.

I waved, and she saw me and let out her breath. "You nearly gave me a heart attack," she whispered, walking over to me.

"What are you doing? You can't even think of going to the toilets alone. I could go with you, but to tell you the truth, if I were you, I'd just head away from the cabins somewhere and—"

"I'm not going to the toilets," she said, exasperated.

I looked at her, waiting.

"Look," she said, "can you keep a secret?"

"I don't know until I hear it."

She scowled.

"Okay, I promise." I said.

She took a deep breath, glancing around, as if someone might have snuck up without us knowing. "I'm going to go and talk to Albert."

"What! Are you *crazy*? Do you know what they'll *do* to you—"

She held up her hand tiredly. "I got it. I'll be okay. He's not a monster."

"You didn't see him just now. He's made weapons that'll tear the flesh off your bones."

She eyed my angle-iron mace.

"They started it," I said. "Why?"

"It's escalating out of control, " she replied, gesturing at my club. "I'm going to see if I can arrange a hostage exchange."

"Ralph for Tim?"

"No. Bugs Bunny for Wily Coyote."

I didn't say anything.

She sighed. "Sorry," she said, laying a gentle hand on my arm. "I'm one big frayed nerve."

"We all are. It's trying times," I concurred. "It's hell, in fact. I wonder what Plath would think if she knew how things have turned out."

"I haven't thought about her in days. It seems like months since they took her away. At least she got out before the dirty bomb."

Trying times call for bold action. I took her hand in mine, and she didn't resist. "I'll come with you."

She smiled a little, took both my hands in hers, and shook her head. "That would only increase the risk. You can't really help me defend against all of them, and they'll be less aggressive with just me—a woman."

"But they could take you prisoner as well."

She lifted her shoulders. "It's a chance I'm willing to take. Two people have died."

"You could be the third, you know."

She looked at me a moment and leaned in and kissed my forehead. Then her brows furrowed seriously. "Don't follow me—promise?

"Just until no-man's zone," I suggested.

"No. Not at all. They'll surely have guards posted. They have to believe I'm coming alone."

I nodded.

"Promise?"

I sighed. "Fine. I promise."

She smiled and took off at a trot. I watched her disappear into the night. I debated. I'd promised, but what good was my promise if I could have saved her somehow and didn't?

My head jerked up when a lone shout rang out through the sullen pines.

I didn't actually follow her. Jeremy had told us not to stick to one spot all night. I just happened to pick the next spot closer to no-man's zone. If there had been any green guards nearby, they had departed with Ellie. The shout I'd heard must have been when they saw her coming.

I listened. And listened. I moved closer, to what I guessed was the very edge of no-man's zone. I thought I heard talking. It sounded amiable enough, no screams at least. The talking was definitely getting closer. I had a sudden urge to run away, or at least hide. Ellie's fate could be on the line. I didn't run away. I hid. I squatted down behind a rock. The voices moved off to my left, and then stopped.

"Make sure Jeremy understands," Albert's voice said.

Ellie's voice replied, "I'll make sure he understands. I can't guarantee he'll agree, though."

"Well, let me know either way. The deal's off after tomorrow."

There was a pause, then Albert added, "No need for Burrows to know about this."

"Of course not. I stay away from him as much as possible." She paused. "I don't trust him."

"It's his show." Yet another pause. "I wouldn't cross him," Albert added.

The volunteered information was an uncharacteristic gift from the normally taciturn green leader.

The sound of footsteps moved off into green territory, and Ellie appeared, walking towards our cabin. I waited until the greens were well gone before trotting after her.

She jumped and spun around at the sound of my approach, then frowned. "You followed me!" she said in an angry whisper. "You promised!"

"I didn't! At least, not until you were already there. I had to make sure you came back okay." I hated knowing she was disappointed with me. "It's okay," I said, "they didn't see me."

In the dim light, I noticed blood on her cheek. "They hurt you!"

She felt her cheek and looked at the small smear of blood on her fingers. "It's nothing," she said. "There was some confusion at first."

"What did they do?"

"It's nothing—really. Let it go. Listen, we have to keep this between ourselves until I have a chance to talk to Jeremy."

"Sure, but what's the deal with Albert?"

She glanced at me, and continued on towards our cabins. I ran to catch up. "Albert's willing to make a hostage exchange," she said, "but he has conditions."

"Conditions? He must think he has the better bargaining position, which implies that Tim is worth more than Ralph."

"Don't you?"

"Uh, sure! I guess I'm just surprised that Albert is willing to admit it."

"Albert's canny. He knows that what he thinks isn't important—what counts is how much *we* value Tim versus Ralph."

"But he's just bluffing. Jeremy could play the same game."

"Is he bluffing? I guess that's the art of negotiation."

"So, what are his conditions?"

"You're going to be surprised."

"He wants you to join them?"

She threw me a skeptical look. I hadn't thought about the possibility until that very second. I had blurted my worst fear.

"No ... they won't harm Tim if we don't harm Ralph—that goes without saying. Here's the weird part—forget the manzanita contest. The blues must agree to use the hazmat suits to leave. The greens will have the option of including one or two of their own people, at their discretion."

"Huh," I said.

"Yeah, 'huh.' Strange, isn't it?"

"Unless Albert's come to the same conclusion about the radiation, based on what it did to Harry."

"Going down—suits or no suits—would be suicide, so force the blues to sacrifice themselves to get help. Maybe one or two of his own group don't believe this, and they'll want to go along."

"Pretty cold hearted," I said.

"On the other hand, everybody's been scrambling to win the manzanita contest."

"That's because they don't understand the danger."

"Maybe it's time to tell them," she said.

"Maybe. Something tells me that Burrows wouldn't be happy about that."

"Fuck Burrows," she said, which placed a definitive period to the end of the subject.

We arrived at our cabins, and I saw trouble waiting. Dana was standing outside, watching us.

"Couldn't sleep, eh?" I said casually.

"You're supposed to be on watch duty—both of you," she snapped.

"We are. We're heading out again in just a minute."

"Why are you together? What's going on?"

"None of your business," Ellie said.

Dana's eyes flared.

"Nothing's going on," I assured. "We just happened to come in at the same time."

Jeremy came around the corner. "What's all the fuss?" he asked.

"These two are goofing off," Dana said. "They haven't been keeping watch at all."

Jeremy looked at us.

"She doesn't know what she's talking about," I said. "What are *you* doing here?"

"Stopped just to check on things. What happened to you?" he asked Ellie.

She felt her cheek again. "A vigilant, over-active green," she said.

Jeremy's brow furrowed. "They came around from the rear? How many? Why didn't you sound the alarm?"

She held up her hand to stem the barrage. "I invaded *them*."

"What the hell are you talking about?"

She looked at me, and I shrugged.

"I went to get Tim back," she said.

He looked like she'd told him she'd just flown over San Jacinto Peak and back.

"I went to negotiate a prisoner exchange," she explained.

As Ellie related the encounter, Dana's eyes grew wider and wider, until I thought her eyeballs would fall out and roll away. When Ellie gave them our theory about why Albert wanted the blues to go down—that the radiation was lethal, even with hazmat suits—Dana broke. "That's a lie!" she cried.

Ellie was taken aback, and just looked at her.

"Doctor Burrows would never send us down if it was as dangerous as that!" Dana insisted.

Ellie shrugged. "Maybe even he doesn't understand the degree."

I knew Ellie didn't believe this, but it quieted Dana. She continued to glower at us, sure we were up to something.

"Well, it was a noble attempt," Jeremy said, "but kind of dumb. What if they'd kept you?"

"I was willing to risk it. And they didn't."

"We obviously can't agree to those terms," he said, shaking his head.

"So, you believe the radiation's too dangerous?"

"I don't know. But I wouldn't want to chance it. Would you?"

The question had been put to all of us, and nobody responded.

"We can ask Dale and Rudy when they wake up," he continued, "but I think we can forget it."

I hated to see that Ellie's efforts—and wound—were for nothing.

"Maybe Albert would be willing to consider other terms," I suggested. "Maybe he was just starting out purposefully high."

Jeremy shrugged and nodded simultaneously. "Nothing more we can do tonight." He checked his watch. "Another hour till daylight. We'd better get out and make some rounds."

I watched Ellie amble off to her rear-guard position. *That's one spunky woman*, I thought. Dana watched her leave as well, but her gaze was pure disdain. She turned her disapproving stare on me as I walked away.

Chapter 25

I opened my eyes to a square of bright sunlight low on the opposite wall. The soft glow of pre-dawn had filled the room when I'd collapsed after my guard shift. I could hear Dale and Rudy whispering. The cabin wasn't large enough to get any distance. They were talking about Sam's schedule.

Rudy saw me. "Uh, oh. Sorry, dude. Did we wake you?"

"S'o-kay," I mumbled.

I considered turning over to go back to sleep. Murders, lethal radiation, and hostage maneuverings flashed through my head, though, like the pulsating strobe of a police car. I knew I wouldn't find sleep until I was thoroughly exhausted again.

"So, what's your conspiracy?" I asked groggily, sitting up and groping for my shoes.

"Dale thinks we should seal Sam's gums," Rudy said, still in a whisper.

I looked at them, blinking. I concluded that sleepy ears had heard incorrectly. "Sam's gums?" I asked.

Dale and Rudy looked at each other. "Guns!" Rudy repeated in a hoarse whisper. "Guns!"

I got it. "You want to *steal* them." I wasn't sure this made any more sense. "Huh?"

"Imagine you're a green," Dale said.

"Okay. I would despise myself," I replied.

"Sure, but now imagine that you've just come back from an encounter with blues ... and they brandished a pistol."

The mist cleared. "Oh, shit."

"What would be the first thing you'd want to do?" Dale asked.

"Either get that pistol off the blues, or ... go for the bigger ones. We need to steal Sam's guns. How?"

Rudy picked up the thread. "It's hard to read Sam. He's so tight-lipped, but there's one thing about him that's predictable. He takes a dump every morning between 9:00 and 10:00."

"You know this," I said as a skeptical question.

"It's a gift."

"Knowing when people take dumps."

"*Observing* when people take dumps. The information doesn't just fall from the sky."

"Rudy, you're a very strange person."

"*You* take dumps either right after getting out of bed, or, if you miss that, then not until after lunch."

"Shut up, okay?"

"You want to know about Dale?"

"I said, shut up."

"Um, sorry guys," Dale cut in. "It's almost 9:00."

He started to get up, but winced and sat back on his bunk, and then, gingerly lay down.

"Still hurts," I observed, voicing the obvious.

"I think it's gotten worse," he said without looking at me.

"You need to ice it," Rudy said.

Dale looked at him sideways. "You're right. Can you go get some for me?"

"I'm just saying."

"Give me just a minute," Dale said, and closed his eyes, trying to find relief.

I looked at Rudy. "We better go," I suggested.

Dale looked at me out of the corner of his eyes, then closed them again. He knew he was down for the count.

Outside the cabin, I picked up my angle-iron mace and handed Rudy the old two-by-four. "What did Jeremy say about your plan?"

Rudy took a practice swing, as though it was a baseball bat. "He doesn't know."

"Why not? Is it a secret?"

"Dana's been hanging on to his butt all morning."

I understood. Stealing from Sam was effectively stealing from Burrows, and she'd never stand for that.

"Jeremy said he was going to check the perimeter," Rudy said. "She's probably with him."

"Well, this may be our only chance. He'll forgive us when we hand him a shotgun."

When we came within sight of Burrows' and Sam's cabins, we paused, watching, trying to discern whether Sam had left. We whispered a debate, and had just decided that we would work our way around between the two cabins and the toilets so that one of us could keep watch, when Sam emerged, and headed off for his predictable dump.

"Rudy," I whispered, "you're a mad genius."

We started forward, but immediately jumped behind trees when someone emerged from Burrows' cabin. It was Dana. She turned to say something through the open door, then walked directly towards us, back to blue territory.

"Crap," Rudy whispered. "What'll we do?"

"Just stay out of sight," I whispered back, inching around, keeping the tree trunk between us as she walked past. I thought about simply challenging her about why *she'd* left our territory, but an inner voice urged caution. For as gung-ho dedicated as she was to the group, the group didn't share a reciprocal loyalty. She was a blue, and we would protect her, but we often whispered when she was around.

She must have been distracted, for she never noticed her two blue colleagues sidling around their hiding places just a few feet away. We waited until she disappeared into the maze of trunks before continuing. We now knew that Burrows was in his cabin, just twenty feet from Sam's, so we had to be quiet. Using hand gestures, I told Rudy to watch for Sam's return, and I entered. The last time I'd been here, Plath and I had talked about Burrows' plan to study group dynamics. No, that wasn't the last time, she'd been delirious the last time. The smell of illness was gone, replaced by Sam's shaving lotion. His toiletries were laid out on the small dresser. He'd piled Plath's books in a corner, and a neat stack of magazines lay next to the bed. Seeing the top one, *Soldier of Fortune*, ratcheted my anxiety up a few notches.

Where were the guns? Somehow, I'd expected a small armament hanging from the walls, or at least a cabinet filled with rifles ready to be snatched. A guy who chooses *Soldier of Fortune* as bedtime reading, I told myself, would keep his guns close—would sleep with them, if he could.

I got down on my hands and knees, and, sure enough, a footlocker lay tucked away under his cot. I didn't have to risk dragging it out, though. It was padlocked.

I glanced out the door, and Rudy looked at me and shrugged and shook his head. Maybe I had time to find the key. I pulled out the little drawer in the table next to the cot. Inside was a wallet and car keys. I spread the keys with my finger, but it was obvious that none would fit a padlock. Thinking he may have pushed them farther back, I felt inside. No keys, just what I took to be a Gideons Bible.

Wait a second. A Gideons Bible?

I pulled out a leather-bound book with an embossed design, but no title.

"Pssst!" Rudy hissed.

I looked up. Rudy was squatting down, jerking his thumb in the direction of the toilets, and rubbing his finger across his throat with the other hand.

I flipped open the book and found page after page filled with cursive writing. Figuring it must be Plath's journal, I slid the drawer closed and joined Rudy. He pointed at Sam, just visible lumbering back through the forest. Judging from Rudy's expression, it might have been hooded, scythe-bearing Death.

"What'll we do *now*?" Rudy squeaked.

I struggled to think, but panic quashed any hope of that. "Run!" I said, and took off.

Running just threw fuel on the panic fire, and I sprinted like my life depended on it, which at the moment I thought it did. Rudy was behind, but closing. He was even more afraid of Sam. I tried to keep Sam's cabin between the soldier of fortune and our mad dash, and once we'd gone fifty yards, I dove behind a large rock, and Rudy flopped down beside me. Peering around it, I saw that Sam had not yet arrived. My breath caught, though, when I saw that Burrows was standing in his doorway, looking in our direction.

"We're cooked," Rudy whispered, as Burrows turned and went back inside. "Oh, man!" Rudy said, rolling on his back so he could stare at the little blue patches of blue sky through the boughs. "That was close. He didn't see us."

I wasn't so sure, but decided not to burst his relief bubble.

"What's that?" he asked.

I held up the book. "I think it's Plath's journal."

"You stole it?"

I looked at him. "I'm not stealing it—I'm saving it."

"From whom?"

"Not from whom, but from what."

"Okay, what's the what you're saving it from?"

I shrugged with my eyebrows. "Accidental fire."

"You stole it," Rudy concluded.

ж ж ж

"I think the cloud's smaller," Rudy said.

"Uh, huh," I replied without taking my eyes from Plath's journal.

"It's strange, though. I think it's moved. Wasn't it, like, over there to the left yesterday?"

I glanced up and out over the miles of pines to the belching black cloud. "Maybe," I said, and went back to reading.

"No. I'm sure. It was over near those humps that look like Hobbiton."

I laid the book on my lap. "Rudy, I'm either going to read this, or we're going to have a conversation."

"Hey, sorry. I didn't realize you were so limited."

"I am. So please be quiet for just a few more minutes."

I was sitting cross-legged on the Potato Chip. Rudy lay on his stomach, chin cradled in his palms as he gazed out over the San Jacinto foothills. I read barely one more page when Ellie's voice called, "There you are! Jeremy's been asking about you."

She walked out along the stone tongue and sat down. "What's that?"

I sighed. "Apparently the book I'm never going to finish."

She hesitated, surprised by my rebuke.

"Go easy on him," Rudy said conspiratorially, "he has limited mental abilities."

"It's Plath's journal," I said, noting the page and closing the book.

"How did you get that?" she asked.

"He stole it," Rudy explained. "When we tried to steal Sam's guns."

Her response was to stare, trying to decide if he was kidding. Suspicion gave way to curiosity. "What's it say?"

"Pretty dry stuff. Mostly observations about our behavior."

"We learn, for example," Rudy said, "that you make excuses to be around Cal."

I felt my face grow hot, and Ellie avoided my eyes, probing at a seam on her shorts.

"I was just getting to the juicy stuff," I explained.

"Do you think it's, like, ethical?" she asked, finally looking at me.

"Under normal circumstances, probably not. But things haven't been normal. Maybe the end justifies the means."

"Like what?"

I opened the book and continued reading out loud.

"I believe that Burrows is taking aspects of his theory to an extreme. Not being a biologist, let alone an evolutionary biologist, I can't properly criticize his ideas, but I find his imagined polarization to be excessive. His premise that, as a result of group selection, we're programmed by evolution to operate in two modes—when there's no danger, we cooperate, resisting strong leaders, but faced with danger, we look to a strong leader—strikes me as plausible ... to a degree. I am skeptical, however, when he insists that the two modes are discrete, with no overlap. Further, he believes that the transition from independent to dependent mode is sharp—binary, as he puts it—and is most often triggered by what he calls a threshold danger."

I paused. "She mentioned that," I said, remembering the conversation in her cabin. "But not in this kind of detail."

"His program," Ellie concurred. "We thought that Sam was the danger he was introducing."

I nodded. "She used a mountain lion as an example, although she may have been joking. In any case, she assured me that Burrows would never introduce a serious danger."

"Ha!" Rudy exclaimed.

"Ha?" I said.

"The dirty bomb!"

"What about it …?" I said. "Wait a second, are you suggesting that he *arranged* it?"

"It makes sense!"

"No," I countered, "it's delusional! Do you seriously think that Burrows, a professor at a university, would—could—create and release a lethal weapon of mass destruction?" I looked at Ellie. "Where would he get his hands on radioactive material?"

"Biology departments often use radioactive isotopes," Ellie said. "Most hospitals have stores of them. It's what they use in cancer treatments."

"I repeat," Rudy said, "Ha!"

"You saw Harry!" I protested. "Do you think that could be done by hospital-grade grade stuff?"

Ellie chewed her lip, and Rudy rubbed his chin.

"I admit," I said, not wanting to appear completely negative, "it's quite a coincidence. The dirty bomb appeared at just the right time."

"It is implausible that Burrows would do something like that," Ellie said reluctantly.

"You're way underestimating the ability for people to be complete shits," Rudy said. "You'll see."

Ellie shrugged. "What else does Plath say?" she asked, pointing at the journal.

I read on, briefly, and summarized. "She comes back to another of his theories, this one even more out there, according to her. Something about how group selection results in the evolution of specific types of leaders."

"What types?"

"More effective. That's all she says."

"What's up with this group selection?" Rudy asked.

I looked to Ellie. "You're the biology major."

"Don't you remember? We talked about this on the bus. A lot of it is an extension of E. O. Wilson's original development of sociobiology. It's the idea that natural selection—survival of the fittest—can operate on groups as well as individuals. It only works on groups that are highly social, where the benefit of being a member of the group outweighs the benefit of being selfish and risking being excluded. It supposedly explains altruism."

"Groups survive better when people give presents to each other?" Rudy questioned.

"More specifically, people have an advantage when they are able to operate as a useful member of a cohesive group. Evolution still works on each individual—it only works that way—but group selection shapes individuals to be better group members. And in the end, membership in the group guarantees better long-term chances of survival."

"Soldiers risking their lives for their buddies," I suggested.

Ellie nodded, thinking about it. "If you risk your life to save a wounded buddy, you're more likely to be saved sometime if *you're* wounded. The idea of group selection was controversial—it still is to some extent. The whole concept became taboo in the early twentieth century when some radicals tried to use it to defend their flawed arguments about racial superiorities."

"Hitler!" I said.

"Close. There was a lot of talk about Social Darwinism. It's not the same thing as group selection, but close enough that as the world rebelled against the atrocities of Social Darwinism abuse, anything resembling it was shunned as well."

"So ..." Rudy said, pretending to ruminate, "Burrows is effectively Hitler."

Ellie rolled her eyes. "Yes," she said sarcastically, "that was exactly my point." To me, she said, "Anything else interesting in there?"

I flipped through the pages. "She writes about xenophobia, but I'm not sure that's connected with the rest. It seems to be a different subject that she's been thinking about." I flipped to the last page with writing. "Hmm."

"What?"

"These last couple of pages. This must be when she was really sick—delirious."

"What did she write?" Ellie asked, looking over my shoulder.

"It's hard to make out. Her handwriting becomes shaky. What's this?" I said, pointing to one scribble. "'Nemlod'?"

"I think the 'N' is an 'H,' and the 'd' might actually be 'ck.'"

"Hemlock? What about this? 'ton glove'?"

Rudy looked at it. "That's 'foxglove.'"

"You think so?" Ellie asked, and then her eyes went wide. "Hemlock and foxglove? They're both poisonous plants!"

Just then we were interrupted by the sound of Dana calling to us.

"What's she saying?" Ellie asked.

We all stood up, listening.

Ellie's face went white, just as I finally made out what Dana was saying.

Tim was dead.

Chapter 26

"How'd it happen?" I asked Dana.

"The greens, of course," Dana spat.

"But how?"

"What does it matter? They slit his throat, just like Viona, then dumped him at the toilets, like so much garbage."

"Holy hell."

Viona, and now Tim. I felt dizzy. Two of our friends, dead. Murdered. Rage swelled in me. How could they be such monsters? I knew the answer: they were greens.

"Are you happy now?" Dana said to Ellie, who just looked at her. She seemed in shock over the news.

"What are you talking about, Dana?" I asked.

"You can't negotiate with greens. You can't trust them as far as you can throw them. Doctor Burrows agrees."

I looked at her. "That's why you went to talk to him? To tell him that Ellie was negotiating?"

Her eyes went wide, but she recovered immediately. "Of course."

"Why?" I asked.

"Why not? He has a right to know what's going on."

"Does he? He doesn't seem to care."

"He *cares*!"

"He doesn't show it." I said. "He stays in his cabin, or just stands off to the side watching."

We'd arrived back at our cabins. Jeremy stood, stone-faced, watching our arrival. Dale sat at the fire pit, his face buried in his hands. From inside the cabin I had shared with Tim, Ralph was yelling, wanting to know what was going on. Jeremy and Dale ignored him.

Dana suddenly grabbed Jeremy's angle-iron mace club and ran to the make-shift jail. Jeremy just watched her. She reached up and took the padlock key we left hanging from a nail. I watched this as I might observe a scene through a window—I had no influence on events.

Ellie shouted, "What are you doing!"

"They're going to pay!" Dana yelled. To the door, she called, "You hear, you filthy green? You're going to pay!"

I knew what she intended to do, but they'd killed Tim. Ralph was a green, even though he'd been locked up the whole time. I wasn't about to hurt him, but the fact that he was going to be hurt seemed somehow justified. It was a gut response.

Ellie's response, however, was different. She raced to the cabin, and arrived just as Dana tossed the padlock aside and entered. Ellie turned and gave us one horrified look before following Dana inside.

That look was like a flashbulb exploding in my face. It smashed the window and suddenly I not only had influence beyond it, but a responsibility.

I ran for the cabin, followed by Rudy. Inside, Ellie struggled with Dana over the club, and Ralph lay on the floor, curled into a defensive ball. Ellie fell back when Dana swung the club at her. Dana lifted the jagged-ended club for another blow, but I caught it on the downswing, and Rudy grabbed her around the waist. She screamed curses, and spit at me, but I managed to pull the nasty weapon from her grasp. Jeremy had arrived, and I held the club out of Dana's reach as she continued to pummel me with small girl-fists until Jeremy pulled her away.

Ellie put her hand out to help Ralph to his feet, but the prisoner just looked at her, paralyzed with fear. "It's okay," Ellie assured. "Nobody will hurt you."

Instead of standing up, the green rolled over on his back and examined his stomach. I saw blood. Ellie stooped down and gently lifted Ralph's shirt. There was a gash near his side, but it didn't look too deep. It oozed blood, rather than gushed it. "I've got the kit," Dale said from the doorway. Ellie got to work rubbing antibiotic cream on the wound, and then wrapping it with gauze and bandages.

"You're wasting your time," Dana growled. "He's a green. They're animals."

"What happened?" Ralph asked Ellie.

She didn't answer, just concentrated on securing the bandage.

"You killed Tim!" Dana yelled, as though he had done it personally, and was trying to deny it.

He looked at us each in turn, shaking his head in disbelief and fear.

When Ellie was done, she helped Ralph to his feet and to his cot. We blues stepped outside, and Jeremy put the padlock back in place. Ellie walked to the fire pit and stood staring off towards the edge of the plateau and the road, where the rest of the world struggled with their own dire problems.

"What're you thinking?" I asked quietly, coming up next to her.

She gave me a quick look, like she might find the answer here. "I don't believe he'd do this," she said, turning her gaze back to the world beyond.

"You mean Albert?"

She nodded.

"That he wouldn't ..."

I couldn't say it, just like I'd had trouble acknowledging Viona's murder.

She took a deep breath. "Yeah."

"Why? Because of his kind heart?" I asked, the sarcasm barely contained.

She threw me an annoyed glance. "He's not stupid," she said.

I'd only been feeling the loss, and with the loss, the rage. "Maybe it was an accident," I said, because I guessed that this might be something she'd want to hear.

What I thought was, *No, he's an animal, like the rest of the greens.*

ж ж ж

The mood at the blues' cabins was silent resolve. We tore apart the rest of the propane stove to make additional battle maces. Tim and Viona, our fellow blues, our friends—gone. We didn't need to voice the conviction, we knew that the greens had to pay.

Except Ellie. She shook her head in disdain at our efforts to manufacture additional weapons. Twice, I caught her gazing off to the west, towards green territory. She looked at us, seeming not to see us, then turned and headed off east, towards the far blue end of the plateau. "Where are you going?" I called.

She stopped, turned, and said, "To pick a burial site for Tim." She then continued on, out of sight.

I looked at the half-formed battle club I was making and then off towards where Ellie had disappeared. I laid down my handiwork and said, "She shouldn't be out there alone." I picked up my trusty angle-iron instead and walked off. When I was sure the rest wouldn't see me, I stopped and debated. I guessed what she was up to, but I didn't know where she'd double back.

That's when I saw movement. She was far off, through the tree trunks, at the very limit of visibility, moving quickly around towards the plateau lip and green country. Making directly for her would take me too close to our cabins, so I had to circle around as well. We were crossing no-man's zone with Burrows' and Sam's cabins on our right before I was finally close enough to call to her without others hearing. I never had the chance. Sam must have seen her coming, and had come out to intercept her. I expected her to turn and run back, but she chose to comply, and approached Burrows' hired gun.

I watched and waited. I was still expecting her to break away after a moment and return to the safety of blue territory. It looked like she was arguing with Sam, though. She kept pointing into the green depths, and I could hear angry words from both sides. When Sam reached out and grabbed her arm, though, I ran forward, calling.

Sam looked at me, and reached into his pocket. By the time I arrived, he was holding Ellie with one hand, and had a knife in the other. This was no Boy Scout pocket knife, but a thick, four-inch blade that reflected the sunlight evilly.

I was standing five feet away, and he said, "Come here," as he glanced around, looking to see if there were any more of us.

"Let her go first," I said.

Ellie was furious, either because Sam was restraining her, or that I had followed her.

He ignored my demand and repeated, "Come here."

"Let her *go*," I implored.

Sam was a man of few words, but clear intentions. With smooth efficiency, he grabbed her hair, pulled her head back, and had the glinting edge of the knife to her throat. "Come here," he said, repeating the only words he'd uttered so far.

Terror froze me. If I did as he said, I'd be within striking distance of that killer blade, and if I didn't, then he might well slit Ellie's throat.

"Why are you doing this?" I asked, but took one step closer to show him I wasn't completely defying him.

In answer, he pressed the knife harder so that her eyes suddenly bulged at the impending consequence.

"Okay! Okay!" I cried, taking another step. "Be careful!"

He watched me calmly, and it struck me that he was entirely composed while Ellie and I were frantic with fear. *This is what he does.*

"Hold it!"

It was Rudy! He'd come up behind Sam, and he was holding his plastic pistol in front of him with both hands.

For the first time, Sam's expression showed concern. He slowly turned his head, keeping his eyes on me to the last moment, before sneaking a glance backwards at the new intruder. He grinned ever so slightly in relief, and turned Ellie around so that he could keep an eye on both Rudy and me. "Nice gun," he observed.

It was obvious he hadn't been fooled, and Rudy let his arms fall to his sides.

But something had changed. Sam looked from Rudy to me. He was unsure. There were now too many of us. Not that we could do anything to hurt him, but at least one of us was going to escape with the story of what had happened. The one thing that gives pause to thugs like Sam are witnesses.

His face relaxed into benign intent. He let Ellie go, and, with a motion so quick I didn't even catch it, he folded the knife and put it back in his pocket. "You have to stay on your side," he said.

I nodded vigorous agreement. He was letting us go.

"Why?" Ellie challenged.

"Ellie," I said, "let's just go—"

She put her hand up to stop me. "Why?" she repeated to Sam.

"Because Mr. Burrows says so, that's why."

She looked at me and Rudy, and we just shrugged.

"Okay," she said, walking away. "I just wanted to hear you say it."

Sam didn't look happy, but he just watched as we walked away behind her.

"You shouldn't have followed me," Ellie said through clenched teeth once we reached blue territory.

"You were going to see Albert, weren't you?" I asked.

She threw me an angry glance. "What, are you jealous?"

Silence.

Rudy looked embarrassed. After a while, he said, "I think he maybe saved your life, Ellie."

She stopped, and Rudy and I turned around. She held her arms out, and we let her wrap one around each of our shoulders. "You guys are my heroes," she said.

"Cal's the hero," Rudy said. "I had a gun."

We looked at him and burst out laughing, then continued on together towards home.

ж ж ж

"I just don't think Albert would kill Tim," Ellie insisted as our cabins came into sight.

"Even if he didn't, one of his greens could have," Rudy said.

"Sure," she agreed, "but Albert wouldn't condone it. He'd tell me if that had happened."

"How can you be so sure?" I asked.

She looked at me, irritated. "I can't be sure. Obviously. But I'm confident."

"You mean you just believe."

"Fine. That's what I believe." She chewed her lower lip, considering. "There's one person who might have some answers."

"Ralph," Rudy uttered what I was thinking.

Jeremy and Dana were out on patrol, and Dale was lying on his cot, resting. He just shrugged when I said that we were going to talk to Ralph. We found the prisoner also lying on his cot, resting his own wound. He looked at me with concern, but relaxed when Ellie came in behind me. I moved off to the background, letting Ellie sit daintily on the edge of the cot, facing him. He smiled.

"Ralph," she said quietly, "you told us that you didn't know who killed Viona."

His smile faded.

"I just talked with Sam," she said, "and he told me the truth."

I tried to keep my face flaccid.

"I know," she said, "that you know."

His brow wrinkled, and he shook his head. "No," he insisted.

"Yes," Ellie countered, nodding hers. "I know you had no part in it, but my companions don't believe me."

Ralph threw a frightened look at me, and I scowled. "Barry didn't do it!" he pleaded. "Honest!"

Ellie threw me a glance. Barry obviously had *some* part in it.

"Are you *sure?*" she asked him.

"He tried to make it *look* like he did it!"

Ellie watched him. I knew she was trying to sort this out. "It was actually Sam," she said, balancing her tone so that her words could have been either a statement, or a question.

"That's not what he told you?" Ralph asked, his words a protest.

Ellie shrugged and sat back. "It's what I guessed. Thanks, Ralph. I believe you." She stood up. "How's that scratch doing?" she asked pointing at the bandages.

"Scratch?" he squawked. "It's a *wound!* That bitch could have killed me!" Even lying down, his arms began flailing. "You're supposed to be following, like, the Geneva Convention!"

Ellie excused herself, and we left, securing the padlock before walking away.

"How'd it go?" Rudy asked at the fire pit.

"He says that it was Sam who killed Viona," Ellie said quietly, staring again off into green territory.

So, it was Sam after all. It seemed like I'd known this all along, even though I hadn't. The pieces fit so well together that, after the fact, the answer was obvious and not really a surprise.

"Sam follows Burrows orders," I stated.

Rudy and Ellie looked at me, waiting for more.

I met their gaze. "It's all his game. Buy why? He's the one with the answers."

Silence.

"So?" Rudy said.

"So, we get the answers from him."

Chapter 27

"We get answers from Burrows," Rudy repeated skeptically.

"Yes," I said.

He threw a knowing glance at Ellie and rolled his eyes. "Cal, my good friend, I'm afraid my toy pistol is not going to fool a college professor."

"I don't mean we get the answers directly from Burrows. I'm betting there's plenty of goodies in his cabin. Didn't you think it was curious that he started locking it from the very beginning?"

"You want to break into his cabin. The one that sits next to Sam, the guy with all the real guns, and a knife the size of Crocodile Dundee's?"

"I was hoping we wouldn't have to break in." I said. "We'll get the key."

"Or, I have another idea. We'll climb to the very top of the pine trees, and wait for the Great Eagles to come and whisk us away."

"What are you talking about, Rudy?" Ellie asked.

I sighed. "*The Hobbit*. The translation is that he thinks my idea is as good as fantasy."

"Well, I like it," she said.

Rudy looked at her. "Like I said—great idea. Let's do it."

ж ж ж

"No!" Jeremy exclaimed. "Absolutely not. No one is to go anywhere near Burrows' cabin."

"But, don't you see?" Ellie persisted. "Burrows must at least *know* that Sam killed Viona."

"I said no!"

"But, why?"

Jeremy sat in his cabin with his fists balled together on his lap, his lips squashed together. I thought he was going to explode. "We have to respect the hierarchy. Otherwise it's anarchy."

"What are you *talking* about?" she shot back. "It already *is* anarchy!"

I nudged Rudy, and we left the cabin. "He's never going to agree," I said.

Rudy shrugged. "So we do it anyway."

I looked at him. "You and me? That's it?"

He grinned. "Do you think Jeremy's going to leave us out to dry? He'll come once we start the ruckus."

I considered. This could be the death of me. Literally. I picked up my battle club. "As my good friend likes to say, 'Let's do it!'"

Rudy grabbed his sack and club, and we headed out for green territory. "You have them?" I asked.

He reached into his bag and revealed the bolt cutters that we'd taken from Barry.

"If you can't find the key," I said, "make sure you don't leave the ruined padlock behind."

"Cal, give me some credit. I'm not an imbecile. If there's no lock when he comes back, he might think he just misplaced it. You really think he'll come to the show, though?"

"Haven't you noticed? Every time there's any kind of confrontation, he's there, standing off to the side watching. No, he won't miss this one."

We reached no-man's zone and continued on. It was strange every time I crossed that invisible boundary. It was like floating out through the space station hatch, unconnected to my umbilical cable.

I stopped where I imagined the green boundary lay and looked at Rudy. He forced a weak smile and nodded.

"You filthy sons-of-bitches!" I shouted as loud as I could.

"Come on, you cowards!" Rudy yelled. "You stinking murderers!"

We continued for a couple of minutes, and I told Rudy he'd better take off. My friend put his hand on my shoulder a second, and then ran away, backtracking the way we'd come.

I kept up the diatribe, and minutes later two greens appeared, angry and ready to fight. I had difficulty breathing, my heart throbbed in my windpipe. "You murdered Tim!" I shouted.

"Go away, blue!" one of them yelled, lifting his face-shredding club for emphasis.

"No! You murdered him, and now you're gonna pay!"

The greens exchanged glances, and then moved apart, one on side of me. This had been very effective against Dale. They were going to beat the shit out of me, maybe kill me.

"Hey!"

It was Jeremy. And Ellie. And Dana. Dale limped along, bringing up the rear. "Dammit, Cal, what do you think you're doing?" Jeremy yelled.

Ellie gave me a look. She'd obviously guessed that Rudy and I would proceed anyway, and gotten Jeremy to come to our aid.

"Here's the murderers!" I shouted, pointing and feeling my feigned rage become real. The greens had stopped their advance at this sudden arrival of reinforcements. "It's time for revenge!"

"We didn't kill him!" they shouted back, carefully retreating back into their own territory.

Jeremy glared at me. He knew it was a ruse, but refrained calling me out. When push came to shove, he had to stick by his tribe. "Go home!" he called to the two greens.

They looked at each other, and then one of them stood up straight and said, "*You* leave—this is our side!"

Jeremy waved his hand in resignation. "Fine. We're leaving!" He motioned for us to follow.

I looked around, but there was no Burrows yet. Rudy needed more time. I advanced on the two greens, screaming about murder and swinging my club. I wondered if my death would be considered an accident or suicide. The greens lifted their own clubs but backed a couple more steps from the hysterical madman, keeping an eye on my companions in case they made a sudden charge.

"What's this!"

Albert had arrived with three other greens. Goody. An all-out rumble would have to attract Burrows.

"We're leaving!" Jeremy shouted. "Cal! *Now!*"

"Hold on!" Albert called, putting his hand up to stop the show. "What're you doing on our side?" He kept coming until he was nose-to-nose with Jeremy.

Jeremy was a few inches shorter, but solid muscle. His breathing came in short snorting bursts, like a bull about to charge. "The last time Tim was alive, he was in your custody," he growled.

This was no show. Jeremy was venting genuine rage.

I realized that I might have set off a powder keg when all I'd wanted was a credible fuse.

Albert responded with one word, delivered directly into Jeremy's upturned face. "Barry."

"That was an accident," Jeremy said. Nobody dared look at Dana. "How did Tim's throat accidentally get cut?"

Albert stared at the blue's leader. He glanced off to the side and then said, "I don't have to answer to you."

I followed his glance to find Burrows standing a hundred feet away, watching calmly. Sam stood nearby.

Got you!, I thought. Time to wrap up the show. "Come on, Jeremy," I said, putting my hand on his arm. "It's not worth it."

Without taking his eyes from Albert, he shook off my hand. At the sudden motion, Albert pushed Jeremy away, and the shorter man pushed back, planting his feet for better traction. Albert swung his arms, throwing Jeremy's hands away, and reached behind him. As though this had been practiced, one of the greens handed him a club bristling with screws.

Seeing this, Jeremy reached out and took the angle-iron mace that Dana handed him.

"*Stop it!*" Ellie screamed, running forward and forcing herself between them. "Don't you see? That's exactly what *he* wants!" she yelled, pointing off towards Burrows, who now frowned.

Jeremy and Albert continued to stare each other down, but Ellie pushed against one chest and then the other until she'd separated them beyond club-swinging distance.

"Don't give *him* the satisfaction," she pleaded, pointing again at Burrows.

The university professor—the pinnacle of Jeremy's hierarchy—suddenly turned and walked away. As though this was the release they needed, the two leaders turned and stormed away as well.

As we walked back to our cabins, Jeremy said to me, "Try something like that again, and I will club you to death myself."

"Got it," I replied.

I knew he wouldn't.

Ж Ж Ж

"Why all the secrecy?" I asked. "Jeremy knows what we planned to do."

"You'll see in a minute," Rudy replied, turning the pages of Burrows' journal until he found what he was looking for.

We were sprawled out on the Potato Chip again. The winter sun was hot, but it was the place we escaped to when we wanted some privacy, which was odd, since it placed us prominently out in open space, in full view for many miles, if anybody happened to be turning a high-powered telescope in this direction.

While he flipped through the pages, Ellie asked, "Did you find anything else in his cabin?"

"Nah," he replied distractedly. "He takes some medicines," he added.

"Like what?"

"I don't know. It's all gibberish to me. There was nothing that read *Take four times a day to reduce violent psychotic episodes*." He flipped some pages, and added, "There was one thick bottle of clear liquid. It had the simplest label—H-SO, or something."

Ellie frowned at that.

"Here's the reason for secrecy," Rudy said, finding the passage. "Backgrounds of both Jeremy and Albert."

"So what?" I shrugged. "He did some checking."

Ellie's brow furrowed. "There's no internet up here, which means he knew from the beginning who the group leaders would be."

Rudy grinned knowingly. "He wasn't interested in their whole biographies, just the juicy parts. Did you know that Jeremy wanted to join the Marines—be a Ranger—but he washed out when he failed a urine sample test? Burrows promised Jeremy a job with some fake Marine training program at the university. Burrows wrote that he could make up some blarney about how the Marines promised him they'd give Jeremy a second chance."

Rudy checked the journal and continued. "Albert's father is Guatemalan, and was killed in a border crossing incident. His mother has MS, and his sister needs a new type of operation—her insurance doesn't cover it. Burrows writes that he could tell Albert that he can pull some strings."

"They've been bought off," I said.

"Here's where it got weird, though," Rudy went on, turning the book so he could read better. "He's writing about how humans evolved through the dynamics of groups, and groups vying together."

"That's nothing new," Ellie said. "That's just regurgitating the principles of group selection."

"Yeah, but he goes on." Rudy scanned down the page. "Here— he says that the effectiveness of the group is dependent on, and proportional to—his words—the effectiveness of the leader." Rudy looked and grinned, then read on. "He says that an important tool of any leader is viable lying—"

"*Viable* lying?" Ellie said.

"That's what he wrote. 'The group must operate within the envisioned world that the leader creates—'"

"Now that does sound like Hitler," she said, indignantly.

"Are you going to let me finish?" he asked. "We haven't even gotten to the best part." Rudy flipped two pages ahead. "He writes about those two modes that Plath talked about. But here he says that in order to ultimately guarantee that the proper leader manifests, the group danger must be appropriately dense—again, his words."

"Dominance and cooperation operating in counterbalance," I said.

Rudy looked at me.

"Don't you remember? Albert repeated that on the bus. He was talking about something Burrows had written."

Rudy nodded and continued. "He proposes—to himself, I guess—that the most effective 'dense' threshold mode-transition danger would involve deaths of group members."

He looked up at us.

Silence.

"You're joking," Ellie finally said.

"I sure wish I was."

"Holy crap," she said.

"I'd go so far as holy shit," he responded.

"That's, like, a confession," she said. "Ralph wasn't lying. It was Sam who murdered Viona."

"Probably Tim as well," I added.

"That knife," Ellie observed.

"That knife," I agreed.

"If you two are through," Rudy said, "we haven't even gotten to the best parts."

Ellie held out her hand for him to continue.

"Let's see … he goes on about how advancement of the species would require emphasis on cheating—the ability to take advantage of the passive cooperators—"

Ellie snorted.

Rudy glanced up, but read on, flipping page after page. "Ah, here. Remember that Plath wrote the word 'foxglove' in her journal? Well, she was right. That's how Burrows poisoned her."

Again, silence.

"*What!*" Ellie woke from her shock.

"Apparently—no, *evidently*, Burrows was poisoning Plath with foxglove. You pointed out the plant to me way back at the beginning."

"Ho-ly …" she looked at us, "shit!"

Rudy licked his finger and flipped some more. "But, my darlings, I've kept the best for last. You're not going to believe this."

"I'm not sure I have any belief left," I said.

He scanned down the page, then put his finger on the spot. He looked at us and paused for dramatic effect. "First, let me remind you that I predicted this from Plath's journal. And, as I recall, I was labeled delusional. Well, guess what? Burrows is the terrorist who planted the dirty bomb."

"Oh, come on!" Ellie objected. "You're making that up."

Rudy looked smug. He handed the book to her, keeping his finger on the spot until she saw. She read the page, jumped up, then flipped to the next and read some more. She looked down at me with wide eyes. "He's right! This is unbelievable! He writes about the best places to locate the 'incendiary device.' What kind of monster *is* this guy?"

"Like any monster," Rudy said, standing up and leaning back to stretch. "Willing to kill to further his aims."

I sat staring at the black cloud billowing from the green carpet of pine forest. "Reason," I said softly to myself.

"What?" Ellie asked.

I looked up at her. "Just before they took Doctor Plath away. I thought she said 'reason.' I didn't understand why she would say that. But that's not what she said at all. It was 'poison.' She was trying to tell me that Burrows had poisoned her."

Ellie squatted down and put her hand on my shoulder. "It wouldn't have mattered anyway," she said softly.

I looked at her and shook my head, dazed. "Don't you see? If the hospital knew what had poisoned her, they might have known how to help her."

She radiated sympathy at my thickness. "Do you really think he was going to take her to the hospital?"

I blinked. "Of course not," I murmured. "He's a monster."

Chapter 28

"I thought it was strange that Sam knew just what to do when Burrows arrived with the hazmat suits," Rudy said. "He got them out of the jeep without being told they were even there."

He was sitting with his arms wrapped around his knees, watching Ellie read.

"Burrows had it planned in advance," Ellie agreed. She was only half listening as she poured through Burrows' journal.

"Remember when Jeremy said that he saw Sam when Viona was killed?"

"Yeah, he was lying," she said, running her fingers along a passage.

"The bastard."

She looked up. "We might not know the whole story."

"What story? Jeremy lied. An important tool of any leader is viable lying—and I quote."

She shrugged and went on reading.

I sat beside them, letting it all sink in. Like when we first learned from Ralph that it was Sam who killed Viona, the revelations about Burrows seemed obvious after the fact. We'd been so busy surviving, we hadn't been able to fit the pieces together on our own.

Ellie suddenly stood up, holding the book. "I'll be right back," she said, and walked off the Potato Chip.

"Where're you going?" Rudy asked.

She looked at us. "I have to pee. Be right back."

"Don't use the pages for toilet paper!" Rudy called after her.

"Hey," he turned to me, "remember when Burrows called Jeremy and Albert off together for a meeting about the manzanita contest, and afterwards, Jeremy looked really upset and didn't want to talk much about it?"

I nodded. I didn't really remember, but didn't want to interrupt my own thought train.

"Remember when Burrows showed up sneaking around in the shadows right afterward?"

That part I did remember. He had frightened Viona when she first saw him standing there.

"I'll bet that's when Burrows bribed Jeremy and Albert."

I put aside my thoughts and looked at Rudy. "That's probably also when Burrows told them they should try to get hostages. He probably didn't say it directly, but they would have gotten the idea."

"Yeah. It was after that when Jeremy started talking about getting 'insurance.'" His brow furrowed. "I'll bet Burrows warned them that Sam was about to head off on a killing spree."

I shook my head slowly. "I don't know. That seems a little far-fetched. I can't believe that Jeremy would have gone along with that." I imagined it. "No," I said with determination. "Jeremy wouldn't have stood for that."

Rudy lifted his shoulders and held them—unwilling to voice a contradiction. "You called me delusional when I figured out that Burrows planted the dirty bomb," he reminded me.

"You didn't figure it out. You just guessed."

"And Sherlock Holmes's brilliant conclusions seemed like good guesses to Watson at first."

"I'll buy you a big curved pipe for Christmas. Hey, what happened to Ellie?"

"Cal, you're losing your mind. She went to pee."

"No, I mean how long does it take to pee?"

Rudy considered it, and then his eyes got big. "Oh damn, we shouldn't have let her go alone."

We ran into the pines, calling for her, but there was no answer. We widened our search and split up, but still no answer. I quickly worked my way back towards our cabins, and that's when I saw that something was going down. Jeremy and Dana stood outside the women's cabin, and Dale sat near the fire pit. Sam emerged, and dumped a box of blue clothes onto the ground. Burrows came out carrying a bag, and emptied the contents next to the clothes.

I started towards them, and Jeremy saw me. He made to raise his hand to stop me, but gave up when Burrows followed his gaze and saw me. The murderous professor nudged Sam's arm and pointed.

"What's going on?" I asked, heading toward Jeremy.

The blue leader looked at me with defeated eyes. Suddenly I was jerked to the side as Sam grabbed me.

"Where's Rudy?" Burrows demanded. He'd lost his cool observational detachment, and his mouth was clenched in angry resolve.

"I don't know," I said trying to evoke disdain.

That earned me a slap across the face, which stung much more than I would have imagined.

"I'm here!" Rudy called, trotting up. "What's going on?"

Burrows nodded to Sam, and the thug shoved me away and went for Rudy who didn't resist. "You tell me," Burrows snarled. "You were the only one missing from that little decoy charade."

Rudy glanced at me—he knew the jig was up. "Don't know what you're talking about," he said.

Burrows took a breath and gave a little wave to Sam, who promptly slapped Rudy across the face. "Shit!" Rudy exclaimed, putting his hand to his cheek. "Damn, that hurts!"

"It was my idea!" I yelled.

Burrows turned a level gaze on me. "Did you take it?" he asked.

When I didn't answer, he turned back to Rudy. "Tell me," he demanded.

"That you're handsome? I can't do that."

Without prompting, Sam smacked him again, this time with the back of his hand, and Rudy came up with a bloody mouth.

"Stop it!"

It was Ellie. She stormed into the gathering, fists balled into their own little mace clubs.

"Well," Burrows said, "Miss Troublemaker herself. Where have you been?"

Her face was flushed and her eyes burned with contempt. "You know very well."

"Off 'cooperating' with Albert, I imagine."

She lifted her chin.

Burrows turned back to Rudy. "Where is it?"

"Your soul? If you don't know, I wouldn't have a clue."

Burrows sighed with impatience as Sam landed another backhand, this time, knocking him to the ground.

"Rudy!" Ellie screamed.

Rudy shook his head, taking a moment to focus on us. He looked at Burrows. "I plan to press charges, you know."

"I took it!" Ellie said. "If it's your book you're after, I gave it to Albert."

Burrows exchanged glances with Sam, who raised one eyebrow, a wild demonstration of emotion for the silent giant.

Ellie was boiling with anger. "Your game's up, you miserable monster! The blue and green war is over!"

Burrows' stare bore a hole through her forehead. "Not at all," he said with calm assurance, which was way more scary than a rant. "The game has hardly begun." He motioned Sam towards her.

"Run!" I shouted and stepped between her and the hired muscle. I saw a beefy arm swing toward me as though in slow motion, and there was impact and flight. And then there was blackness.

ж ж ж

I wasn't out for very long, but I was too disoriented to get up. I remember somebody bending over me and announcing that I was okay. I was too weak to argue. There was a lot of shouting and then talking, and then I was half helped, half dragged along into more darkness. I saw that I was now inside a cabin. Seconds passed and I wasn't being jostled anymore, so I let myself go to sleep.

It seemed like seconds later, but it could have been minutes, that somebody was gently shaking me awake. "We should keep him awake," Dale was saying. "He might have a concussion."

I sat up, and then fell back as the room spun. I tried again, more slowly, and managed to get into a sitting position. The back of my head throbbed. I must have hit a rock when I fell.

Jeremy, Dale, Rudy, and Dana were sitting and standing in the small space. Sam and Burrows had made such a mess searching for the journal, I couldn't even tell which cabin it was.

"What happened?" I asked.

"*You* should ask!" Dana yelled, giving me a shove, which sent my head spinning again. Her anger surprised me, but I realized that as Burrows' protégé, she would see me as the criminal. "You ruined everything!" she shouted, and struggled against Jeremy's hold.

"I ruined everything?" I said, holding my aching head in my hand. "I ruined being trapped in a game of horror?"

"He let the mice out of the maze," Rudy said.

Dana whirled to him. "You! You had no right stealing Doctor Burrows' personal property."

"Let's call it state's evidence," he suggested.

Dana went for him, but Jeremy held her back. "Stop it!" he exclaimed.

Her respect for authority was unshaken, and she stopped, but continued to glare.

"What'll we do now?" Dale asked.

"Nothing we *can* do," Jeremy replied. "Sit and wait."

"Um," I said, "what the hell happened?"

"You were there," Jeremy replied.

"Hardly."

"They took Ellie?" he said—the question was whether I remembered.

"Where?"

"No clue. Probably locked her in Sam's cabin. Sam came back, and shoved us all in here. They took Ralph away as well."

"The door's locked?" I asked.

"No. Sam politely asked us to stay in here."

I looked at Jeremy.

"Sorry," he said. "It's been a bad day."

I sighed. "I guess I did cause all this trouble."

Jeremy shook his head. "No. It was overdue. I couldn't go on much longer."

"It's not like you could just leave," I reminded him.

"No, I mean the deception. Burrows had us over a barrel."

"Us?"

"Me and Albert. He threatened to have Sam continue killing people if we didn't cooperate."

"Cooperate? Doing what?"

Jeremy looked at me a long moment. I realized he was trying to figure it out himself. He finally shrugged. "Continue being a leader. Protect the group—*defend* the group. Take hostages as insurance."

"We, um …"

"What?"

"In the journal. We thought that Burrows …"

"It looked like he'd bought you off," Rudy finished for me.

It took a moment for Jeremy to understand. "That nonsense about a post at the university? Training Marines?" He shook his head. "Nonsense," Jeremy snorted. "Burrows tried to convince us that true leadership—when the group's in danger—requires deception."

"Viable lies," Rudy offered.

Jeremy looked at him, perplexed.

"It was in the journal. He wrote—"

Dale put his hand up. We all heard it—footsteps—and got to our feet. The padlock jiggled, and the door swung open to reveal Sam holding a shotgun. "Let's go!" Burrows called from somewhere off to the side.

We filed out, and Sam herded us away. "Where we going?" Jeremy asked.

"Your embassy," Burrows replied. "The games, as Ellie calls them, are getting into gear."

We stumbled along. I was still a little unsteady, and the others were tripping over each other's feet. When we approached the perimeter of the plateau, Jeremy suddenly stopped, and we piled into him. There, high on the embassy tower, Ralph was tied, arms wrapped backwards around the trunk, looking down on us with fear.

"What's this?" Jeremy asked angrily.

Burrows held out a pistol. When Jeremy didn't take it, Burrows shook it a little, as though maybe Jeremy didn't see it. Our leader finally took it from him. "What's this for?"

"A little bargaining."

"I don't get it."

At the sight of Jeremy with the pistol, Ralph's face contorted in terror, and he struggled against the tie wraps binding his wrists.

"It's simple," Burrows said. "You've lost two members, while the greens have lost just one. It's time to even the score."

Jeremy glanced at Sam, who gave his head a little shake. Jeremy would be dead before he had a chance to aim the pistol. He tried to hand the handgun back to Burrows. "You're crazy."

Burrows didn't take it. Instead, he lowered his head and looked at Jeremy through serious eyes. "You haven't heard the whole deal. You either kill Ralph, or I'll let the greens kill Ellie. Your choice."

"They won't do it," I said.

Burrows turned his Satan gaze on me. "You're willing to gamble that? I had the idea you were quite smitten by that fawn."

I clenched my teeth, aching for the pistol so I could shoot him.

"It's time to become a true leader," Burrows said to Jeremy.

Jeremy glanced at the pistol in his hand, and then at Burrows. As though reading his mind, Burrows grinned and nodded towards Sam, who stood pointing the shotgun at Jeremy.

"The life of one of your group is on the line," Burrows prodded. "A true leader will do anything to protect his group."

Jeremy just stared at the gun in his hands.

"Are you a coward, Jeremy?" Burrows asked mildly.

Suddenly, Dana screamed in rage and grabbed the pistol from Jeremy. She turned, and, holding it in both hands, lifted it, aimed, and as we watched, frozen in horror, pulled the trigger. I jerked at the explosion. Ralph twitched once, and then went limp. A red hole at the base of his neck trickled blood.

The gunshot echoed around the distant slopes and melted away—we were left standing like statues, a sculptor's rendering of a frozen second of horror.

A rustling off to the side broke our spell. It was the greens leaving. They had watched the whole thing.

Chapter 29

It was our turn to watch. Once again we stumbled ahead of Sam's shotgun through the pine forest that a week before had been our playground. The flag game had seemed such a serious endeavor, and now it was like a remembrance of childhood frivolity.

When the green's embassy tower came into view, the nightmare took on a sharp, undeniable reality, and I gasped, falling to my knees so that Rudy had to help me up before the prodding tip of Sam's shotgun. As Ralph had been hung for sacrificial display before the blues, so now was Ellie for the greens. She held her head up, denying Burrows possible satisfaction at watching her squirm, but I knew those eyes too well. I could see that they struggled to hold abject terror at bay. She would have heard the gunshot that killed Ralph, and would understand full well the meaning of having her fellow blues lined up along the side as unwilling witnesses.

Burrows stepped forward and walked up to the tree, looking up at the bound sacrificial prisoner. He shook his head, as though gazing upon something pathetic. "I had hopes for you," he said. "I thought I saw a strength back at that bus stop. I even compromised and let *that* come along." He gestured vaguely in my direction. "But I was mistaken. You are no leader. You live inside the fantasy of democratic cooperation."

He spat those two words.

"Ah, well," Burrows said, turning away, "it may be that women are just not genetically capable of leadership."

He motioned for Albert to step forward from the group of greens, and handed him the pistol.

"No!" Jeremy shouted. He took a step, but Sam raised his shotgun, and placed Jeremy in the sights. "You said it was either Ralph or Ellie!"

Burrows observed Jeremy. His brow wrinkled in disapproval. "The deal was that you shoot Ralph, or Albert shoots Ellie. You did not shoot Ralph. Because of *your* cowardice, you're about to lose one of your group. Let that be a lesson."

He turned, and added, "Besides, lying is part of leadership." To Albert, he said, "You ready?"

Albert stared at him. "My sister?"

Burrows nodded. "She'll be taken care of."

Albert nodded in return, took the pistol, and turned to Ellie.

My stomach dropped. I realized that a second opportunity at a career in the Marines is nothing compared to the life of a sister.

I heard something low and guttural, and realized it was Jeremy. He was muttering the word "coward." Suddenly, he shouted and ran at Albert. The green leader spun around, gave one quick glance at Sam, and then raised the pistol and shot. Jeremy tumbled to the ground, holding his leg. Albert had shot him in the calf, and Jeremy moaned and rolled back and forth in pain.

Burrows was watching Jeremy's suffering with satisfaction, whether because he was happy that the man had finally showed some courage, or that he simply liked watching the pain, I couldn't tell.

Albert was looking at me. Intently. Everybody was preoccupied with Jeremy, and he was staring me down. I had a fleeting thought that maybe, inexplicably, he was going to shoot me, too. But then, weirdly, he winked. He then went back to staring at me, his face as cut in stone as ever.

That wink. I remembered. On the bus to Idyllwild, he'd given me that same wink when tussling with Dana's snobbish bragging. I hadn't been sure afterward that it had actually happened.

He was still staring at me. When he was sure he had my eye, he gave a quick little glance in Sam's direction and then returned to staring at me. He gave the slightest nod.

Oh shit, I thought. *Oh shit, oh shit.* I suddenly knew what he was asking of me. *Why me?* I wondered. *Why not ask somebody brave, like ...*

I didn't think I could do it. How could anybody voluntarily face the blast of a shotgun? It was just not possible. I glanced up at Ellie. If Albert didn't shoot her, I knew Burrows would have Sam do it. If I didn't do this, I'd have to stand here and watch Ellie die.

The scream that issued from my mouth took even me by surprise as I launched myself directly at Sam. I saw the thick neck turn, and the face, calm as ever, gaze at me. The shotgun barrel lifted and steadied so all I saw was the dark hole from where death was about to blow my face away. The hole jerked as the explosion enveloped me, and I fell heavily to the ground.

I felt no pain. None. I wasn't shot, I had tripped. I looked up to see that Sam had dropped the shotgun. He stared straight ahead, looking confused. He held his hands on top of each other across his chest, as though making a spiritual offering. His face relaxed, his hands fell, and I saw the hole in his chest as he slumped to the ground.

Burrows looked on with wide, shocked eyes. It was the first time I'd seen him taken aback. He turned his stunned gaze from the fallen Sam to Albert. The green leader stood, holding the pistol pointed at Burrows, who stared at the gun, trying to understand what it meant.

"Burrows!" Albert called.

The professor raised his gaze from the pistol to Albert's eyes.

"Sometimes leaders have to lie," Albert said, and pulled the trigger.

I winced at the second shot, expecting it this time. Burrows fell like a puppet whose strings have been cut.

The gunshot echoed, and finally dispersed into the swelling return of the birds' chattering. A thump as the pistol hit the dirt seemed to be the release everybody was waiting for, and the forest filled with a cacophony of shouts and chatter. Albert walked over first to check on Sam, and then to Burrows, prodding him with his toe as though suspicious that he might be faking.

I saw Rudy trotting towards the embassy tower. *Ellie!* We'd need something to cut the thick tie wrap. "Hold it," I called, and ran to the prone Sam. I hesitated just a second before reaching inside his pants pocket. Sure enough, I found the huge folding knife. I dashed over and handed it up to my friend. Rudy looked up at Ellie, smiled, and held out his hand towards the base of the tower. "The honors, sir," he said, bowing.

I shook my head at his silliness, but couldn't hide a smile as I jammed the knife between my teeth like Tarzan and climbed the tree. When I reached her feet, I could hear that Ellie was sobbing quietly. In order to reach the tie wrap binding her wrists, I had to continue climbing until we were face-to-face. Her eyes were filled with tears, and she kissed the tip of my nose, which took me by surprise. She laughed and I laughed, and I almost dropped the knife. I unfolded the blade carefully, blindly behind the tree, and worked, sweating, seeing with my fingers, to cut the tie wrap without slicing her wrists. She was crying again, and I heard her whispering. "So many, so many."

I tilted my head back and looked into her eyes again. She met my gaze and said with heartrending remorse, "That was Ralph, wasn't it?"

"Yes," I said, and went back to my task.

The tie wrap finally came loose, and Ellie wrapped her arms around my neck and buried her head under my chin. I wanted us to remain that way for hours, but my arms were getting tired. I let her turn around so that she was facing the trunk, and then I climbed down. I waited as she came down, and we turned to face the crowd together.

The chatter of blues and greens had gone silent minutes before, but that fact registered only now as I saw why. Dana had picked up the pistol, and was swinging it back and forth, trying to cover everybody at once.

"Dana!" Ellie exclaimed, a reprimand. "Put that down. Don't you see? It's over."

Dana swung the gun to point at Ellie's chest. The young woman's eyes were wild, flicking back and forth.

Dana was more dangerous than Burrows or even Sam. She had killed twice, in front of witnesses. Both times, her victims were immobilized, clearly not a threat. It was indubitably murder.

She has nothing to lose.

"Careful," I said quietly to Ellie.

The wild eyes settled on Ellie and locked on her, like targeting radar. "It's all your fault," she snarled. "You interfered from the very beginning."

"Dana," Ellie coaxed reasonably, "Doctor Burrows was insane. There was no way any of this could have ended well. We've all been under extreme duress. Everybody has done things they're sorry for. The important thing now is to go forward on the right track. The rest will take care of itself."

I wasn't sure Dana was even listening. Her eyes narrowed. "You teased him."

"Dana, believe me, I did no such thing. And he truly was insane."

She shook her head, denying this to herself. "You enticed him. I watched you. You coy bitch!"

I knew she was going to do it. Subtle changes in body language signaled the end. I watched her trigger finger move even as I heard myself shout and jump, knocking Ellie out of the way. I didn't have nearly enough time, and Dana pulled the trigger.

There was a click as I slammed into Ellie, sending her tumbling. No gunshot.

I rolled over to see Dana pull the trigger again, and again, her eyes getting wider with each fruitless attempt. She swung her arms out to the sides, and screamed at the sky, a blood-curdling cry of despair. Suddenly, she stopped and scanned us, as though we'd magically appeared out of nowhere. She turned and sprinted off into the pines. Seconds later, a howl echoed through the forest. It was the cry of something wild and terrible, something trapped even though it ran free. Nobody said anything. Moments later, another howl issued forth, this time farther away.

Silence.

"*That* was weird," Rudy said.

This broke the trance, and the greens' perimeter again erupted in chatter.

I helped Ellie up, and Rudy came over. "You okay?" he asked Ellie.

She gave me a shove. "Watch it mister!" she said angrily. "Who you pushing around?" She couldn't maintain the farce any longer, grinned and fell into my arms.

Chapter 30

"Burrows didn't really trust Jeremy *or* Albert," Rudy said.

"The four bullets?" I asked.

"Yeah, I'm surprised he even put four in the gun. He only needed one for Ralph, and a second one for Ellie."

"Maybe he figured the first shots might miss."

Ellie spoke up. "You're trying to understand the mind of a madman," she reminded us. "He might have thought that four was his lucky number."

"In which case," Rudy said, "he couldn't have been more wrong."

We were walking across the plateau towards the road. All of us. The greens had started off first, and the rest of us blues followed. Ellie had tied my shirt around Jeremy's calf to slow the bleeding. Dale could barely walk, so it was mostly Rudy and me helping Jeremy limp along. But then Albert came back with one of his greens, and they took over. Nobody had spoken the decision to go to the road, it was just a natural migration. We let Burrows and Sam lay where they had fallen, as well as poor Ralph, still hanging from the blue embassy tower. The terrible task of dealing with yet more corpses would have to wait.

Rudy glanced back at the greens and Jeremy, and frowned. "Albert was lucky he didn't kill him," he said.

"If he hadn't shot Jeremy, Sam would have," Ellie said, "and he wouldn't have missed."

"I know. I just can't imagine taking that risk—shooting at somebody and hoping you don't kill them."

Ellie sighed. "That's why Burrows didn't pick you as a leader."

Rudy snorted. "Burrow's two requirements for leadership—willing to lie and to shoot people."

Ellie stopped.

Rudy and I turned. "What's up?" I asked.

We were passing Burrows' and Sam's cabins.

"That thick bottle you saw in his cabin," she said to Rudy. "Is it still there?"

"I guess," he said. "I didn't take it."

She headed over, and we followed, Rudy picking up the boltcutters he'd dropped earlier to cut the padlock.

Seconds later Ellie entered the darkness of Burrows' haven, and returned with a small jar sealed with a conical glass stopper. She held it up for us to see. "This is our freedom," she proclaimed.

"Um, mass suicide?" I asked.

She shook her head. "This would be a very nasty way to go."

"What is it?" Rudy asked.

She eyed him. "You of all people should know. What does the label say?" she asked, holding it out for him to read.

"This is the one I saw before. It says 'H SO.'"

"Does it? Look closer."

He peered from just inches away. "Ah-ha! It actually says H_2SO_4. The little guys are all faded. So, what is it?"

She wasn't yet ready to tell us. "Hold this a second," she said to me. "Carefully!"

We heard her rummaging around inside, and then she reappeared, carrying what looked like a slab of plastic.

"The Phial!" Rudy exclaimed, taking it reverently from her. "Burrows—the bastard—took for 'safe keeping' at the beginning. Where'd you find it?"

"There's a box-full of our stuff in there," she said. "You must have missed it in your rush as a burglar." She pointed. "How long would it take to charge this?"

"Depends on what function you want."

"The radio."

His eyes lit up. "That takes almost no juice. It'll run on the power directly from the solar cells, assuming they're in full sunlight."

"Well, let's get it into full sunlight."

That didn't take us long. As Rudy used the metal bolt cutter to nudge the tuning through the Phial's polyurethane covering, Ellie explained that the little bottle contained sulfuric acid—concentrated.

"I don't get it," I admitted. "How is this our freedom?"

"It means we can go down off the mountain," she said.

"It does?"

"What was Burrows' most convincing evidence that the radiation down there was dangerous?"

"Harry," I replied, and then I saw it. "Oh. My. God! Burrows used this *acid* to create the blisters on Harry?"

"How many blisters were there? Wasn't it mostly, like, melted skin?"

I nodded, shuddering.

"Just what you'd expect from concentrated sulfuric acid," she said.

"That's *horrible*! He must have been in unbelievable agony—"

"I doubt he was still alive at that point," she said, shivering herself. "What have you got?" she asked Rudy.

He had his ear pressed against the plastic. "One downside of hermetically sealed functions," he mumbled. "Nothing really."

"Can't get any stations?"

"No. I get stations, but no news. Mostly just AM talk shows."

"Isn't that exactly the news we want?" she asked.

He froze and looked up at us. "Holy cow! You're right!"

I was getting it. "If it was really a dirty bomb, it would be all over the radio, day and night," I concluded. "Then, what's making all the smoke—"

Rudy held up his hand for quiet. "Here's a news report." He listened carefully, then looked up again, eyes wide. "They're calling it the Lake Fulmor Fire. They say it's ninety percent contained. All evacuations have been canceled."

"A forest fire!" I exclaimed. "Of course! Shit, but he was one clever madman."

"Be careful who you lionize," Ellie warned. "He was a murderer, first and last."

We were quiet until she added, "I'll spend the rest of my life wondering if there wasn't something we could have done to have Viona and Tim with us now."

"And Ralph," Rudy said.

"And Ralph," she agreed, her eyes watering up. "Oh hell," she said, tears streaming down her face, "Barry, too."

ж ж ж

The three of us plopped the cardboard boxes down on the ground next to Burrows' Jeep. Greens sat together on their side of the Jeep, and blues on the other.

"What's that?" Albert asked.

I picked up one of the boxes and dumped the contents onto the pine needles.

"Our clothes!" came an excited cry from the greens.

Minutes later, jeans, T-shirts, slacks, and blouses were scattered about as we tried to sort out what belonged to whom. Green shirts were flung aside, blue pants kicked away, leaving white legs below undershorts. Once we were all dressed again in our street clothes, caressing the sleeves lovingly as though feeling cotton for the first time, Rudy gathered together all the discarded uniforms.

"What're you going to do with those?" I asked.

He was stuffing them into the empty boxes. "To the fire pit." He stopped and looked around. "Anybody object?"

The boos and no's were deafening.

Ellie explained Burrows' dirty bomb ruse to the shocked group.

"No keys in the Jeep," Albert informed us. "Did you see them in his cabin?"

"No," Ellie replied, "but I wasn't really looking for them. They might be in his pants pocket."

Albert nodded. "I'll check."

"Well, I'm going down," I declared.

I hadn't decided this until that very second, but now that I'd voiced it, I could hardly wait to get started.

"You walking down?" one of the greens—one of the former greens—asked me. "I'm coming along."

"I think it's, like, at least five miles," I warned.

"I don't care if it's twenty. I'm outta here."

Soon everybody was going along, except Jeremy and Dale—the wounded ones—and Rudy, who offered to find the keys and drive the other two down.

The first stretch was steep, and we slipped and slid, raising a choking cloud of dust, but soon the dirt road angled more gently as it wound back and forth through the switchbacks. Albert came up next to Ellie and me. "No more blues or greens," he noted.

I glanced around. The street clothes had transformed us back into just a bunch of Americans stumbling out of the wilderness. Burrows had known what he was doing with the uniforms. A thought struck me. "Burrows' study was supposed to be about how danger to a group changes the dynamics," I said.

Albert threw me a glance. "Yeah, I got that."

"We guessed he was going to introduce a danger, and at first we thought it was Sam. "But then," I continued, "it seemed that maybe it was the dirty bomb, which in retrospect was kind of ridiculous, but nevertheless."

"But it was the groups themselves." Albert said.

"Yeah—right! When did you figure it out?"

He shrugged. "I didn't really figure it out. It just slowly dawned on me—the purposeful contention over the meals and baths, the fact that he encouraged cheating and rough play during the flag game, that he didn't give a damn that we were stealing desserts, that he told Barry and Ralph that the hackberry tree was manzanita—he *knew* that would get one of them captured. It goes on and on. Now we find out that the competition over the manzanita was fabricated. He had Sam kill Viona and Tim to ratchet up the tension. It was all orchestrated to set the greens and blues against each other. It was why he hated you, Ellie, for your attempts towards cooperation."

I sighed. "You know, Dana was right about that. You did completely ruin it for him."

Ellie didn't reply. She seemed deep in thought. "Tribes," she said.

We walked along until she looked at us. "Burrows was playing on our deepest instincts," she said. "Loyalty to the tribe. After a million years of group selection, we're programmed to identify with a tribe—a group—and defend it, to the death if necessary." She shook her head in disgust. "It served us well as small bands of hunter-gatherers. It created virtue and altruism, but it also turned us against anybody not of our tribe. And now entire populations are repressed, and even slaughtered. Evolution gave us the gift of xenophobia."

"Muslims against Christians," I offered.

She ticked off on her fingers, "Jews against Palestinians, Muslim Shiites against Muslim Sunnis, Christian Tutsis against Christian Hutus, Christian Nazis against Jews, the Khmer Rouge atheists against anybody they could get their hands on. It goes on and on and on and on. There's always an 'us' against 'them.' I have to tell you, I get uncomfortable at high school football games, listening to the students—the parents even—booing the opponents. It's like kindergarten training for the next ethnic cleansing."

Silence.

"I got a little carried away with that," she admitted, then looked at me. "Burrows wanted you out, not because you were desperate, but because he heard you say how you couldn't fit into a group."

"The Pod?" I scoffed. "That just meant I was sane."

She shrugged.

"Right," I said. "Sanity wasn't a factor in Burrows' world."

Albert kicked a stone, his hands in his pockets. "And still," he said, "I think that the whole group-against-group was itself just a means to an end."

"What end?" Ellie asked.

"Effective leaders," he replied. "Jeremy was a miserable failure."

He grinned, an unusual form for his face. "I am complimenting Jeremy. Burrows' ideal leader is one who handles deceit adeptly. To him, a leader is a manipulator of his people, a puppet master. Jeremy's ideal is almost the exact opposite. From the beginning, Jeremy was a continual disappointment to Burrows. If it weren't for the threats that Burrows rained down on us—food, cabins, hazmat suits—Jeremy would have walked away from it all."

We strolled along, until Ellie finally said, "So, what about …"

"Me? Ah, I'm a pragmatist. I played along, biding my time. In the end, Burrows needed Jeremy and me to kill so that we would be completely committed, by our crimes. In retrospect, though, if I'd acted on an idealism such as Jeremy's, perhaps it never would have gone as far as it did."

Ellie glanced at me, and then at Albert. "But in the end, it was you who defeated Burrows."

He stopped and put his hand on her shoulder. "No, I killed him, it was you who *defeated* him."

He walked on, and we hurried to catch up. I could see that Ellie was blushing.

"Hey! Smoke!" a former green shouted, pointing.

We turned around. A pillar of gray rose from up-slope and sped off east as it was caught by the wind. "It's Rudy," I said. "He's burning the uniforms."

Ellie grinned. "They're all the same color now."

I heard a gasp, and turned to look. It was Sheryl. She had fallen to her knees, and buried her face in her hands. She sobbed uncontrollably, her shoulders rocking in rhythm. After a moment, one of the green men approached her. I recognized him. It was Danny, her husband. I had the idea that they'd had a falling out at some point. He stood, seeming unsure what to do. Sheryl suddenly grabbed handfuls of dirt and threw them into her face, as though it was water. I realized what she was doing when she began rubbing her cheeks, the dirt mixing with her tears to produce smears of mud. She was trying to rub off the painted warrior lines. Danny finally knelt down next to her and placed his hand on her shoulder. She stopped, and looked at her filthy fingers, then at him. An instant later, she wrapped her arms around his neck, and he returned the desperate hug.

Wordlessly, we all continued walking in order to give them a little privacy. The shared mood was muted, the festive feeling of release from prison now moderated by memories of fallen companions. Thoughts of karma and consequences of deeds done must have weighed heavily on some. For others, simple niggling guilt sufficed. I probed through the events of the last weeks, searching with trepidation for actions I should regret. The process would continue for a long time.

We came to the end of one of the switchbacks, and had a view upslope. Above, a small stone tongue stuck out at us, as though bidding us good riddance. "Hey!" I said, "Look!"

A tiny figure stood at the tip of the rude appendage waving its arm back and forth over its head. Ellie returned the wave. "It's Rudy! He looks so small from here."

She turned to me, seeming suddenly serious. "Do you think we'll ever be able to come back here? I mean, after all that's happened?"

I raised one eyebrow. "You mean after the police drag us back for a detailed, step-by-step recounting of the sordid events?"

Her serious expression turned to horror. "Oh no! This is going to be one of those stories that make the news show rounds forever. Oh lord, we're never going to have any peace!"

I lifted my palms in resignation. "There's no getting around writing a book and heading off on tour."

"Oh pooh," she said, sticking out her tongue.

"In fact," I said, "they'll probably turn this into some kind of macabre tourist park, like they did where the Donner party spent their cannibal winter."

"If they do," Albert joined in, "they will have to call it 'Green Tribe Park.'"

I looked at him, and saw the glimmer of a grin.

Ellie looked at him and then me, and she made her face into an exaggerated scowl. "Never! Blue Group Park, or it's a fight!"

"A fight it is, then," Albert agreed.

We both slung our arms over her shoulders, one on each side, and walked on down the mountain together.

Ж   Ж   Ж   Ж   Ж   Ж

About the Author

Blaine C. Readler is an electronics engineer, inventor of the FakeTV, and, of course, a writer. He lives in San Diego, where people come from all over the world just to be there.

He encourages you to visit him:
http://www.readler.com/

www.ingramcontent.com/pod-product-compliance
Lightning Source LLC
Chambersburg PA
CBHW060316260626
47160CB00007B/2629